THREE HILLS

The Borderer Chronicles

(Other titles in the series by the same author)

Devotion and the Devil

On Solway Sand

MARK MONTGOMERY

THREE
HILLS

For Nora Charlotte, a mother who gifted me a little black
and white dog, who in turn preserved my sense of life.

.

THE BORDERER CHRONICLES

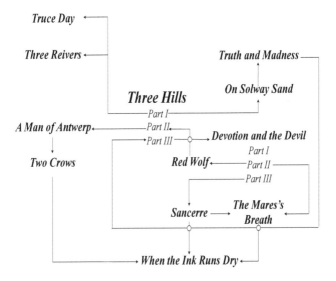

The German
Ocean

✝ Leith
EDINBURGH ✚

Scottish East
March

BERWICK ✚

✳ Flodden
Field

Scottish
Middle March

English
East March

✝ Hawick

Scottish West
March

Langholm ✝

The
Debatable
Land

✝ Dumfries

Caerlaverock Castle ✝

English Middle March

Orchardton
Tower

✝ Solway
Moss

NEWCASTLE
✝

✚ CARLISLE

The Solway Firth

✝ Kircudbright

✝ Allonby

✝ The Traquere's Tower

Workington ✝

✝ Cockermouth

English
West March

The Borders

The world of John Brownfield

Prologue

M any years ago I was fortunate to have a friend. He was a good friend, one who shared a little of his life with me. He shared his time with me, his family, his friends, and sight of his possessions. But unlike the most of us, his possessions were not a reflection of him exactly, but a reflection of a hundred other lives. Lives left in boxes. Boxes of objects and artefacts he had acquired from innumerable house clearances. Articles not deemed precious enough to keep by those families who grieved the loss of a mother or father, sister or brother. But items fascinating to those who value the history of a person, and the stories they leave behind.

One dirty and ragged cardboard box contained a number of antiquarian documents. The papers in this box included a will, an inventory, a few letters, and what seemed to be a few charred and torn pages from a journal. All, but the inventory and some of the letters, appeared to be in the same hand; their rhetoric texts barely decipherable to us; we who were not versed in archaic forms of composition.

The largest document was the will, dated 1601, of a man called John Brownfield, who announced himself in the record as, '*A*

Border Horseman, from birth to death, neither Scot nor Englishman.' He bequeathed all his considerable fortune of fifty-five thousand, six hundred and fifty-four pounds (considerable because it would equate to around two to three million pounds today) to a family member called Catherine Brownfield, which included cryptically, *'Three hundred pounds outstanding monies due from a stipend awarded by a man of Antwerp'.* There was no mention of what relation Catherine was to John. So we did not know if she was his wife, daughter, niece, sister or even mother. Also within John's will, but barely legible, was an entry in Latin, *'per aspera ad astra',* which my friend was told translated into *'through difficulty to the stars',* and we assumed it was a family motto.

With the will, there was an inventory of belongings, which we concluded John was leaving to Catherine. Amongst the list of personal effects, such as glassware, books, various receptacles and clothing, were a number of more noteworthy items—things of war, items in precious metals, and items of seemingly personal value. They were strangely labelled and identified John as a soldier and perhaps a lover. They included weapons and exotic artefacts; *'a stick named Knocker; a tall axe—late of Henry Musgrave; two oriental swords; a rapier of fine steel—gift from a Frenchman; a silver button—gratuity from a lady; a length of gold chain; and a silver locket—with a lock of red hair within.'*

With the inventory, there were also a few letters and a few charred pages, probably torn from a journal. The contents seemed to be mostly private thoughts shared, again cryptic to us at the time in their meaning. But they seemed to indicate observations and events surrounding our John Brownfield, as both a boy and a learned man.

The evidence before us led our imaginations on, and both being keen on history, but not being historians, we attempted in our amateurish way to research the history of this man.

The location of the documents, and the reference to John as a Borderer, led us to seek him out within well-documented *Anglo/Scottish Border* history. We hoped to tie him in with the infamous *Border Reivers;* men who spent their years making as best they could, amongst the strife inflicted on the Borders under ambitious Royal warrants, during the time of the English Tudor and Scottish Stewart kings and queens.

Many Borderers attained their wealth through felony and opportunity, and we hoped to link John into some nefarious historical activities and thus generate some greater monetary value in the ancient documents in our possession. But John's name did not appear in the list of those noted 'Names' of famous families that occupied the Borders in the sixteenth century, and despite our lengthy search we could not find record of property or marriage, birth or death. We were left in mystery to who this man was, and where he lived and died. It seemed inconceivable to us that John, with all his wealth, was not a member of a noted Border family, and the riddle of the man remained unsolved.

Unfortunately I lost the friend, and therefore sight of the documents some time ago, and the routines and more pressing challenges of life replaced my quest for the history of John Brownfield. So now in my later years, I have invented his life from the scraps of past that remain in my memory. Of course, this story from my pen is all, and can only ever be, complete fiction, woven into the history of his time, as all historical fiction is. This story created around a few journal entries cannot be the whole tale; there will be many others. But for now, it is a core of a greater chronicle of a man who was a Border Horseman, from birth to death, neither Scot nor Englishman.

Three Hills

Your own destiny lies over three hills. Three peaks to climb and descend. The first peak is childhood. It moulds your spirit, and its vigour runs you to the top and you ardently descend its fall, eager to reach the next hill. Wounds are taken lightly, scars heal quickly and worn bravely.

The second peak is youth, with decision how the rise of the hill should be taken. Easy and difficult paths are there, fortune and ruin. The descent is a path few relish, for it leaves behind the strength and hopes of youth. Wounds are harsh and scars never heal.

The third peak is middle age, and is an arduous climb with the burden of responsibility, made difficult by the tally of wounds. Descent leads one to decline, and the finality of the journey.

But I hear you say, what of birth and death, infancy and old age?

Discount them, because one has little influence over their shaping, as one's fate is in the hands of another, governed by their direction and care.

But surely old age has the gift of wisdom?

Discount old age most of all, as it is a rare gift given only to a few, and a curse for most.

John Brownfield, MDXCV (1595)

PART 1

'childhood into youth'

Chapter I

I was a man in my fancy. A man riding amongst men. A man with his brothers, uncles and father to the fore. I was going to put blood on my dagger. I was going to put a smile on my father's lips—hear him salute me as a man. I can remember how joyed I was to be part of it. My pride was hoisted, and no chide could dampen my spirit, and no mockery by my brothers could lower my head.

We had joined the army marching southwest from Edinburgh, at Langolm, from its muster at Fala Moor, with some seven hundred men from the Scottish West March. Local men keen for requital against the ruin wrought on Scotland by the forces of the English East March Warden, Robert Bowes. Some of the men we knew as kith and kin, some we knew only by reputation, most were strangers to us, but all were armed. I had never seen so many men and horses, so much steel and leather.

The ride towards the border and Carlisle, amongst so many, was exhilarating. We kicked up so much dust and dirt as we rode, and by the time we approached the border with England, some said we were fourteen thousand, some even said it was more like twenty.

My father would speak of times like this, in earlier days, as we sat around the evening fire in our tower. After we had eaten supper and the day was nearly dead. But to be here proper, was so much more than his descriptives had ever offered.

And now as we travelled, my father spoke to my brothers, and even though the din of so many hooves and feet deadened his words, I would ride up hard behind him to listen. I could hear my father complaining about the indiscriminate burning and looting as we marched. He said some were using the ride to settle local scores on the Scottish side of the border, and it had little to do with our cause against the English Warden. I was proud of my father. To listen to him chastising the wicked amongst that noble venture made me feel noble too.

During the day I rode amongst the men, cannon and carts in order to see them all; lowland soldiers and riders, carrying spear and stave, in armour older than the wearers; foreign mercenaries in handsome red and blue liveries; highlanders in saffron and mail, with great claymore swords fastened at their backs; Irish kerns, light foot troops, dressed as my daddy would say, 'In nightshirts and barely a decent blade between them.'

I cannot recall what excited me most, but I remember mixing my pony in with a host of banners, flying proudly in the November air. I can remember my head held high. My eyes lost in their flight—in their colour against the sky. I can remember so many banners, but most of all the blue and white standards bearing the St Andrew's Cross. The thrill of it all made me bold, and I ran my pony into a column to pluck a red feather from a soldier's cap, to place in my own bonnet, to mark me to the English as one of the splendid Swiss. Yes, I remember the Swiss men, so brash and formidable in their Germanic delivery of rousing drinking songs as they marched.

On the road, I spied blue on the ground and dismounted quickly to pick it out of the dirt and mud. My prize was a cloth badge, bigger than my outstretched hand, and it showed the St Andrew's Cross—*my St Andrew's Cross*, and I clutched it tight.

'What have you there, boy?' demanded my father, as he pulled his nag alongside my pony, with my brothers, Thomas and William, in escort.

I replied, '*A saltire*. I found it on the road. It must have fallen off one of the men's jackets.'

My father pulled at my fist to open it. Examined the cloth badge within, and closed my fingers back around it tightly. 'Aye, easily done… especially when they're stuck on wi' spit.'

Thomas added sarcasm to my father's observation. 'It's amazin' how badges get lost from jackets in the thick of a losing battle… and this one's nae even lost yet.'

'Ye'll no doubt find as many a George Cross on the inside of this army's coats—ready tae be turned inside oot,' added William.

My father turned from me to ride close to Thomas, slapping a hand gently on his back, drawing his gaze with a smile and a heartily delivered question. 'What of oor own men, Thomas, are they ready tae turn coat?'

Thomas answered, 'Two of oors had the English badge sewn on the insides of their jackets. I stripped them of armour 'n' arms, and sent them home.'

My father endorsed my brother's action with a nod. 'There's much woeful rumour and foul discontent runnin' through this venture. Many would rather of stayed by the fire.'

Will, seeing my sad face at the loss of our father's attention, shifted on his mount so he could put a gloved hand easily on my shoulder as we rode. But his hand meant mischief, and he snatched the bonnet from my head.

He held my bonny blue bonnet and plucked free the red

feather, holding it high to tease me. 'Dinnae worry, *Da*. I suspect there's a few *men* amongst us, with fire in their belly fer the fight.'

Will's mocking produced amusement amongst all but me. But my father quickly curtailed the mirth, perhaps to save me from ridicule, more plausibly for the sake of making his own observation.

'I noticed *Slack 'o' Jack* in the rank 'n' file. I thought he was excused service because his weddin' day approached?'

Thomas laughed and smiled. 'He was. He was tae marry Meg Bell. He was caught stealing her da's cattle a while ago, and her da offered him either his daughter's hand… or the hangman's noose. He thought livin' was better than dyin'. But methinks he's with us today because dyin' may be a better option after all.'

My father slapped hard his thigh and laughed. Actions that caused his nag to bolt a little. He showed a rare loss of horse-control, but it was only for a moment, and he steadied his mount expertly, exclaiming, 'We must be damned if that idle sod chooses fightin' over shaggin'!'

'No, it's Slack 'o' Jack who would be damned… Meg's uglier than a coo, with grace and manners tae match,' announced Thomas gleefully.

We all joined in with laughter, at both Slack 'o' Jack's predicament and Thomas' wit.

Poor Slack 'o' Jack, I thought. His acutely self-serving and lazy nature prevented him from being an esteemed sergeant-at-arms amongst my father's horsemen. His soldiery skills lost amongst his deficiencies. His shiftless spirit guiding him to censure rather than preferment. My father saw the merit in him and he often singled him out from all his charge for his attention. But reward for his trust was never repaid. Slack 'o' Jack remained a feckless man; subject more to my father's punishment, rather than his praise.

It was a rare time to be with my father and brothers together.

To be, as I thought, as equals. And even though in terms of armour and weapons I was deficient; them being so well attired with lance and sword, steel bonnet and shield, I did that day feel an equal. You see, to be the youngest was to be favoured by mother as a child to coddle, and to be disregarded by father in matters of manly responsibility. So I was keen to take any given opportunity to impress my father, headsman of his clan, keeper of his people. I longed for him to acknowledge me as he did Thomas and Will; *warrior men.*

'*Da*, I noticed some highlanders in the fray men. I hear when they charge, the ground shakes 'n' trembles.' I looked for response from my father, but none came. 'They charge with a frightenin' scream and withoot fear of shot 'n' arrow. Is it not good tae have such heroes in oor midst?'

My father smiled, and I was pleased to have his agreement. But instead he quickly challenged my opinion. 'Heroes are fodder fer fiction. Good fer stirrin' up the men in a fight… but only disciplined strategy wins battles… and highlanders have neither respect fer discipline nor strategy. They think war is a game of ball. They run at the opposin' side yellin', in the hope they unsettle their opponent. A plausible policy against a disinclined militia, but a witless one against seasoned troops.'

I nodded to show contrition for my misunderstanding. In the domain of knowledge givers, my father was not to be questioned. He was never wrong, always right. His wisdom was without equal amongst my tutors.

'*Pa*, it is likely we'll be takin' the fight tae the garrison at Carlisle… Perhaps laying siege tae the castle? Will we be stormin' the castle wi' ladders? The lads say that's how it's done—ladders and grapplin' irons… I hope I'm first up the ladder.' I hoped my enthusiasm would impress, but I was met with a vicious scold.

'Now dinna pish yerself, Jack m'boy. Keep yer mind on yer

tasks and nae on the fight. Do as yer brothers ask. Keep the pistols loaded. Mind the nags and oor baggage. Most of all… keep yer heid down.'

My father's harsh delivery caused me to flinch, but I heeded his instructions carefully, and nodded in obedient response to all that he asked.

'If me and yer brothers get into trouble, and things look bad… drop yer blade… head fer the baggage train and the women. Be careful boy, running away… don't get cut doon by oor own men.'

I was nettled at my father's suggestion that I would be running away like a coward, and even though I was wounded and subdued by his harsh counsel, I hit back. 'No, *Pa*, I wont be runnin' away. I'll be fightin' at yer side.'

My father's face showed red. He was not pleased at my childish boast. His reply designed to cut me down and keep me compliant. 'There's nae honour in death boy. If something bad happens to yer brothers 'n' me, I need you tae return tae yer ma and look after things… If things go bad, there will be a terrible reckonin'… just as there will be if you disobey me, *boy*.'

My ardour lay defeated, and I thought on the man who was making me subject to his will. In a rare moment I stopped thinking of him as my father, and instead as others saw him. He stood out from the other gentleman in the field. He put his integrity before his purse, prudence before the sword. He paid and trained his soldiers well to keep his people safe. Many said he was the last knight in Scotland.

As day turned to dusk on the evening of the twenty third day of November, 1542, my father was forty-four years of age; my brother William, seventeen; Thomas the oldest, was twenty-two; I was nine years old.

I did not feel the winter cold that November night as we rode. It was not the extra shirt my mother made me wear. Or the thick oversized leather jack, or jerkin, cast off by my brothers, Thomas and William in turn. It was my pride and delight of my presence in such a wondrous gathering.

All the while we travelled, we anticipated the King's arrival, but no news came. Chatter spread amongst the men. Grumble. I listened. I heard protest. I heard them complain, and I would nod in learned agreement, even though I knew nothing of their grievances—nothing about disunity and disenchantment.

By early morning, the army had reached the ford on the River Esk, and beyond lay the Solway Moss, a massive stretch of shifting bog. In the morning air, thick with the smell of burning farms, the sight and sound, the very taste of it, frightened me. It was not the cold on that morning that made me shudder, but the sight of the land—such an expanse of water and tall marsh grasses, featureless and cruel in its winter mantle. Then there was the sound of the men. No fervour, only complaint, because all the while the men's chatter had grown into rumour that the King was too ill to travel, to ill to lead—and the men were very unhappy.

My pony took some cajoling to approach the river, and I needed to dig my heels firm to move her forward. She whinnied and whined, and her pain made me grit my teeth to silence my own scream as we entered the icy water. Our travel in the water was laboured, and all I could hear was the other men and horses complaining as we crossed the chilled Esk, swollen by November rain. As I splashed across, I could see riders about, coming down from a hill, and those around me talked of our own skirmishers returning from firing the local land and rejoining the column, but others called out they were English skirmishers attacking our forces. By the time I had crossed the ford, soaked in cold and discomfort, rumour had grown to agitation.

We still waited for news of our commander. Many thought it likely that able *Lord Maxwell*, the Warden of the Scottish West March, would take charge. Then news arrived and spread that another had been given command of the army in lieu of our sick king; *Oliver Sinclair*, a fop of the King's court and no general. Agitation now turned to alarm amongst the men, and they were shouting, all in different voices, but all sounded the same dissent.

I struggled to see the head of the column and the riders coming down from the hill, but the numbers of men around me grew and my sight was impaired. All the while the column of men and horses were struggling to find firm ground in the Moss. Cannon and wagons glued into the ground, and those men working desperately to free them, forced other advancing men to go around them deeper into the bog, and they floundered too.

My father had tried to keep us together, but he was now ahead with Thomas trying to direct the men and wagons onto better ground, and even Will was lost to me as I struggled to keep my pony moving in the mire.

Then alarm turned to fear. Distress. I heard desperate shouts from terrified men. Men caught in crowds stuck in the bog. Men caught exposed on the edge of the column, without command or protection.

'*Thousands of lancers, horsemen… Prickers!*'

The English army was attacking the column.

Our army was caught. It could not move. It could not organise and without leadership, or firm ground on which to manoeuvre, fear quickly turned to panic, and those retreating from ahead magnified the woes of us caught in the bog.

The mass of men coming together was unbearable, and those pushing past my pony unnerved her and she lost her way, and I fell into the viscous ground. It sucked me down. I tried to free myself. I tried to breathe, but the watery earth had swallowed me, and it held me firm. I tried again and again to sit up, but again and again I was pressed down. I could not understand it, and through my terror, I could feel the pressure of being forced further in. I gasped for air, but all I found was water and mud, and I thought I was dying. But then… I could feel a force stronger than the ground that held me, and this force pulled me free, and I could see and breathe again.

Will's hand was firm on me, pulling me up and out.

'The boys were usin' ye as a steppin' stone,' Will said, wiping the detritus from my eyes.

I spluttered, 'Th… thank thee, Will… thank thee!'

'Yer troubles are nae over… The army is in flight, and the English are aboot. Ye need tae move.'

'Where's *Pa*? Where's Thomas?'

'They're ahead. Fightin' the English I think, but all is lost, and ye need tae get back over the river.' Will picked up his sword and shield out of the mud, and began to push his way through the suffocating crowd of men clambering away from their fear and the fight.

'Where are ye goin'?' I shouted.

'To lend oor daddy a hand.'

I did not argue. I was not brave. I did not think of rescue for my father or brother as Will had done. I ran. I crawled. And I swam my way out of the Moss, and over the river.

By the time I had reached the opposite bank, my wool hose and gown were thick with mud and soaked through. They hung low and my sodden leather jack weighed heavy. I had no dagger, no pony, and no one to guide me except the mass of fleeing men. So I stripped off my jack, pulled up my sodden hose and ran with the rout.

A hard and desperate run had brought me to the wagon train, breathless, heart pounding, streaked with mud and soaked in fear. They were already preparing to withdraw. Fortunately they had been held steady by a large troop of our own retreating horsemen; mustering men to bolster the existing baggage guard against any following English attack. I ran desperate from wagon to wagon, looking for familiar faces, but found none. All the time other men and horses ran by, looking to put distance between themselves and an expected English assault. I can remember the sight of the Swiss and German mercenaries so resplendent in their colourful livery on the march to the Esk, not so noble as they ran away. I felt my plight was increasingly desperate, as panic stole reason from me. And without my father or brothers to guide me, I looked to escape it by running more with the retreating men. But I couldn't. My strength had given way to fatigue. My resolve had broken into tears. I stood amidst the panic, *lost*.

'Cu-cum on lad, up here.'

I looked up to see a man on a horse, and I thought the English were on me. I squeezed my eyes tightly closed and I cowered, ready to be pounded bloody into the earth.

'Cu-cum on lad d-divvent waste time.'

The assistance in his voice quelled my fear of death, and I wiped the tears from my eyes and saw him true—an ally.

'T-t-take ma hand lad, we'd better m-m-make time away from this mess.'

A large gloved hand reached down to me and I took it, and with a broad sweep he lifted me onto his horse to sit behind him. He smelled bad, but I did not care. The horseman turned to look at me, but his face was hidden beneath dark dirt and a darker beard that was thick with neglect. But as he spoke, as he introduced himself, it was his eyes that calmed me—piercing bright green eyes.

'Ma name is W-W-Willy.'

'Mine's Jack, Jack…'

Willy interrupted me before I could finish. 'No clan names, Jack m'lad. I m-m-might not like it… and wished I left ye fer the E-E-English.'

I did not question my deliverer. He was the second man to save me that day, and I obeyed his stuttered instructions to the letter.

'If it's fine wid you lad, I'm h-h-headin' north-east, but I'm p-p-puttin' a spurt on.'

'Aye, Willy, the English may not be far behind.'

'N-no so much the E-English lad. I d-d-dinna think they're followin'. But I've not long thieved this nag… and its former owner were as b-bigger bastard than I've seen t'day. Wid a p-p-pair of fresh legs and a good p-p-pace he'll be on us in a wink.'

Willy skilfully guided his stolen horse through the chaos of a fleeing army, looking all the time for a better route to take, away from the flow of panic, as men followed men.

'B-b-best stay away from the roads, J-J-Jack. It'll b-b-be a rougher escape, b-b-but a safer one.'

'Why's that, Willy?'

'Th-the Scottish Marches are no a safe p-place for a Scottish army. Th-there's too many wi'oot affection for King James and his cronies. T-t-too many Scottish border families looking to f-f-fill their stores with spoils fr-fr-from a spoilt Scottish army. There'll be no safety in numbers this day.'

Willy took us away from the main force and the fleeing groups of men, to find harder, quieter paths to the northeast and *Liddesdale*. He would kick his nag as we headed up high into the fells and

19

forests to avoid people, and away from any shelter the habited world could offer. The going was hard and often difficult, and we needed to rest the horse often to save him for more difficult journeying ahead of us.

As we rode, we talked. Sometimes Willy would answer my questions. Sometimes his stammer would not allow the release of words from his mouth to reply. So even though we talked to ease our journey's day, our conversation was often ill at ease, and silence often preferred to lengthy discourse.

Willy foraged well. He made good camp with shelter, food to eat and fire to warm. All welcome while the weather was at its wintry worse. Strong winds, cold days, icy nights and forever wet. I fretted over my woes; a boy separated from his family; not knowing of their fate, or my future. I thought the worst of it. But Willy kept me occupied; snaring rabbits, building camp, and scouting areas around our travel. Many tasks he devised. Many more I thought were simply to divert my self-sorrow onto more practical matters; those concerned with survival. And as we rested, we talked of home.

'Where d'ya call home, Willy?'

'I have no home under roof lad… I live were I find ma'self. B-b-but I was b-born and lived most of my life south of the b-border.'

'What did you do in England?'

Willy ran a stick through a rabbit, stripped and prepared for the fire. I could see he wanted to answer my question, but could not free the words from his lips. The poor man tried to conceal his strained utterance by covering his mouth, feigning a cough and turning his head away from the fire. But I knew his actions were to hide his embarrassment from me. The long pause uncomfortable, as I willed him to win and to speak. Finally his words burst forth.

'E… E-E-E-England, lad? There's no England, only the

Marches. Ye have t-t-to travel a long way south to find yerself in E-England.'

Willy placed the rabbit over the fire. I did not wish to think on Willy's stammer. I did not want to show him that it bothered me. So I looked on Willy's handiwork applied to my rabbit proudly caught. I thought Willy had stripped the rabbit without a single thought directed to it. It was prepared expertly, and set above the fire in a moment. But as I took my eyes off the rabbit, I could see Willy was caught in his own thoughts; his eyes lost in the distance. His next words came more easily, but sore they were, so difficult for him they were to speak.

'I had a family once, and I worked the land. B-b-but I lost most of it t-t-to one more thieving raid than I could recover from… I lost ma wife in the last one. N-neither coos, nor ewes did they leave me for milk. No w-w-wet nurse. T-too proud for charity I was. N-n-no… m-m-milk for the b-baby. The b-b-b-babe… d-d-died soon after.' Tremendous grief filled Willy's eyes.

I wished to change the subject, to escape my unease with Willy's display of sorrow. 'How did ye end up fightin' at the Moss?' I asked.

Willy seemed relieved to change the subject.

'I t-tagged onto the wrong army hoping fer some spoils of my own. N-n-never could pick a winner in a cock fight neither.'

୫୬

Three days ride brought me to within a walk away from home. Three days made difficult, as Willy skillfully avoided any trouble brought about by the border clans and gangs inhabiting Liddesdale—opportunists who poked and prodded the shattered strings of a fleeing Scottish army. Three days and countless hills climbed, rivers forded and forests travelled. An entire sea of green navigated by a good pilot, evading the dangers of the Marches and those peoples that would do us harm.

I was sad when time came to part company. Willy had been a good soul, and I was grateful for his keep on the way home. He had maintained my safety and provided kindness without reward. He had eased the distress in me and brought me out of danger by means of his generous and selfless fellowship. And behind the dirty face, hidden beneath an unkempt beard, may have been a damaged man, but his benevolence remained bright. It shone through his piercing green eyes.

We said our farewells on a good morning, on a far sunnier day than it had been for quite some time. I was sad when my escort turned his stolen nag southwards to journey to a different place; one far away from my journey's end. I asked him where he was going. He mentioned places I did not know; names of towns and villages I had not heard spoken by kith or kin. I cannot recall the names of the places. I tried to. I wanted to, so that I could seek him out some day to thank him again. But I could only remember one place he mentioned, one name—*Utopia*.

Chapter II

It had been raining for ten days without abate, and the world was a foul, dark and wet place. No comfort existed for man or beast those weeks after the disaster on the Moss. Spirits amongst the men were low. Voices in the inns and meeting places quietened. And angst stretched out over our sodden realm.

No man wanted to talk about the shame of that day. The shame of a few hundred English sponsored horsemen, who put an army to flight. Who poked and pricked our forces into submission, taking many prisoners. No one could reckon how much life was taken by the hand of men, and how much by the Moss. By the bog and river that devoured men whole in the rout. Little was said of our King, he who died in shame leaving a newborn babe, a girl on his throne. Many said much. Few knew fact. But none knew the fate of my father and brothers.

My mother posted extra watch throughout our land-holdings, and kept the men at arms ready for reprisal attacks by the English, or opportunistic reiving by local and the not so local families. Even I was given a spear and a sentry posting. Although I suspected my mother wished me safe, because it was the softest lookout in our kingdom with, as I complained to my mother, *'Nowt but chickens and hogs tae watch over and fear.'*

Pinchback, one of the guards assigned to the tower house, was the one to fetch me from my uncomfortable sentinel stand to the comfort of the tower's hall. Where my mother and uncle waited. My mother did not speak. My uncle addressed all.

'Jack, we have news of your kin. The English March Warden offers return of your father and brother.'

My face made a smile long absent since Solway Moss that, by its design, fashioned a smile matched by my mother. She seemed to move forward, as if to hug me in an emotional release, but my uncle stepped on, and gestured to stop her interruption.

'The Warden agrees to release your father and brother, for a pledge of loyalty to his authority.'

My smile turned to indignation at the thought of such an ignoble ransom, and I yelled, 'The English have no authority here.'

But my uncle arrested my angry retort with a gentle finger to his lips. He pressed on. 'No, Jack. He suggests a bond of cross-border co-operation against those who would perpetuate lawlessness and turmoil. He releases your father and brother on the understanding that a pledge be lodged in his keeping. A hostage if you like. One to ensure our family adheres to the covenant proposed by the Warden. He offers this in lieu of ransom.'

At first I had little care to the notion of hostages, but I grew anxious with my uncle's reference to *brother*, instead of brothers, and thus I reasoned either Will or Thomas was to remain captive, so I enquired, 'Who is to be hostage, Uncle? Will or Thomas?'

My response brought tears to my mother's eyes, and my uncle bowed his head. Then in a lower, more measured tone he continued, 'It is you, Jack… You are to be the pledge.'

৪০০৪

I never saw my father. There was no news of my brother, Thomas, and we feared the Moss had interred him deep within her viscid black earth. But with a pledge signed, within the week Will was released, to return home to bring me to the English March Warden's quarters at Carlisle.

We exchanged little by way of discourse on the ride to my own incarceration. I thought Will was hurting, because his liberty was paid for by my own detention. But I was not unhappy. I held in my mind that I had delivered Will and my father. And I clung to my childish expectation that they would storm the English stronghold with a thousand warriors to set me free.

Our ride together ended just beyond the border, on the road to Carlisle. Where six English garrison men with halberds (the combined spear and battle-axe common amongst foot soldiers) stopped us on the road, and took the English Warden's warrant for my internment from my brother.

As Will and I parted, I remembered his words. 'Mind yer manners. Keep yer pride in check. Learn aboot yer keepers, and ingratiate yerself in their keeping. The road tae manhood is short Jack. Yer road is shorter still.'

And as we said goodbye, my eyes checked tears. But before he was gone, he turned his nag to me. He cast his eyes for a last look at his young brother. He shouted for my benefit and, I think, for the garrison men too, 'The English have the upper hand now, Jack, but we'll restore oor honour... We'll soon be kickin' the English arse.' Then he wheeled his mount and kicked it hard. And as he rode away, he galloped that nag as fast as I had ever seen.

My journey from the border took me, under guard and horseless, to Carlisle, and the office of the English Warden in the great castle. The walled city smelt like pigs. Its streets no better than the floor of my porkers' pen. At *Rickard Gate* we stopped at an inn, so my keepers could quench thirsts long outstanding since they left their sentry posts. Well drunk, they continued my humiliating march to the Warden, witnessed by townsfolk, some with pity in their eyes, but most with a sneer on their lips and insults to throw. One kinder faced old woman pushed past my guard and reached out to me. I thought it was to offer a benign hand to ease my discomfort, but it lashed out at my face and she spat, 'Look the spawn of the reiving scum, *ladies.* Come to meet the gibbet's knot.' Her cruelty and the realisation of my predicament grew a fresh fear in my soul, and a new terror entered my mind.

As I had seen Carlisle Castle before, it was no wonderment to me. But inside, through the gates, were new visions. Although frightened, I could not help but appreciate the sight of them on the way to my journey's end. The castle was immense. The curtain walls made me feel even smaller in their shadows. But within the castle walls, was a beast, and its gates swallowed me up, to throw me down deep, dark corridor. The castle's stone gullet furthered me down into its gut. I expected to travel further down into the bowels of the castle, and to the dungeons, and to horror. But after a while, we ascended into brighter places. Travelled along finer corridor, until I stood outside the Warden's quarters, between two new guards, who did not speak, or even acknowledge me.

One of my deliverers entered the great oak door to announce my arrival. After a while, a short man, furnished with a quill behind his ear and an ink stain on his cheek, came out of a nearby door. He hurried past, laden with paper and leather folders, and I assumed him to be the Warden's clerk. Soon he returned, still with his bundle, but now nervously leading a gentleman warrior; a gentleman, because he dressed as such in fine green velvets; a warrior, because he wore a fine decorated back and breast, or a cuirass if you please, blackened and gilded. His well arranged beard highlighted his vanity, and all was topped with a helmet; a Spanish *morion*, styled to match his armour. Both men stopped to look at me, and the gentleman's voice addressed my guard, while his eyes addressed me.

'You can leave the boy. He'll not be going anywhere while his father remains our guest.'

Then they left me standing, to enter the Warden's quarters. Without a guard to obstruct me, I overcame my exclusion from the room and from the meeting, by affixing my ear to the empty keyhole in the door.

'I beg you sir, not to inflict upon me a runty. An unschooled stripling Scot, who will unquestionably infect my household and corrupt my three young daughters.'

'Captain Traquere. You will maintain my will. You will lodge this child and keep him safe.'

'Surely sir, ransom is more tangible. Gold in the hand.'

'Captain Traquere. I will try reluctantly to understand your displeasure with this commission, but I beg you to understand mine. We prick and poke at the Scots, but we do so at our peril. For it is not England and Henry that will suffer for the deficient war we wage, it will be we with monies and lives to lose. We the unfortunates, who either own borderlands, or are commissioned to protect them... *God help us*. Bad King James, may have seen his army put to rout on the Moss... *God rest his soul*, but this is not the end of it. English gentlemen may prefer the profit of ransom for Scottish prisoners, but it will be a purse repaid tenfold by our English border estates, through endless reiving and looting by the Scottish.'

There was a pause in the voices, and I was feeling the castle's cold. But through the chattering of my teeth, I could hear footsteps pacing the room. I gripped hard my mouth to deaden the sound in my head, to hear more of the conversation and to assign the vocalists.

'My esteemed companions around me believe that we need more tangible agreements with captured Scottish gentlemen, before we release them. All are disaffected with the Royal boot on our necks. It is certain the only loyalty in this realm is assured by family and friends. This far north, we do not have the comfort of the King, unless we kiss his backside and fill his purse.'

'It appears milord, this poor land is a commission to either endure, or enjoy fighting, and not for increasing one's wealth.'

'Surely, Captain Traquere. Warring fattens one's purse, only if there is fat to fill it.'

'Yes, sir.'

'And are we clear on the boy?'

'Yes, sir.'

'I will stress again. Ensure he is kept safe and well treated. To this end, lose his name. His name could be a danger to him here. There may be grudges against his kin, or even friends to see him free.'

'I have a distant border cousin, Brownfield his name. He is a man of little consequence, far away with few friends or funds. I shall say this boy is a bastard son of his, sent for a better future within my retinue.'

'Then, Captain, call the boy, *John Brownfield*. Ensure he uses his counterfeit name, and that he understands his real name will mean his certain death.'

Chapter III

My incarceration was not what I had expected. There were no chains or lodgings in the dungeons of Carlisle Castle. There was no proper watch over me, and I was not subject to mistreatment. There was only indifference. But despite this soft gaol, during the first two years as a hostage of the English Warden, I felt who I was—*a prisoner*.

In those first years, I never saw the English Warden again, let alone the inside of his castle. Instead, I was lodged with his Captain, *Walter Traquere*, some distance away. A subordinate whose continuing resentment of the Warden's charge of my care presented itself in the total exclusion of me from his presence, his sight and his immediate home.

The Captain had acquired a large estate, complete with its tower house, curtain wall and gatehouse by fortuitous marriage. All had been much strengthened by the Captain over the more recent years of his occupation to make safe his treasure; his wife of thirty years of age, rumoured to be his fourth in a procession of wives.

His current wife, Anne, who had inherited the border property, and also larger landholdings in Hampshire from her noble born father, was much aggrieved that she and her husband were forced into occupation of their poorer northerly estates to safeguard their modest yield. She did not favour northern ways, or the people, or the climate.

It was said, despite her disfavour, Anne Traquere was indeed most fortunate. It was so said, because all the Captain's previous wives had been deficient in their production of children, but not negligent in their efforts—all to the dear cost of their own lives. It was rumoured that this was the root of the Captain's prevailing periodic melancholia, and of his current wife's periodic disaffection. However, despite her rude home and desolate husband, Anne Traquere counted herself most fortunate to survive the birth of three cherished daughters. Three daughters, no sons—all younger than myself.

The Warden had agreed, whilst I was held, to educate me. I was given schooling along with a few other boys of richer local landowners, by the Captain's own tutor employed by him chiefly for the benefit of his own children. Religious instruction and Latin were given by the Captain's own priest, a religious man of such extremes that if his wishes were to be granted, every non-conformist, boy or baby, would be burned alive.

The Tutor, in contrast, was a bold, handsome, reasonable man. I was told he was born in London and educated at Winchester College. He was young and an attraction to many of the women in the villages surrounding the Captain's home. Married or unmarried, their lustful eyes would follow him as he passed. He knew of the women's attentions, his eyes would reveal his delight in it, but his applied consideration always seemed to be on his scholarly appointment.

In matters of schooling, my tutors seemed pleased at my competence for education. I already had aptitude in grammar, dialectic and rhetoric from my mother, who herself was well educated against the convention of our homeland. But new to me, such as the sciences, including geometry, arithmetic and astronomy, were a wondrous new discovery that I was keen to digest. Learning seemed easy to me, and I was grateful for the gift of it. Although in truth, the Tutor was weak in sciences and astronomy, and I sought the knowledge of the Captain's priest in these subjects, who was easily coerced with immoderate flattery and a pious performance of such fiction that I thought myself worthy of the theatre. However, in matters concerning music tuition, I was less than a competent student. I appreciated music in terms of understanding form and composition, but when it came to practice and delivery, I was a boy wishing for a dark prison cell––locked away from it all. I hated those instruments, nearly as much as I hated the Tutor's rendition of song by them, or worse by his painful vocal delivery.

Outside music, my tutors appreciated my triumph in learning and thus took greater interest in me to the detriment of the other boys, feeding their irksome dislike of me into a deep gluttonous hatred.

When I was not at the convenience of my tutors, I was charged with looking after the Watch while they lodged in the guardhouse. The Watch being ten of the Captain's troop of eighty horsemen assigned, by twos, to watch the roads lying to the west of Captain Traquere's charge. Ten during the day; ten during the night. Although, if the day Watch ended their duty with a jug or two of ale, they would remain to be joined by the night Watch, and together, would drink copiously into the early hours of the next day, ensuring poor delivery of their duties well into the following morning and, more often than not, well past midday.

My chores were dictated by the Watch's needs, whatever they may be; often this would be running a circuit between the guardhouse and brew house, to keep the ale jugs filled, and to stand at the guardhouse door as look out whilst they gamed and drank.

The guardhouse was on a road leading into a village of slight consequence and slighter amenities; a small collection of fortified bastle houses and a number of poorer timber and turf dwellings with barely a stone course amongst them. The villagers called their home, *Trþenoh*, my gaolers cruelly called it a *Trþig-oh*, because porkers outnumbered the people, and wandered freely as masters of the village to snuffle their way into every house and hut. There was many a time, as I ran the circuit with a full jug of ale, a pig or two would take dislike to my presence (or a like to my ale) and with great zeal charge me down, and I often had to take cover in the very pigpens that should have ensured their safe incarceration. Those pigs were almost feral creatures, with an appetite for flesh, and thus to be feared, but they were selective in their belligerence, directing their warmongering only to those outside their intimate knowledge, thus often provided better watch over the houses than the Captain's own guard, too often finding themselves at the end of an angry snout.

Despite the poor houses, there was a stout church and a small manor that housed a local landowner, once richer than he is—poorer than he was. But it was the presence of the brew house that suggested to me why the position of the guardhouse was chosen. Although, to the village's credit, it was not too far from the Captain's home and therefore probably why it was chosen for my quarters, so the Captain could hide the fiction from the Warden that I was under his close watch.

The guardhouse itself was a bastle house; more substantial than the other bastle houses in the village, due in part because of its isolation and therefore vulnerability to attack. This stone and tiled former farmhouse had shown signs of its purpose. Deep charring around the door lintel and deeper scarring around the small barred windows revealed its past defence of its occupants. Its ground floor storeroom once used to secure livestock from raiders now housed the guard's supplies and provided stabling for their horses, mostly *Galloway Nags*; small horses some fourteen hands high, bays and browns with clean black legs. These were the horses of my kindred, the horse of the border rider, the horse of my father's men, rapid and surefooted, ideal for the mountains and bogs of the borderland. I would tend to the horses needs when stabled and when penned in the paddock behind the guardhouse. And if not watched, I would improve my horse skill by riding bareback at pace up and down an adjoining field cut into the expansive forest, and into the greenwood that surrounded me; an entire land of bark and leaf, bush and thicket, and narrow trails that covered the whole region south of Carlisle.

Above the storeroom was the meagre windowed upper floor living area, accessed only by ladder. The original occupants, farmers, were evicted many years ago when the Warden increased the defence of the area and garrisoned more troops in the people's homes. My quarters had few amenities, and ever present was the stench of the guard, which remained in my nostrils, tainting the food that I ate and rendering habitation within its walls almost unbearable on warmer days. Dirty, for none of the women would clean it, and I would only do as the guard instructed me. Even if this was contrary to my own wisdom to employ my own labour, if the labour was to my own benefit.

My guards were the men of the Captain's troop, although they did not guard me, because to guard would imply I was subject of their attentions, but their scrutiny of me was as scant as their watch duties following a night of considerable drinking.

I was on occasion allowed to share their drinking, and as a result I was often in my bed longer than my duties allowed. My bed; a luxury not known to me—a bed of my own. Not shared with my brothers, or taken away from me when guests stayed at my father's tower. No… I had my own bed. Meagre it was, but it offered me a place where I could retire. A place to escape the waking hours, into my own world created behind closed eyes, or fall into after sharing and stealing the Watch's ale.

I could hear a sound, *boots on the stone floor*. I kept my eyes closed in the hope I would not attract the attention of the sound. I feigned sleep. But sensing the sound may be watching me, seeking signs of waking and not sleeping, I turned over to hide my face. Hide from the sound; the noise of boots approaching close. Finally the sound found its voice and a cruel sound it was.

'Your bed not comfortable, not to your liking, *my prince*… perhaps the straw fill needs changing?'

It had taken me a long while to get comfortable, and his dull wit was not welcomed in my world of the closed eye and sweeter thought.

'It would be mair comfortable withoot the stink. I wish ye'd wipe the dung from yer boots afore ye enter the guardhouse. I thought a porker had climbed the ladder and found its way in.' And I opened my eyes to put a form to the voice, to confirm its owner.

Francis was a man's head on a boy's torso; a slight man of ignoble bearing; mean in body; mean in nature; he spoke clear without dialect; he spoke poor without kindness. He put his boot up on my bed and reached down to pull a single errant blade of dead grass from the toe. He affected a polishing action with his hand, rendering his dirty boots no cleaner. Then he wiped the sole of his foot across my blanket, leaving a rich brown stain. He sniggered and then changed feet to wipe the other boot across my blanket again.

All I could do was watch.

Francis leered at me as he spoke, 'Sorry, *my Prince of Scotland.* My boots were indeed dirty, but now they are clean. No, I am mistaken. I've wiped them on a bigger pile of Scottish dung. I will need to polish my boots again, or better still, you can clean them for me.'

I gritted teeth and remembered my brother Will's counsel. But I was me, and I was seething. 'Sorry sir, I was dreamin' o' Scotland. But now I see yer boots, I am reminded of the reek in here, and the fact yer boots will always leave dung in their path, because ye're made o' dung yerself.'

Francis scowled and raised his hand as if to strike me, but thought again. The Captain's rule about my care was cruelly enforced, and Francis did not like a thrashing on top of a fine for disobeying orders. He simply smirked, turned and walked away without further retaliation.

I was vexed at Francis' retreat. I would have welcomed his fist if it meant my nettling had provoked strong reaction. But as ever, it was my captors' indifference that maintained my frustration. In fact it was only the youths of the village, my only physical tormentors, which allowed my frustration of being kept to ferment into a rich and excellent fury, which I dispensed with fine fist and foot whenever their numbers would allow a fairish fight.

I was often subject to the boys' abuses and their ganging up against me in greater numbers, but they did not outwit me. I never gave them the opportunity or the satisfaction for ambush, because I ran everywhere. I say I ran everywhere—this is not the truth. I ran everywhere except to Church, because tardiness resulted in my place in church being at the door of a full house. Thus my surreptitious exit was assured, and I could steal away into the surrounding trees and hills, whilst the tedious sermonising of the locals by a pious priest kept my young persecutors out of my way.

ഇ◌ര

In those early years, I was greatly sorrowed by the separation from my family. But to ease the pain, the Captain allowed me to write to my mother once a month, addressed as Brownfield, under the watchful eye of the Tutor. I was instructed to reveal nothing in my letters that would compromise my alias, and the Captain would censor the letters carefully. But cruelly, I never received letters in return, and as the years passed and my disappointment grew into detachment, my letter writing faded.

More tangible were the infrequent visits by my brother, Will, sponsored by the Captain within the terms of the covenant of my keeping, to assure my health and good treatment. These were days to look forward to, and my delight, estranged by separation from my family, returned for a while. Will would relay the humour of day-to-day events in my homeland and stories of deeds I thought too fanciful to be real. However he never shared the harsher side of the home life I was excluded from and, despite my persistence, he never talked about his time on the Moss or his subsequent capture and imprisonment.

I always held the expectation that it would be on one of his visits that the news would come of my release, so he could return me home as he had delivered me. But no news came in those early years, and my expectations of release diminished.

Still, I was pleased that the Tutor was instructive in the shifting politics of Scotland and England, and I was mindful that changing situations would test the agreement between the English Warden and my father, so escape was never far from my thoughts. But so too was the agreement between my father and the March Warden. My mother would welcome me home, of that I had no doubt, even if no letters from her would confirm it so. I thought my father would also, perhaps, open his arms, but that would be accompanied by dishonour of an agreement broken by a honourable man. So with a young head filled with sober thought, I made it my purpose to stay in my prison and to live out my time as best I could.

Mistress Brownfield. Forgive my ill writing and poorer manners if I address you incorrectly. For your much loved son, John, has been remiss in instructing me of your correct title, status or rank you may hold.

It is with the utmost regret that I report that malice has been prosecuted by my master, Captain Walter Traquere, against your son, John. I am to understand that your correspondence to your dearest son is not to be released for his pleasure. I am also instructed not to inform John of my Captain's malignity. I am also prevented from passing on your words to John, by way of letters from your kindest person to myself, your humblest servant. But rest assured your son is well and of such fine learning as to render him my finest pupil, mature beyond his years.

I see sadness in a boy parted from his mother, but I have long counselled against the mothering of children beyond the age that mother nature decrees men are men and women are women, that is to say when procreation is able and boys ambitions for liberty of parentage is evident through a question of authority. It is therefore my earnest expectation that your son will quickly overcome his childish bonds to better except his cruel fate.

Your humble servant, Edward Hendon, Tutor,
MDXLIII (1543)

Chapter IV

The strangest of the Watch was Henry Musgrave, although he never was called as such. He was a man not treated like a man, but as a ruined creature. Often mocked within the walls of the guardhouse, he was a man deformed of anatomy and because of it, deformed of spirit. His birth could not be more blessed, born of good parentage, prosperous in fortune. But nature bred crueller fortune, and he was born a runt and grew into a twisted man, a hunchback. The Church blamed his mother's demon lover; *a mare—an incubus—a night demon*, one who visited her in lieu of her own husband. But those who knew better, blamed a history of immoral union within family members.

They said God took pity on his wretched form and built him as big as a beast and twice as strong, and it was also by God's good grace that he found his way, by favour of the Traqueres, into the Captain's troop instead of into beggary or occupational foolery. Those he called familiar, called him Bendback, or Bendback Bob. Others simply called him Big Bob. Few called him friend, but I was one of them.

At first I feared Bendback, for his appearance was one of such frightfulness that one could only imagine it in terrible dreams. Then I avoided him, because I feared his association would bring more ridicule on myself from the local boys. Then after a time, I saw beyond the corrupted form, and through to the gentleness and intelligence that revealed itself only when not in the company of the other men. To the men in the troop, he was simply a war beast, a tool to wield when they felt fit, and as such he was largely ignored, simply endured. Not endured however, was his capacity for emptying the food stores and ale jugs, and the lack of victuals was a constant source of irritation for the men.

Even though bent and twisted he stood as high as Robert and he carried twice the steel of the other riders. He carried no sword, bow or pistol, but instead an ancient tall battle axe; property of his ancestor, reported to be a great knight of the day; and a lance, half a length longer than the standard eight foot. All of this atop of a large bay Flemish horse of sixteen hands named Mars, after the Roman god of War, provided him a fearsome spectacle.

Bendback's tasks were allocated him under two edicts; tasks the other men did not like to do and tasks the other men did not want to do. This meant poor Bendback was assigned task upon unpopular task without respite. His soldiering duties thus involved escort and protection of anybody and anything that did not offer the other men reward in terms of bonus or recognition. If Captain Traquere's tenants, or the local landowners requested escort, Bendback was there, his great tall axe on his back and great spear in hand to deter the petty criminal, who lived by thievery and thrived on opportunity. Any disagreeable labour to be assigned, anything that needed exertion or discomfort without reward, was allocated to Bendback. If it was moving, whether it was supplies moving over muddied road, or carriage over rutted track, Bendback was there to move it, his great horse doing the pulling, whilst he was doing the pushing.

And so we were on the road from the Captain's hall to the guardhouse after tutorial. The Tutor took the ride with us for the air after a heady day with the Greek classics. Bendback, as always, was the escort assigned for the journey to ensure my safety on the road. My companions with me were a welcome pair that day, because at that time they were all I could dare call friends.

The track through the forest was at its narrowest, green in the spring, well shaded in the summer. A path for horse and foot, not for wagon, and Bendback led the way with the Tutor to the rear. I constantly turned to view my teacher, to catch his attention, to talk and learn more about the greater world around me. In those days, I was hungry for any knowledge that dwelled beyond my sphere of understanding. But the Tutor was not for illumination, only for contemplation that day.

I thought the Tutor a man of very good humour, never quick to temper and not subject to outward signs of melancholia. He was a man consistent in his advice, full of self-control and pleasant discourse. A man better for it I thought. The women of the area, those that knew him to converse with, thought him all that too; he with the added benefits of a handsome face, shapely leg and a tongue well oiled with flattering sounds in Latin and Italian; languages he used in fact to hide his true words; his remarks often delivered to tease rather than to flatter. Oh how I pitied all those poor women who foolishly thought they had caught his eye, those poor women ignorant in Romanic languages.

The Captain's priest thought well of him too, with the addition of a respect for his scholarship and for his piety, deep thought and understanding of the Scriptures, as well as his apparent devotion towards the Pope and proper faith. His learning did however, irk those amongst the Captain's retinue who were deficient in learning, and therefore felt intimidated by his knowledge and rhetoric. Francis, in particular, disliked the Tutor. *La'al Francis* (a name I gave him in thought to make him seem less odious) viewed himself the scholarly type, simply because he was the only one with a better degree of learning in the Captain's troop; one who benefited from a priest to educate him in a land where true priest, chapel and school were few and far between.

The Tutor's face was in the air, his eyes skyward. I joined his gaze to see what he was watching, but the pleasing lattice of new spring leaves, filtering the sun obscured my view, so I returned my eyes to the direction of our travel.

The Tutor breathed in deeply then exhaled, letting his words flow on his breath, *'It is good to be outside on a day this good. With good sky and good forest to shade the eye.'*

I smiled at his lyric and joined in his pleasure, *'Good Tutor, do you not get out to see welkin this good, goodly travel in green and wood?'* and I turned to see his reaction.

The Tutor smiled at me and laughed warmly, 'Well done, John, your music making might frighten the pigs, but your words are sweet enough.'

I enjoyed his compliment.

The Tutor let out another sigh and said, 'I'm afraid my tuition and my writings keep me from fresh air, John.'

'Surely sir, they cannot take up all yer time?' I replied.

'I'm afraid any time outside my duties is not for my leisure. So many responsibilities have I, but it matters not. I'm outside today and enjoying the spring green and leafy lane with my favourite student.'

'Thank thee sir, fer yer favour, I'm favourin' you too.'

The Tutor took both his hands from his reins and clasped them together, squeezing them so hard they shook, announcing, 'Then we both shall be friends in bondage of different sorts.' He then released his hands but did not retrieve his horse's reins, preferring instead to let his mount amble at her own pleasure. He then asked, 'Have you thought of entering the Church as a vocation, John? You have a capacity for understanding the universe that does you credit.'

'I'm sorry sir, what I have seen of priests disappoints me. They are either men of extremes, or men of poor morals.'

'Yes, John, they are men, but being men they are imperfect. Only our Lord, the Almighty, is perfect. So forgive imperfect men, even if they are priests. The problem is… in this realm priests are unlikely to be priests at all, but men pretending to be priests.'

Meagre provision of spiritual care in the Marches was a problem long concerning the Church. Counterfeit priests, self-serving men masquerading as godly men were everywhere, opportunists to be loathed for their immoral behaviour and impropriety towards those in their charge.

The Tutor's disappointment showed a little on his face as he continued, 'If the Church does not excite you, John, where will you go when your release is given?'

I replied, 'Back tae my father's home, tae work my father's land, serve his will, marry and strengthen his clan.'

'Those are ambitions of your father. But what of your dreams and aspirations, John?'

I dared not mention my mind to the Tutor, for it would have dishonoured my father, so I posed another question to avoid giving the truth. 'What have I tae hope fer?'

The Tutor smiled at my avoidance and said, 'You seem unexcited about your future, young Scot. I wonder, does the country life not dwell in your soul?'

'I am too young tae think of future. I live each day as it comes. My future is only the next day, sir.'

'Then my young warrior, I will endeavour to look into the next week, to see if I can see a brighter future for you.'

I did not understand his meaning, so I curtailed our conversation by turning away.

The track to the guardhouse continued to be no more than a footpath through the trees. Tracks to local villages, outside the main roads between Carlisle and Penrith, Carlisle and Cockermouth, cut through the forest and thus were sheltered much of the way. They were ancient tracks, well worn and a little more than a wagon wide at best, and they were worse most of the way. They were worse still where they skirted hills, the run off after strong rain creating bog that was a challenge to pass. That ground never dried out, and Captain Traquere pressed any beggar and displaced person into the maintenance of the paths, cutting drainage and installing timber crossings to ease the way.

Outside the condition of the tracks, the green was a pleasure in the spring. It had new form and new life, but it was also a danger to consider. Woods people dwelled deep within the green, their occupation often illegal, but tolerated when it supported the production of charcoal for the benefit of those in authority and those who sought profit from the King's forest. Many poached the deer, but many were called into petty thievery to supplement their own meagre living from the wood, especially if they were lacking in terms of woodcraft.

I thought on this danger many times as I travelled, but to think too hard on danger is only to actualise the fear, and prophetic thought often becomes reality. So I wiped it from my mind. But I was too late. And three such miscreant men appeared from nowhere—three men ahead with evil intent and bows pointing our way.

Bendback dismounted. 'The name is Henry Musgrave. Make way for the boy and his tutor, or I'll be breaking heads.'

The three men stared at each other, and waited for one or another to make comment regarding the big man's request. Finally their faces broke into laughter.

It was the taller and therefore perhaps the bolder of the three men who arrested his mocking hysterics, and faced the hunchback. 'Henry Musgrave is it? Strange name for a devil.'

'Make way little man, you're blocking the road,' ordered Bendback.

'Ye're needin' to pay a toll to pass,' replied the bolder man.

Bendback stood firm. 'You'll get no money from us, thief.'

'I think ye'll pay. Ye might be big, but we're three against ye… Ye and a boy, and a booky on a nag.'

All three men were dirty. They were men no doubt without roof, nor women wed, nor family, nor priest to shape their lives and appearance better. These were the lowest scum and they would not be shy of murder for a few groats, never mind a few shillings.

The Tutor rode up to put his horse between the men and myself—to protect me more than support Bendback, I thought. Bendback wouldn't be for yielding, it was not his way, but a tall axe faced three men with bows, swords and no doubt daggers hidden from view, and the Tutor and I had no weapons to aid him, or skill, or even courage enough I thought to make a difference. The three men did not move and their arrows were drawn to point at Bendback, and I feared for him more than myself.

'Hey you… *booky*, I know you,' shouted the dirtiest of the three men, as he removed his aim from Bendback and turned it to the Tutor. 'Get off your nag and let me see your pretty *fyace* better.'

The Tutor obliged the man. He did not hesitate. He did not seem scared. He simply handed me the reins of his horse as he dismounted and walked up to the thief, straight past the point of the man's arrow to within a nose of the man's muddy face. The gesture was bold and it drew all the arrows aim from Bendback onto the Tutor. The thief facing the Tutor was angered by his audacious move, and his growing violence was apparent. Then the

45

man's façade changed, softer with his recognition of the Tutor.

The thief opened his mouth, 'Brother…'

But before he could utter further words, the Tutor brought up hard, a hidden dagger from out of his sleeve to uppercut the man's chin. The blade disappeared into the man's head. His eyes widened with shock then rolled with death. Immediately the two other thieves let loose their arrows at the Tutor, but the Tutor had pulled back, shielding himself with the dead man still skewered on his knife, and their arrows were deflected. Bendback's action was as swift, and drawing his axe from its harness fixed about his broad back, he ran at the bolder thief as he fumbled with another arrow. Bendback's swing was smooth and clean, and the poor man did not live a moment longer, cleaved heavily by the hunchback's downward blow, leaving a deep furrow of blood and flesh running from his shoulder to his gut. The third man ran; he had no stomach for requital, no courage against greater numbers. Bendback did not have the legs for chase and the Tutor any commitment to further exertion.

'A good cut, Tutor. Was he kin?' asked Bendback as he wiped the blade of his axe on the rags of his dead thief.

'Certainly not, Henry. Only a loon would mistake me for his sorry brother.'

Bendback returned his axe to his back and returned to me to check my condition, to see me well. I was calm, impressed by my escorts' action in our defence. I shouted to the Tutor, 'It was a bold move, sir.'

The Tutor returned to his horse, not smiling. As he mounted he seemed unsatisfied with his actions and our assured safety. He shot me a glance then looked away and said, 'It was nothing, John. The men's dirty clothes told me they were not successful thieves. I concluded they would be poor bowmen also.'

Robbery was always a risk on the highway, but as we continued our journey that day; a journey not meant to be special; a simple journey between hall and house, I felt a new admiration for my Tutor, but also a new fear for a man who was more than he seemed. More secure was I in my procurement of friendship with the other man, not seen as a man but a beast, who was as good a warrior as I would come to know.

ഇൗൽ

Just as I found fellowship in Bendback and the Tutor, there were other men that I was keen to have in my association, either because of their wit, demeanour, or growing kinder attention. The first and uppermost was Robert, or Scottish Rab to his fellow troopers, although I never called him such. He was a young fighting horseman of exceptional skill and command. His charge of ten men, all mounted troopers, respected him deeply, and stood differently from the other men in the Captain's force in their commitment and competence towards their duties. Yes, if any showed any interest in me, Robert did, and because of this, his men did too. Their occasional teasing reminded me of my brothers, Will and Thomas and their often relentless taunting designed to provoke me into scrap and my inevitable trouncing. I would be happier when it was Robert's watch. I would be sadder too, when it occurred to me that Robert and his men might have been amongst the English Prickers, the cavalry that inflicted so much humiliation on my army at Solway Moss and the death of my brother Thomas.

Robert was an economic fugitive from Scotland in an English army, fighting for better money and the companionship of his men, all Cumbrians except Finn who was Irish and by far the insanity that unsettled reasonable conversation. Tom was the humour that fuelled the Watch; Tom Kemp, or Tom the Flirt to his friends. Many a time I could hear the men recite Tom's ballad as they drank and gamed:

Tom who loves the land mair than his wife,
loves his wife mair than the women he loves.
He is so tight of funds,
he'll never use an arrow he can'na retrieve.'

Tom was a fine Cumberland man, a man who smiled away any indignation, and would ruffle my dirty blond hair at every opportunity.

∞

It was my true acceptance amongst the men of Robert's Watch that was a prize I much desired, simply to make my incarceration bearable and honest discourse achievable. Thus I was glad of those days where my presence amongst the men was more than mere inconvenience.

And so it was on such a day amongst days, when the men of Robert's Watch were in the stock field behind the guardhouse, playing at ball.

But they were nine, and I was watching...

'Jack, di'ya play ba'?' shouted Robert.

I returned Robert's call, cupping my hands around my mouth to amplify my shout. 'Aye, I've played with ma brothers.'

'Then come and stand with Tom tae make up the numbers.'

'We'll break his bones. The Captain will be none too happy if we cripple him,' offered Tom as he broke up the group to stand away.

'Din'nae fret Tom, the lad is tougher than he looks,'

replied Robert.

Tom shouted as I ran to join the men, smiling to counter his wicked taunt, 'Tough… I'm not persuaded. But the boy is fast… I've seen him flee from the village lads afore.'

The game was set between two trees, one at either end of the stock enclosure, chosen as our markers. Five players each side, the winners to score best of three, the losers to supply five jugs of ale. We stood the circle around Bendback, holding a ball of leather, stitched around a pig's bladder and filled with dried pulses to give it weight. All the men stared each other out. I joined in the stare, but no one caught my eye, no one thought me a threat to tackle. Then the ball was tossed high in the air, Bendback's great strength apparent. The ball rattled as it flew tall and all the men clashed fiercely together to collect it as it fell.

It was a brutal affair and neither side gave quarter, as each won and lost the ball in turn. The ball stalled a long while in the middle of the field while the men fought over it; such was the equal will of the men.

Robert's team played a strategy, and Bendback was its name. If they won the ball they would pass it to the goliath, who with head bowed would force a way through any men trying to stop him. We brave enough to tackle him, met his fearsome great-outstretched hand as he swatted us away, and Robert and his team would spare no violence in removing any man found hanging on, or blocking their battering man.

The men would laugh as Francis mounted Bendback and hung around his shoulders, and they shouted, *The heifer mounts the bull.*

And, within a bloodied and breathless while, each side had struck their opposers' target with the ball, and the final goal was sought and victory.

Throughout the game, and despite my courage in tackle and tussle, the men never passed the ball to me as they fought and fell amongst the melee. So I won it through swift wits and swifter deed, and I intercepted the ball as Bendback, halted in his charge to our marker by the weight of men on his distorted shoulders, passed the ball to Robert. I had caught the bladder well and drew it in tight, as if by a miracle my puny young frame could protect it from the charging men. I ran as if my life depended on it. I kicked off tackle and slipped through their vicious defence. I pushed on through... Yes, and I ran and ran towards their marker tree. I held breath and burst my heart as I outran the chasing men... and the game was won.

I did not feel the pain of my wounds as Robert lifted me on his shoulders, as Tom hailed my name. The smiles of the men were all for me, and I felt my acceptance amongst them was well won. Nothing could blunt my triumph that day, or take away a new joy found. Not even the gross discomfort and pain of twisted limb and a body bruised could dampen my spirits.

That evening, Robert doubled the prize to ten jugs of ale in honour of my victory. New drinking songs were composed and old ones sung—they all fuelled our high spirits throughout the night. As for the prize, it was well drunk, and well deserved it was.

Robert's men from that day looked on me differently. They sought to include a lad they once ignored, and none would look upon me badly. They even smiled at me when Captain Traquere fined them considerably; a penalty for causing me injury on that playing field.

My dearest Mistress Brownfield. I write to you in lieu of your dearest son John Brownfield, whom I assure you is well, but has been of fever of late and thus confined by it with regards to his responsibilities. I write so you should know this and so that you may not be alarmed by any lengthy absence of correspondence from your son. I must labour that his life is without serious threat, but merely suffers a fever that has rendered many of my master's troop indisposed. Rest assured he bears his pains well and is in the highest of spirits.

There are those who record the exploits of men, whose deeds are of interest to the King, or those of power and good grace. There are those who have gold enough to chronicle their lives. I believe your son is destined to have such a chronicle that will be great amongst accounts of great men.

Your humble servant, Edward Hendon, Tutor,
MDXLIII (1543)

Chapter V

The water was hot, the pain not welcome, and I screamed like a girl to escape it. Meg was not for listening, and she held me in its burning grasp with the strength of a dozen men. No, Meg, the Captain's flinty housekeeper was not for compassion. Her effort was tireless. I was simply another dirty floor to be cleaned, and she scrubbed me with the same endeavour, hard and unrelenting.

Hardly breaking a breath, she said, 'The Master wants ye clean, so shut yer gob and let me wash yer scrawny hide.'

I was not for compliance and I screamed, 'But it burns bad you bitch!'

'Delicate you are, but if you cuss me again, the taste of soap will flavour yer bath worse. Have ye never been bathed before?'

'Aye cauld ones. I've never been boiled.'

Her hands had no restraint or modesty as she flayed the skin from my body with a hard brush that coloured my skin blood red. She took no pleasure in my body, only in the pain she could inflict under order from the Captain. Pain came upon pain as she doused my raw flesh again and again with freshly boiled water, and shock upon shock as she rinsed me with icy cold water, brought fresh from the outside cistern by two giggling maidservants. The icy water put the fire out on my skin and the cold shock finally gave me the strength to jump free of Meg's hold, straight into embarrassment at the sound of young girls squealing at the sight of my upright naked body. But fortunately a man's voice behind me quickly removed my mind from my humiliation.

'Is he clean, Mistress Meg?'

I did not hear or see Meg's response, and I looked to the direction of the voice and saw the Tutor, dressed well and grinning widely.

'You are fortunate it was a hot bath, John. A cold one may have presented your manhood less favourably to these delightful young ladies.'

Meg laughed. 'But Master Tutor, his balls are still hidin'. No, this poor babe has no manhood to please a lass.'

Meg's chuckle was to my ears, merely a deformed cackle, and her observation did not help locate my mislaid affection for her.

Caught by the handsome tutor, the girls giggling chatter turned to hushed sheepishness and they rapidly retreated out of the room along with Meg, drying her hands on a towel I think was meant for me, because I was left cold and naked. The Tutor bowed to the retreating women, and seeing my discomfort snatched up a blanket from a nearby stool and threw it to me as I stood in my watery wood barrel.

'Meg has put some clean clothes for you in the next room. Go and get dressed.'

'Master Tutor, what's this all aboot? Am I goin' home?'

'No, Jack, you have been brought to the Captain's home because we travel today with him to the Warden's lodge, to dine and to stay a while.'

'Why?'

'I suspect Captain Traquere wants to reassure the Warden that you are well in his keeping. So I strongly suggest you comply with this confidence.'

'A bath in the Captain's home, a visit to yon Warden, must be rare important?'

'Perhaps. I am to watch you, to make sure you do not embarrass the Captain. Make sure you do not embarrass me my young Scottish warrior. Speak little, drink less, or I shall inflict Mistress Meg on you again every day for a month.'

The Captain's home, pleasantly situated in Inglewood forest, somewhere between the two main roads leading into Carlisle from the south, and west from the coast, showed much sign of recent renovations. Indeed, it was said there wasn't a single day when scaffold wasn't present, or a builder wasn't plying his trade in the construction of the improvements. The barmkin wall was greatly enlarged with new sections to enclose a larger hall, a new gatehouse, kitchen block and a far grander lodge built to house the mistress of the house and her three daughters. The Captain's quarters were in the square pele tower, the inside of which was a mystery to me, as I was never allowed to enter his home, and I felt perversely privileged to have taken a bath, although painful, in his kitchen.

₧ʘₛ

The Warden's lodge was a contrast in stone and timber, part ancient castle, part recent hall, extended by him and previous wardens; men appointed by the Crown to watch over the Borders and keep meagre justice in a belligerent shire. It was a place away from Carlisle Castle, a place for the Warden to indulge in hunting and to entertain without the City or the King's eyes upon him.

Captain Traquere was not shy on the journey in vocal resentment of the presence of the compound, because he had the price to pay for its upkeep. It was an ancient law to maintain a hunting lodge for the King, and Inglewood Forrest by Royal Commission, was a Royal forest, full of such lodges for poor landowners to maintain for the pleasures of the King and their deputies. Many of the trees were cleared for the accommodations, many more for the extensive gardens laid for the pleasures of the ladies that sometimes would accompany the hunting party; women of better birth; all with immoral fancies; all with husbands at home.

It was a few years after my visit there, a stay of fourteen days, that a terrible fire devastated the lodge. Arson was suspected, because the fire leapt from building to building against all probability. The Captain was never amongst the accused, but I remember his soldiers, Francis and Finn, being out on the night of the fire, and the stench of tar and smoked clothes filling my nostrils in the guardhouse all throughout the following day.

The main hall of the Warden's lodge was set for a banquet, and I was standing small against the maturity of the other guests; men and women, finely attired and not in the functional modest costume of my knowing. The table was set for thirty and the food presented could have fed thirty more. Birds of every size, meat of every type, fruits and breads, jugs of liquids; ale, wine and other liquors that I would come to know better and come to love more. Playing cards were laid out on side tables ready for gaming. Candles lit to brighten the room. The aroma of good food was a better perfume than I had grown accustomed to, and I was thrilled by it.

Captain Traquere had observed me enter the hall with the Tutor. He quickly excused himself from another guest and walked over to where we were standing.

'Tutor, make sure the boy's tongue is sparse in word.'

'I will make sure he does not compromise you, sir.'

The Captain nodded, and without favour in his eyes, or kindness in his voice, spoke to me, 'Boy, that man over there is Sir Thomas Wharton, the Deputy Warden of the West March. He sponsors this party… partly at my expense. He is a loyal servant of King Henry and no friend to the Marches. He beat your army on the Solway Moss and conspires with lesser Border families to feud with greater ones, with promises of land. Because of this, the Marches are further filled with blood, as neighbour erodes neighbour, and Scotland is robbed of its powerful border families. The rewards are great for our noble knight. He is now a Lord, the first Baron Wharton. Mind him well young man.'

The Tutor took me to my seat, positioned in the middle of the table, accompanied with consoling words, 'Do not mind Captain Traquere. He has no love for Wharton. He has precious little love for anyone these days.'

Amongst the seated guests, one could not help but notice a fop, most excessive in his manner, preened and puffed in white. His jewels glittered in the candlelight, more so than any other, their quality obvious. His fingers bore so many heavy gold and jewelled rings I thought it a miracle he could raise a cup to his lips. He was a man I thought around thirty years old, not of this country; his fashion said so. His brown hair was cut in a strange fashion, curled, and his beard was coloured redder than his hair, unnatural in its shade as if it was painted. He drank from his own cup, a fine Venetian glass, and ate his food with a fork, an item I had not seen used before in the consumption of food.

I watched Captain Traquere study the foreigner, deep in conversation with Wharton, as if to probe for a weakness. His study made him absent for a while and he missed several conversational punts that required his return. The Captain missed all as he studied that foreigner, *or perhaps it was Wharton he studied?*

Finally the Captain caught the foreigner's eye, and he asked in a voice designed to be heard above the room's din, 'Are you a Catholic, sir?'

The foreigner broke from his conversation with Wharton to look at the Captain proper. I thought the Captain had delivered the question like an insult aimed at provoking the peacock to offence. Instead the foreigner turned to the Captain and smiled.

'I am what it pleases me to be. I am what my company wishes me to be; Catholic, Protestant, Papist, Heretic or Politic, it bothers me not. I am a convictionless whore. I sell my principles to blend into my company.'

I could see the answer did not please the Captain, if it was an answer. I thought the Captain's question was simply parried away.

The Captain thrust again, 'I cannot believe, sir, you blend. To be as you are in such a violent land of clans, patriots and zealots, without a cause or flag to stand under surely invites death. You must declare yourself, sir, King or clan, Papist or Heretic. What's it to be?'

'You are misguided, *mon ami*, to have a flag or cause in this land only assures one's death. But if it pleases, you may call me a commercialist, without allegiance to country or king. Catholic, but sympathetic to the reformed church, for I feel it sits more comfortably in this esteemed company.'

Sir Thomas Wharton had been listening keenly to the exchange and interrupted, 'Traquere you should be careful not to upset our guest. Monsieur Hueçon is an excellent swordsman and if you put a blade in his hand… you *will* bleed, sir.'

The Captain, in acknowledgement to his superior, bowed his eyes in response to Wharton's rebuke. His discomfort however was short lived, as humiliation took its place, furthered by a small monkey dressed royally in a banded purple and gold velvet jacket complete with matching feathered cap, which appeared at his shoulder to tug at the Captain's jewelled necklace.

I had seen monkeys before in the street markets of Edinburgh, an amusing and far better beggar tool than deformity or amputation, but this one surprised me because of its presence at this fine table and its confidence in its surroundings.

One guest shouted out, 'I see King Henry joins us for dinner!'

Wharton seemed to take offence at the comment and corrected the misplaced wit of his guest, 'No, sir, finally Captain Traquere has a son,' and amused by his own wit, Wharton continued to tease the poor Captain. 'Does he seek his share of the family jewels, Walter?'

But the Captain was not amused, and failing to free his necklace from the monkey's grasp, he drew his dagger.

The foreigner's tongue rushed to the ape's defence, and he exclaimed, 'Kill the monkey, *mais non*, he is the most fashionable here this evening!'

All the room erupted in laughter, the noise scaring the monkey from his thievery, to retreat to the corner of the room pausing only to relieve some fruit from a bowl and a jug, which he dragged noisily across the oak floor. I suspected the jug contained wine, because that monkey was absent for the rest of the evening.

To my surprise, Wharton, who had not acknowledged me all evening, lightened by drink and satisfied by his own drollery, brought me into his conversation with the foreigner.

'Henri, may I introduce you to John, a guest here tonight, or Jack if you prefer, for I know John prefers it.' He swept his hands and head to me and announced me in turn, 'Jack, may I introduce you to Monsieur Henri Hueçon, a French merchant of wines and fine goods. He fills our table tonight with his wares; wines from Burgundy and brandies from the Charentais.'

Discovery of that foreigner's nationality drew a mental epithet into my mind—*Frenchy*.

The Frenchy bowed his head to me in introduction. He then pointed to the beaker before me, filled with sweet, strong liquor that had dizzied my head and would eventually hasten me towards complete inebriation.

'*Jacques*, the *vin-de-liquer* in front of you is an exceptional Charentais grapes blend added with *eau-de-vie*... a new favourite of mine.'

The explanation of the spirit was lost to me. Much was that night. The Frenchy seeing my likely response dulled because of my age and probable ignorance, and blunted because of my state of sobriety, sought quickly to end his education of wine.

'*Jacques*, the Lord Wharton does not offer your full title as introduction. May I enquire your family name?'

I was about to answer the Frenchman true, drunkenness casting my counterfeit name away from my conscious thought, when a bosomy serving girl appeared between us, bending to refill the wine jug, and distracted by the handsome Tutor, spilt wine over the Frenchy's lap.

'*Bastaard!*'

The Frenchman jumped up and added a string of muted curses to his loud exclamation. I thought they were curses for they were delivered as such. But although my French had improved greatly under the expertise of the Tutor, both the Frenchy's accent and words were unknown to me. Conversation was at an end. He was too busy fussing the serving girl to find solution to his stained costume, and I turned my attention to the Tutor sitting next to me.

The Tutor was engaged in conversation with a man of fine features and apparent good manners, who sat on his right side. The gentleman, who had not been introduced to me, seemed well acquainted with the Tutor and they talked like old friends in hushed tones. I heard the Tutor call the gentleman, *Ruskin*, and all the time while they spoke both men would glance at a lady which sat across from them—a very fair lady.

'Ruskin, how goes your campaign with the fair married Anne?'

'I visit her after church services while her husband games,' replied Ruskin.

'I take it she is no longer the virtuous Anne?'

Ruskin's smile grew broader and his voice softer into the Tutor's ear, 'I fear her husband cannot fill her belly with a brat. I suspect she sacrifices her virtue for her own gains… and my *learned* seed.'

'You are so kind to provide such good husbandry.'

Ruskin laughed loudly, which drew a glance from the Lady Anne's male companion, who I learned was not her husband. Ruskin recovered his composure and again lowered his voice below the ears of the guests. 'I try to spread myself carefully, sowing in only the right fields. Good crops only grow in good ground.'

'Do you think the lady's husband will wish you well for this service?' asked the Tutor.

'I think she finds a pleasurable solution to their predicament. But I doubt her husband will see the merit in it.'

The Tutor looked to Lady Anne's gentleman companion. I could see him too, a man caught in the Tutor's gaze, and by his eyes and feigned smile, I could tell he was well aware his lady companion was the subject of the men's mockery.

The Tutor raised his observations of the man with Ruskin. 'I suspect Lady Anne presents her haunches to another stag. She must be fond of her husband to work so hard to guarantee the production of a brat.'

Ruskin smirked and shook his head. 'He has not had the pleasure of the rut with Lady Anne. She dangles him for gifts and favours. Besides, she is already well ploughed and seeded.'

'How do you know this?'

'I'm bedding her personal maidservant too. Who tells me her lady's sheets no longer show monthly blood… She also tells of her morning nausea.'

The Tutor's face beamed admiration for his friend. 'You have worked hard, Ruskin, and it will be your added pleasure to know your bastard will inherit well.'

The Tutor sharing in Ruskin's carnal boasting was a surprise to me. I thought the brandy had muddled the men's conversation in my head. But I heard all correctly. The Tutor was indeed a man hidden within another man.

Ruskin then leaned forward on the table and looked beyond his conversation with the Tutor, wine beaker in hand, to look straight at me. 'And who is this spy who eavesdrops on our private conversation?'

The Tutor turned to me, put an arm around my shoulders and gathered me in. 'He is my student.'

'I have heard of Master Brownfield, the Warden's hostage… and do not fret the reveal Tutor. A secret in this noble company is like woman's chastity, pursued and badly kept.'

Ruskin was drunker than I thought, evidenced as his mouth missed his beaker, but the contents of it did not miss its mark, staining his white collar red. The spillage bothered him little as he turned again to me, this time leaning further forward on the table, so as to exclude the Tutor from his words.

'Ah… education is a path not accessible to the masses. You are lucky. Learn well, *Scot*.'

The gentleman, dizzied by drink, amused me. But the spirit too had its way with me and my boldness had grown in this company of men, and I asked, 'What would you teach me, Master Ruskin?'

'I would teach you to polish your eavesdropping. You are too easily caught listening in to other people's private and *indiscrete* conversations.'

'Sorry sir. I did not mean to listen.'

'No young one, you did not *mean* to get caught.'

The Tutor looked on, smiling to reassure me. Then without further warning Ruskin stood up and raised his spilling beaker to the room, and with raised voice against the chatter shouted, 'This boy asks what would we teach him?'

From one corner came a voice, 'Gamble only that you can afford to lose.' To this the party raised their beakers to their mouths. From the Frenchy, who raised his fine glass, came Latin words, *'Per aspera ad astra,'* and the gathering responded with a repeat, all except the Tutor who uttered different words as he raised his beaker, *'Semper paratus, semper fidelis.'* From another corner came, 'Religion is a chain that will hang you,' and this only raised a few cups and disquiet in the room. Wharton was forced to counter the unpopular toast with his own salutation, 'Keep your steel clean and your genitals cleaner,' and his coarse address caused the room to erupt with laughter and applause, from all except Captain Traquere.

Much of the rest of that night was lost to me, by means of drunken stupor. I recall the Tutor removing me to the guest lodge before the night was over, saving Wharton's guests and the Captain's humiliation from the presence of an intemperate juvenile.

∞∞

The next day, was a day moulded in discomfort, as I recovered my senses and lost much of the contents of my belly and bowels through violent release. However my poor state was fortuitous for the Captain, as he used my malady to excuse me from the hunts and further feasts for the rest of our stay.

Chapter VI

There had been only a few days during my incarceration to spend time at my own leisure, and my exclusion from Wharton's hunting, gaming and feasting at the lodge gave me such an opportunity. It was good to be on unfamiliar ground, without the constraints of the Watch or scheduled tutelage. I would spend time at the river; to fish in better waters and lie on the clipped grass of the Warden's extensive gardens. On those days, lying on the green and looking up at the blue, I could imagine myself in a better place, in a better time, and my disappointment and torments of internment could be hidden for a little while.

It was about four days into my stay at the lodge when the Frenchy came upon me, as I was daydreaming along to the music and motion of the water running the rocks in the river.

'It is a fine day, *Jacques*, is it not?'

The Frenchy's interruption startled me at first. Then I was bemused, not by his question, but simply because he actually seemed to care about my opinion. So I replied, 'Yes it is *Monsieur Hueçon*. The weather suits this fine garden.'

The Frenchy grimaced, and the disdain was clear on his face. 'Is this a garden? *Non*. This is a poor patch of green in a poorer landscape. I have seen gardens that define what a garden should be. Alas this is not a garden.'

I was amused by his contempt, at his manner, and in slight awe of the fact that there existed in this world better gardens than the haven I had labelled my *Eden—my perfect place.* I sat quiet, tongue tied, afraid that I might offer up other opinions to insult the sensitivities of this Frenchman.

However the Frenchy did not allow the silence to last long, because sensing my unease, he spoke again, 'Ah, *Jacques,* you are a fine looking boy, I suspect you have the ladies' eye… *non?*'

I was embarrassed by the Frenchy's flattery. 'Not me, sir, I do not think so, sir.'

The Frenchy thought again on his observation and laughed. 'Ah perhaps not… you are too plain… But there again you have something about you that sets you above the ordure living in this country. So I will gift you with lecture on my world-wise wisdom.'

At first I was resentful of the slur against my neighbours and kin by this peacock, but then charmed by his adulation and engaged by the possible direction of his commentary.

'In civilised society, away from this wretched land, fashion is a tool to attract the eye of a rich widow… or at least a girl with a father's lofty position, or rich vocation to fall back upon. Skill with the blade, although valued by women with virtue to defend, will not impress the gentile woman who will perhaps look upon a man who can dress with… how do you say it?' The Frenchy paused for a while as he looked skyward to find his words, and then returned to his disquisition with words located, 'A more fanciful and *accommodating* eye.'

The Frenchy's self-satisfied look on his face nettled somewhat; so much that I lifted my own head skywards in imitation, and in hidden ridicule to find my own words to describe it. I found only one—*smug.*

The Frenchy still pleased with himself, continued, 'To this end, *Jacques*, a gentleman must have at least two suits. The first one, his daily attire, must be of good riding quality, serviceable and of course fashionable. Burn your hose, *Monsieur Jacques*, because believe me, Venetian breeches will be the newest thing. Hose are so unfashionable regardless of the opulence of their cut.' The Frenchy raised a finger. 'But above all… choose your boot maker well.'

The Frenchy seemed to take his attention away from me, as if a person had called his name. But despite my own careful scrutiny of the surrounding tree line, I could not hear or detect anything that would catch the Frenchy's interest, and wishing him to return his attention to me, and to appear interested in his lesson, I asked, 'What of the second suit, Monsieur Hueçon?'

The Frenchy smiled, then he suddenly twisted to the side, and raised his arm as if he held a pistol ready to shoot into the trees. I scanned the point of his aim to the far right of our position. On the opposite riverbank was a deer barely discernable and silent in its activity. Hueçon kicked up his arm as if he released a shot.

As I thought on his feigned shot, too far for a pistol, but not too far for the Frenchy's arrogance, he returned to his discourse, his smugness continually evident.

'The second suit, *Jacques,* must be fit for a wedding or a royal court, and in truth, it will cost a modest man a year's wage. Of course include shirt of silk with a collar that is as elaborate as modesty allows. If you are in funds, *Jacques,* and funds allow, invest in your clothes.'

At this point, the Frenchy finished with a flourish of his hands rolling down his own attire to end in a courtly bow. With the gesture, I thought he had completed his instruction, but he continued.

'Now regarding hair. You are still too young for manly hair

about your face, but I tell you this, beards are a matter of personal choice. The King wears the beard, so it is the fashion for beards. But regardless of face or fur, see to it that your grooming is of the highest order, with beard and hair cut, *parfaitement*.' The Frenchy thought on his language slip and was quick to correct himself. 'Sorry, excuse my French… I meant perfectly.'

I listened to his address on fashion, but I felt his sermon was badly placed in this poor realm. I thought awhile for a clever riposte, and with newfound boldness spoke out. 'Surely sir, a peacock strutting about this land would bring robbery upon himself?'

The Frenchy simply smiled at my proposal and responded, 'In this bandit country, a finely dressed gentleman may indeed draw unsolicited attention. But those who would perpetrate foul deed may think on again, in case the fine gentleman be well connected and their robbery attract appreciable unwanted attention.'

I was silenced by his reply, unconvinced of its reasoning.

He continued, 'Your dull tunic and gown may serve you well in these bogs, woods and barren hills, but at Court, a shorter, richly embroidered sleeveless cloak with a high collar worn from the neck will serve you better. Remember, *Jacques,* your wits will further your cause, your sword will safeguard your honour, but manners and clothing will always maketh the man.'

My previous boldness in my questioning was short lived, and I returned from ill deserved peer to humble student. 'I will never be at Court, I will never be worthy enough to meet the King.'

'There are many courts and many kings. Titles can be bought, so can places in the courts of kings and nobles. I can see a future for you in many, if you fit the part.'

The Frenchy looked me up and down with careful thought and measured consideration. He seemed to dress me in his imagination. Finally his eyes rested upon my short dagger hanging in front of my waist; allowed for reasons of self-defence by Captain Traquere after the affair with the three thieves. After a few moments, he put his forefinger to the side of his face while resting his chin on his thumb and after a few moments more, exclaimed, *Je l'ai!*

The Frenchy then removed his own sword belt and handed it to me, along with a long knife and its scabbard, which he seemed to produce from nowhere.

'The sword is a newer development of the *spada ropera*, a dress sword. It is a rapier; longer, lighter and thinner than your Scottish and English swords, more fit for the trust than the slash, it will give you distance between you and your opponent. The hilt, you will notice, is swept back in the Italian fashion, which in my opinion flatters the cut of one's suit. It is the sword of a gentleman, and I will teach you how to use it. Use it correctly and it will serve you well.'

I could not believe such kindness, and I could not find words worthy to express my thanks for the gifts. I just looked at Henri Hueçon and my eyes told all.

Hueçon, seeing my emotion, interjected to save my further embarrassment. 'The knife is a Venetian stiletto of the finest quality, easily concealed; stealth and surprise its virtues.'

I held the blades in my hands, and felt the world had been given me, and finally I found some words for Henri Hueçon. 'Such fine offerings, I have no money to pay you or value to reimburse you.'

'Worry not, John Brownfield. I suspect one day you may become a man of means, perhaps of great position. Then you can repay me in deed, or even in service, as I have gold to spare, but am in constant deficit of friends in these foreign lands.'

I did not think on his words. I did not think on their implication, nor that he had used my name proper to seal the transaction. I had a sword. That was all that mattered. I had delight in my hands.

Henri Hueçon was true to his word, and over the following week he taught me to use the rapier and stiletto in the *Bolognese fashion*. He was with great skill, taught to him, he claimed, by the Italian master, *Achille Marozzo*, a name, at the time of my youth, alien to me. I learned how and when to defend and attack, and how to wear a sword properly as a gentleman does. He also clothed me in finer cloth, not as he would wish, but in the best the merchants in Carlisle could provide. Captain Traquere would mock Hueçon for such displays of lavish generosity, but Hueçon would often dismiss the scorn with indifference.

'Allow a man with gold, but no progeny, to fuel his fancy.'

෫෬ඏ

I was pleased to have Hueçon's attention, and was delighted when Henri pressed Sir Thomas Wharton to have his invite extended to include a visit to the Traquere's home. And despite Captain Traquere's vehement protest, it was given. The Tutor told me that the Deputy March Warden coerced Captain Traquere into agreeing the request simply to vex the Captain, and it was apparent to me that there was something between these two men other than mere dislike.

The Captain, in disgust, refused to return home and instructed the Tutor to accompany Henri, and instruct his wife to make Hueçon, *'As uncomfortable as she could manage.'* Of course she did the reverse, Henri's charms not lost on a woman who mourned the loss of a more civilised life in diverting company. Henri's perfect flattery and compelling stories were a gift that Mistress Traquere felt was long overdue, but try as she did to monopolise Henri, he made sure of my inclusion within his schedule, and thus my education was not neglected.

༄༅

It was a fine afternoon, the weather warm and the sun clear in the sky, and Henri insisted I take a walk with Mistress Traquere and her three daughters, to improve my polish with regards to discourse with ladies. So I called on Henri, lodged in the great hall, accompanied by Robert as my watch, Bendback being excused duties that may bring him into contact with the gentle dispositions of three young girls.

As we waited within the boundary of the barmkin walls of the Traquere's tower, Robert kicked his heals and shifted his body uncomfortably in clean clothes and a borrowed cap.

'Dressin' for the ladies is nae ma callin'. Was it that Frenchy's idea?'

'It was, Robert. He suggests we should be clean around the ladies. He is a fine gentleman.'

'A fine gentleman indeed, he poses gud enough. Ye'd think he was havin' his portrait painted.'

'Methinks you aren't too fond of Henri.'

'That Frenchy is nae what he seems. He's like an actor on a stage, convincin' his audience he's somethin' he isn't. Him with accent and dropping French words amongst his perfect English.'

I leapt to the defence of Henri. 'He has been good to me, Robert.'

'Perhaps so, but a man like him only woos those that can dae him favour. What can ye dae fer him that warrants such of his attention, Jack?'

'I think I make up for an absent son.'

'I am nae so sure, Jack. I think ye be his fancy. Watch yerself, the price he request may be more than ye wish tae pay.'

I was unclear to Robert's meaning, so I chose to close the conversation and to ignore Robert's advice.

It was long past our rendezvous before Henri appeared, escorting Mistress Traquere and her three daughters. Greetings were proper, and Henri's attire was perfection in the deepest black velvets, and silks with an indigo hue that shimmered in the sunlight. Mistress Traquere too, was a picture in brownish-crimson, a display far less grand than Henri's, but one I thought designed to attract romantic attentions.

As they approached closer, when gently spoken words could be heard comfortably, Henri removed Mistress Traquere's hand from his escorting arm, and in turn framed his own arms to direct my attention to his escort.

'Isn't Anne a jewel, *Jacques*? Her dress reminds one of good claret in a fine Venetian decanter. The wearer of this dress would never need to introduce herself as a woman of quality—the dress does it all. The richness of the cloth and the opulence of the cut, dress her most royally. I would wish to drink every drop of her in this dress.'

'Monsieur Hueçon, you turn my head,' fluttered Mistress Traquere.

Robert was far enough behind to utter words hidden from the ears of the women and Hueçon, but not from me. 'He would turn mair than her heid, more like turn her over fer a shaggin'. Or perhaps he prefers tae bugger boys… eh Jack?'

I chose to ignore Robert's quip, not wishing to upset Henri or the women.

Mistress Traquere was still responding to Henri's overplayed flattery. 'Monsieur Hueçon, it is of greater blessing to have civilised company within these poor estates. Oh how I miss my home in

Hampshire. Oh how I want to live in a house without walls around it, to see green fields at my doorstep, to smell southern air and touch chalk in the earth.'

Henri adjusted and delivered his flattery perfectly. 'You are a woman with passion, and your daughters are beautiful. I can see you in all of them. But only Eleanor and Edith have their father's looks in them I think.'

'Mary is her father's child. You will see it if you look hard.'

Hueçon turned to look again at Mary, he studied her a while, and turned back to Mistress Traquere. 'Yes, madam, I can see her father now. It is obvious she is the daughter of her father. A noble man indeed.'

To hear the two rich colours speak about Mary and her sisters, also drew me to study Mary as she walked ahead of Robert and myself. Mary did not share the nature of her mother or her father. She was a child of individual attitude; not guarded in her words; one that spoke what she meant, even-tempered and ambitious for herself. I had not paid her heed. She did not have the beauty of Eleanor, or even the prettiness of Edith. But she did possess a spirit more than the other two, and the heart of a man, not to be subjugated.

But as I observed the girls, my ears surveyed the discussions of the leading couple, not quiet or discrete in their dialogue.

'Why is your husband absent from your side? I cannot imagine any company more worthy of his presence.'

'My husband is annoyed with you, Henri… you take him at cards.'

'Yes, the cards favoured me during my repose at Monsieur Wharton's pleasure.' Henri raised his right-gloved hand, spreading his fingers and alternated his palm and backhand under his gaze. 'There again, any hand would look good in these gloves.'

❧❦

Henri Hueçon left the Traquere's home soon after that day, and Mistress Traquere mourned his leaving for a few days after that. She was not the only one, I did too, but we were the few. Robert, and even the Tutor, who originally championed my time spent with Henri, seemed to be much relieved by Henri's departure. I believe even Captain Traquere, on his return, forbade his name mentioned within his home. I thought it all to be simple jealousy of a man. A man more than a man should be in a dour society. However, despite Henri's censure, he maintained his friendship with me secretly, animating my education. He claimed to understand my situation, and with great sympathy maintained his kindness towards me, hiding our relationship from the others, so I would be spared criticism and calumny. I liked Henri, but I never admitted it to others, and I always played down my admiration for this man.

A boy is lucky to have a good father, a worthy mentor. Internment abates a father's influence, but even before that, I was the youngest son, so I never really attracted the attention of a mentoring father. So it is little wonder I unconsciously sought out a man with much to teach of the wider world—an artist who understood the colour of life and how best to paint it. Actually, Henri once told me he was as great an artist as any of the great Italian artists—his material, flesh and the human condition, rather than stone, clay or paint. He recalled new works he had recently seen by *Tiziano Vecelli* and *Jacopo Robusti;* different works in colour and form that had impressed him greatly. He said like them, he too would be the great painter. I would be the paint, and he would help me become a fine painting. I thanked him for that. But I ask you, when does the paint ever have a say in what the artist paints? And even then, great artists rarely work by their own commission.

Chapter VII

Into my third year of captivity, and after the anniversary of my eleventh year had well passed, I found myself more and more settled in my surroundings. All those around me who had frustrated me with their indifference were less mindful to why I was lodged with them, and slowly I became a member of their close community. No one more so than Robert, who had adopted me into the troop as a kind of apprentice, who he tutored in the ways of a Border Horseman, ways that I already had measure of because of my father's training. He improved my riding, and taught me better sword craft and other weapons handling, from horseback and from foot. There were now more days that gave me substance, none more than those when Robert would have me join the Watch, and from the saddle, accompany him with his men on patrol.

During my time lodged with the Captain, the peoples around me—the farmer, woodsman, farrier and labourer, were spared much of the privation that affected the Marches. But there were always constant reminders of the poverty and hardship that other souls suffered. There were days that it seemed an endless stream of refugees, from burnings and lootings, walked through the territory from the north; people with little to their name; wretched peoples seeking sanctuary away from their wasted homes, their belongings bore on the back because beasts had been stolen; crying children, the old and the infirm, women but fewer men. The men stayed to keep safe their stewardship of ruined lands, their families sent south to relatives for safer keeping, or just south away from impoverishment.

Although much of the raiding and looting was outside our watch, poverty did visit the Captain, sponsored by raids to his property in the north, denying him revenue from cattle and crops. Also the spiralling cost of maintaining a standing guard to keep his family safe, as well as his onerous military commitments to the English March Warden were showing. The Captain, in a shrewd move to hold on to his own troops for the sake of his own security and still provide his commitment to the muster, pressed sixty dispossessed and unskilled men and boys into service with empty promises of good pay. He dressed them like regular troopers with old helmets, spears and worn out jacks, and sent them on my troopers' nags, with the poorest of training, to be under the command of Sir Brian Layton, as he ventured to fight the Scot.

I heard many died at *Ancrum Moor* fighting the Scottish army, including Layton himself. Many on the English side pointed accusing fingers at the Borderers, and denounced them for their poor fighting. Condemnation was particularly directed at the Scots Borderers for turning coats on the English who had contracted them to fight against the Scottish force. Robert even said it was some of my father's men committed to the English Warden under the terms of the pledge, who turned on the field at Ancrum; I did not believe him.

However, the Captain's ruse was well discovered by the English Warden who fined him considerably. After that his coffers and resources were so lean that at one point the Captain's troopers were without new nags, and proper pay and victuals for some considerable time.

It was without mounts that we were on the road early, one hour before daybreak. We were on foot—five men and boy on our way to the eastern hills, an area on the border of the Captain's charge. There had been reports of troubles around that area—reports of raids by reivers. Stolen beef and a local church had been looted. The intelligences, reported after the raids, said the raiders were on foot, which had discounted theories of incursions from further outside our territory. There had also been sightings of tinkers lodged within a natural defensible land skirting the eastern hills. A wild area covered by wood, and only accessed by difficult entry.

The cool of the dawn turned into a warm summer's day, and on the road we made good of our footwork. Robert and I spoke a little. He kept my thoughts alive of my home and Scotland, encouraging me to recount my visits to Edinburgh and Stirling with my father and brothers. I appreciated his interest in me, even if I was saddened to discuss things long gone. But being one so young, I felt comforted by his fellowship.

I remember my spirits being high that day, and although the march was onerous, I cannot recall feeling any fatigue. The time passed without time being felt, because our discourse filled my mind and closed my eyes to the sight of long roads, and softened the hardship of long climbs. All I can remember of that time was discourse filled with humour and delight, more so as Tom joined us for a long while, and conversation with Tom always put a smile on one's lips and new intriguing notion into one's thoughts.

'How d'ya like yer march, Jack?'

'It's fine Tom, how's ye coping yerself?'

'I'd feel better on a pony. Ma boots are wearing badly.'

Francis, the smallest man in our company and recently recovered from a bout of fever butted in, 'Aye, Tom, if you would spend a few more funds on your attire and less on the women, you would not be complaining about your feet.'

Finn, happy for spending time out of the saddle, joined in the scoff with his own poorly composed and off-key recital of Tom's Ballad, in his thick Irish brogue:

'Aye, Tom loves his purse more than his wife.
Loves his purse more than the women he loves.
He is so tight of funds he'll use a stone instead of an arrow.'

As ever, Tom smiled against the scoff. No man outside Robert was better respected in the troop. Even Finn respected him. Finn once an Irish kern, contracted to fight the Scot. A mad man with a temper hot and violent, poorly hidden under an easy charm. Born and bred a kern, a light and mobile foot soldier, he was not suited to the horse and he would prefer to dismount at the gallop to loose his bow with deadly aim. The men would tell me tales of his savagery. Told, I suspect, to frighten me, spiced with barbarity to keep me quiet at night when they played at cards or dice. Yarns I thought to keep me mindful of retribution if I spoke badly of them to my counterfeit kin—Captain Traquere.

But for all the troop's wild tales, I knew Finn's madness was real. I had seen him cut himself—to paint his face in his own blood, to stand out at night, naked to howl at the moon. If a man in the troop unsettled me, it was Finn McCuul, more so than even *La'al Francis*, with his bitter and often brutish manner. I never knew if Finn's untroubled smile was real, or simply a show to hide his wanton violence, and his contempt of anything not from his own green and boasted isle.

I had composed my own ballad for Finn. A ballad to remain in my head, for I would never dare to utter it:

'His look was wild and wary,
his wit dull and dreary.
Finn was a scare, son of an Incubus mare.'

Bendback Bob brought up the rear. Big was he, but slow on foot. His joints stiff, his breath laboured under effort.

As we walked and talked, Tom did as Tom always did, fluffing my hair in a kindly manner, but it annoyed me and I suspect Bendback felt my discomfort, because he approached Tom to speak, and it was rare for Bendback to initiate conversation.

'You'll take the gold from his head if you rub any more, Tom.'

'The lad dis'na mind, Big Bob, he's got plenty of hair on his heid to rub.'

By mid morning we turned off the Roman road, and by noon we had reached an inn on our way to the eastern hills. Beyond was a great moor that opened to Northumberland and a forest that skirted its border. Robert suggested we should take comfort of a drink or two before we journeyed on, and he elected to remain outside, preferring his own company for a while.

The inn was dark, but cleaner than most I had encountered. Well-worn tables crowded the room, obstructing easy movement across the floor. We all gathered around the largest of the vacant tables and drew up what stools were around—four only, none for me. Chatter about the inn quietened as the occupants there studied our entry and then enlivened when they recognised us as Captain Traquere's men—local and therefore deemed friendly.

Francis looked at me lost for a seat, slapped some coins on the table and said, 'You're standing, *boy*. Here's some coin. Go bring some ale. But be aware, the innkeeper here is slow to serve.'

I found the innkeeper skulking behind a partition pretending to sweep, whilst through twisted neck he kept his eyes and ears open, not for his customers, but for female sights and sounds in the kitchen. Nagging noises from an angry wife.

It was a ruder interruption I needed to break the innkeeper's guard against his wife's hostile threat, for two politer ones had gone unheeded. But the innkeeper brusquely acknowledged my request for drink, and put down his broom to fill four mismatched pewter beakers with golden liquid from a large clay pitcher, setting them down on a wooden tray. The beakers were full, and with easy travel impossible amongst the scattered tables, I concentrated on not spilling a drop of the precious liquid.

As my eyes were fixed to the ales, a stout dirty hand reached onto the tray and took one of the beakers. I looked to the owner of the hand. Sitting at the table I was passing was a broad man, dirty faced and as ugly as an old pig. He sat with two other men who were half his size but twice as dirty.

I dubbed the broad man, *Pig-fyace*, for he reminded me of my old porker, *Sweet Fyace*—my grand old boar back in Scotland. Uglier than a pig should be, and often to be found dressed by Will and I, in one of my brother Thomas' shirts, to his distress and our childish amusement.

Pig-fyace looked up at me, and a broken toothed mouth grunted, 'Boy, ye're a drink short fer yer mates.'

Although parted by a few feet, his fetid breath managed to fill my nostrils, and my face twisted to escape its sharp and penetrating stink. *Pig-fyace* certainly looked a brawler; an ugly brute showing the scars of many an inn melee with broken nose, cabbaged ears and a brow deep and swollen. I looked at the three beakers remaining and the four men across the room waiting for their ale. I did not want to lose face in front of my men, even if it meant a thump from this brute. But I determined he wasn't looking to fight, after all, I was just a lad, and I supposed he only wanted to humiliate me whilst obtaining free ale. I looked at *Pig-*

fface and weighed up my options. I had no more money for ale. I could ask for the ale back, or simply take it back, as the beaker was on the table unguarded by the man's hand.

Decision made, I put my hand down and reached for the beaker, and as quick as I reached, the man grabbed my wrist snarling, 'Wouldn't steal a man's ale would ye?'

It took all my effort to keep balance and secure the tray with the remaining beakers on the table next to *Pig-fface*, who smiled and looked to his two cronies sitting about him.

'Looks like this little snot has bought us a whole round o' drinks, lads.'

Just then Tom appeared by my side, with a smile and armed with friendly discourse.

'Is my boy giving you cheek, lad? Forgive him. Why don't you crack wi' me instead? Well I say me, I mean me and my friend… *Knocker*.' As Tom said that, the broad ended stick he always carried in lieu of a sword was brought down gently to rap the table twice.

I could see *Pig-fface* thinking on the stick and Tom, who I surmised he knew to be no dunce with regards to fighting. He was not fooled by Tom's affable manner. He knew violence was likely if the most courteous of apologies was not delivered. But to apologise would be a significant loss of face in his kingdom of the inn and other drinking dens of the surrounding villages. His free ale was at risk if he couldn't pay for it by intimidation, and his cronies would disregard him if his presence did not assign protection to them. He shifted uncomfortably on his stool and grunted noises that only he could understand.

Tom not hearing a coherent response from the man spoke again, but this time hostility lightly shaded his voice. 'Knocker needs to knock. Will Knocker knock thee?'

The indifference of the other inn occupants to the exchange now had changed to one of absorption in the proceedings between the two men and the stick. Violence was imminent. Everybody knew it.

Suddenly Robert burst into the inn, breathless.

'Men tae arms!'

The shout broke the tension in the inn, and I briskly left the encounter to gather up my equipment as quickly as I could. The other men of my group hurriedly donned steel before rising to depart the inn with Robert. All except Tom, whose stance remained fixed on *Pig-fyace*, still sitting but now glaring at Tom. Finn, seeing the stolid Tom, interceded to break up the encounter, putting his steel peaked burgonet on his head with one hand and putting his other on Tom's shoulder saying, 'Come, Tom, ma bonny lad, you heard the order, to arms.'

Tom looked to Finn and acknowledged the instruction in his voice and stepped from his encounter to quickly gather up his belongings, joining Robert and the other men outside the inn. I held the door for Tom as he left, smiling and tousling my cap-less head.

As I looked on Finn to join us, *Pig-fyace* rose from his stool gathering words to recover his respect and he sneered, 'Just as well ye're leavin'. I was aboot to ram yer friend's stick up his arse.'

Finn simply smiled at *Pig-fyace* and without any alteration to his demeanour, without any warning at all, brought his steel peaked head forward in harsh contact with *Pig-fyace's* already broken nose. *Pig-fyace* reeled back, his nose marked by a terrible gaping wound, and then he dropped like a sack of grain to the floor, unconscious.

Once all were outside, Robert addressed our party.

'A rider has come in from *Melmerby*. Tinkers… a canny number on foot… They're in the village, lootin'. They've cut a few people, and the farrier has been killed. With spoils and a killin' tae run from, they'll head north back towards *Ren'ick* and their rabbit hole. We can cut them off… waylay them afore they can melt intae the forest.'

Tom broke in with opinion. 'Better we haste to Melmerby… snatch'em while they're ravagin'. There's no guarantee they'll run to the forest with the fells on their toes.'

Francis was quick to oppose Tom's suggestion. 'They'll not be long enough in the village for us to catch them, and the fells offer little cover. They don't know we're on the chase, so with loot weighing them down they'll be keeping to the trail for their return to their forest camp. We can steal ahead of them if we cut over country.'

Tom arrested his argument, turned to look at the way to Renwick and started up towards a deeply wooded hill. All the men followed, and I followed too, at pace.

The sun indicated two hours after noon when we reached the wooded trail to Renwick and the forest; to a stone wall that lined the track. I watched Robert breathing hard, looking far down the track towards the direction of the stricken village, and then down the rutted way that led towards to the great forest. Robert told me later that he remembered that place. He knew of the stone wall penning livestock on both sides of the track that would funnel his target into his ambush, and in turn would give his own men solid cover. He also knew of the trees that would hide the forthcoming violent affair from, as he put it, *the perfidy of outside eyes*.

Robert walked amongst us as we recovered from our hard and rapid journey, and still with broken breath he addressed us all. 'We've made good time… The path disnae show signs of recent hard 'n' heavy travel… Perhaps within the hour the tinkers will pass by… We'll give'em two… If I'm right we'll take'em here. If I'm wrong we'll head back intae Melmerby and try tae pick up their trail.'

He then ordered us behind a good solid and unbroken section of wall to one side of the track. All we could do was nod in agreement, too breathless from our hard travel to question.

A while passed by and we lay whisper quiet, finding comfort in our hiding place. But the sounds of other men and metal entered the quietness of the wood. I took the lead from the others and quietly shook off my comfort and drew myself ready for the forthcoming assault. I was, in my own way, prepared for the fight even though in terms of weapons I was grossly lacking, having my sword, the gift from Hueçon, confiscated by a spiteful Captain Traquere and placed in his safe keeping. But although I was *ready*, I was prevented by order from Robert from taking part in any actual fighting. Even so, my hand was on my knife.

Robert, who had positioned himself nearest to the travel of the oncoming tinkers, signaled us to the ready. But no column of men came marching by, instead the band of men came to rest around twenty yards away from our position on the opposite side of the track. Robert, sensing the halt of travel of the men, and to clarify their identity, peered though a small gap in the rough stone wall to count; fifteen that he could see, all at rest, but still standing with their spoils on the ground, some relieving themselves; passing water against the trunks of trees, whilst others relieved their thirst and passed stolen ale amongst their group. Robert gestured to Tom next to him with his hands indicating ten with fingers spread, then five fingers more. Tom in turn passed the signal on to the rest of the men, but Francis, who had found his own squint hole, held up ten fingers, then seven more.

Robert sat back to the wall and reviewed the situation. The angle of assault was oblique and a little far for us to bring our ranged weapons to bear without deficiency, but to wait would invite discovery and the loss of surprise. Robert remained at his wall listening for a change in the raiders exertions, noises that would indicate them moving on, or possible alarm to our ambush. I could see him hesitate for a moment as he urged, with silently mouthed profanities, the raiders to take up travel again, so as to pass our own position full on. We looked on to our leader and knew his lead would be the signal for action, but we were increasingly nervous at being discovered and losing surprise.

And so it was. Robert made his decision and he rose to his feet stretching his crossbow arm over the wall and his dart found its target, squarely in the middle of a tinker's back, dropping him to the ground. Then almost immediately, Tom and Finn's bows appeared and directed arrows into the enemy. Wheel lock pistols then rang out, but only delivered noise and smoke; shots running wide, with the exception of Francis next to me, who with a wheel lock in each hand, put a shot firstly in the left eye of the only tinker that was facing our position, and with the other pistol, shot wide and left into a tree and de-perched a fat pigeon in a cloud of feathers.

The fourteen tinkers still standing after the first volley quickly rallied to respond, but another two arrows from the wall side reduced their able numbers further. The twelve remaining without injury or still fit to retaliate, not knowing the strength of their ambushers, thought better of a hostile response, panicked and took retreat leaving their loot behind as well as their dead and wounded comrades.

Seeing the flight of the men and sensing a complete rout we climbed over our wall—our hardcover, and crossed the track to the fallen men and their scattered chattels. All except Bendback Bob, whose frustration at his inability to climb the wall resulted in him shouldering the wall and knocking down a good two yards of stout dry stone.

I could see Robert, as he crossed ahead in staggered line with us, counting on his fingers; three obvious wounded and incapacitated, and two apparent dead. He looked onto the direction travelled by the retreating tinkers and I figured he was thinking on what their reaction may be. We could not follow, with surprise gone, there were still too many tinkers to assure our own safety.

I could hear Robert berate himself as he considered the poor execution of his own actions. Poor, because too many had escaped and justice would escape them. Poorer, because the tinkers may regroup quickly and return to reclaim their booty and challenge Robert's four men and a boy. His annoyance at himself was so apparent that he paid scant attention to the pleading and cries of mercy from the wounded as he reached Francis' kill. He studied the grotesque black smudge that was once an eye and he marked his fascination with the strangeness of the wound with a tilt of his head. Then he looked at the pile of pigeon feathers on the ground to the left of the fray. Robert then raised his observations with Francis who was close by.

'A perfect shot, Francis, but the other astray, seems yer fever stays with ye.'

Francis joined Robert at the corpse and shaking his head said, 'Not perfect at all. I was aiming for his right eye, it was the one that had his daddy's glint.'

'And the bird?'

'I was thinking about my dinner. Fancied pigeon, with greens from the field over yonder.'

Robert smiled, as he knew Francis' claims were not fallacious and all his shots had met their intended targets.

I avoided looking at the fallen and wounded tinkers, because I was frightened by their distress and wounds, and instead watched Robert look about himself at the carnage. He then instructed his heedful men without a word, but with a forefinger drawn across his throat. And thus he ordered the butchery of the wounded; broken men, low born, without kin or clan to see them worth a pound or penny in their saving. No value in life had they, so a prompt death was a better road to maintain thrift within the law's purse; better than rightful trial, and the keep of such pitiless souls in death's waiting—only to dangle regardless, on the gibbet's knot.

Francis, Tom and Finn took their positions over the three wounded men, and I looked away from the murder scene. Suddenly the audible pitch of a choked scream alerted my ear to the activities around me. I could not help myself and turned to see Finn smiling, kneeling over the recumbent body of one of the wounded men. Finn's left hand was roughly lifting the poor man's head by means of the collar of his tunic and his right hand was slowly slotting a dagger into the poor man's mouth, which erupted red to a chorus of blood tuned gurgling. I could see the sight of Finn's amusement of the execution disturbed Robert, but he held back an immediate chide as he was always careful to choose the time to rebuke his men.

Instead Robert left his position and travelled to stand over Finn, as he bathed in the blood-scented air of his slaughter, pleasured by the sight of his victim's pained and horrified eyes. Robert with disenchantment in his voice said, 'It does me poor tae see ye enjoyin' killin', Finn.'

Finn turned from his butchery and replied to Robert's disappointment, 'He called ma mammy a whore.'

Francis, who had joined Robert after despatching his charge, interjected with a quip, 'Your mammy was a whore, *ye sad-Irish*.'

Finn nodded and withdrew his knife, wiping the bloodied blade on the jacket of the dead tinker and replied, 'Aye, perhaps so, but he was in no position to call her such to my face.'

Tom dragged his wounded prisoner to the base of a large oak tree and propped him up against its wide trunk, wiping the dirt and hair from the man's clean-shaven face. He then drew and held his dagger to the frightened man's throat.

'Rab, this one's a *Kemp*, one of my family. I recognise him from a gatherin' years back. I am saddened to see him here.' Tom stood back to look away and then dropped his head soulfully. 'This bastard land breeds broken men, turns good family men into clanless thieves.'

Robert looked to Tom, and I could see he sympathised with him and even the Kemp kinsman held under Tom's knife.

'We're all thieves, Tom, but we've a headman and a warrant tae kill thieves. These poor bastards settled on the wrong pickin's. Dae ye want me tae let him go?'

Tom looked at the tinker. 'Nah, the farrier was a gud man,' Tom hesitated a little not taking his gaze from the fallen man, 'Never liked his side of the family anyway.'

For the first time since the fray, Robert looked at me, and then he studied the wounded man in Tom's charge. He looked back at me with a look that frightened me. No… it terrified me. I had never seen a look so monstrous on Robert's face before. Robert just stood, glaring, and then broke his gaze on me to look onto the other four dead tinkers.

He then looked at me again, deep in mournful consideration and said, 'Have ye ever killed a man, Jack?'

My eyes widened and I could only reply, 'No.'

Robert's demeanour towards me was hostile, as if I was to blame for the scene around us.

'Did yer daddy teach ye how tae cut a man clean?'

The fear of what was coming wiped my memory and again I could only reply, 'No.'

Robert softened his voice a little and said, 'Well if ye are tae be a man in my company ye better wet yer knife.'

Robert walked over to me, pulling me harshly towards the

wounded tinker and he knelt by him ripping open the man's jacket and shirt, whilst maintaining his strong grip on my arm. An arrow protruded from the tinker's stomach and he was bleeding profusely. It was a bad wound.

Robert commenced his instruction. 'The greater the bleed the quicker the death. Cut the main arteries and he'll fade faster and die quicker.' Robert then pointed to the arrow. 'Holes tae the stomach are unreliable unless ye can rip a bigger cut, never a quick death… painful and slow. There may be enough strength in him tae cut ye back.' Robert then looked into the tinker's eyes. 'Isn't that right, Tinker Kemp?'

The poor man could barely acknowledge Robert, because even though his eyes were open, I suspected him to be nearly unconscious to his surroundings.

Robert continued, 'Jack, there are six good cuttin's on a man,' and as he said this he pointed out the arteries on the neck, shoulder, heart, arm, wrist and thigh. 'Cut in these places and cut deep… and ye'll kill yer man. Now draw yer dagger.'

I drew my knife and my whole body shook and trembled. Robert then roughly guided my hand and knife to the man's chest and jabbed the point of my dagger into the man's skin, just below his heart.

'Push up and push hard, Jack. Put this poor bastard oot o' his misery, because alive or dead we're stringin' these worthless tinker-beastie-thieves up on the trees, so their friends can see the English Warden means business. Send him quickly tae Hell… and save him the waitin'.'

I looked into the man's eyes. I could see he was fading further into unconsciousness through the loss of blood from his stomach wound. But as Robert forced my hand harder into the man's chest, his eyes widened and a sickened scream issued from his mouth. My head started to spin, blood hot in my veins. Sweating accompanied nausea and fear fronted my own near fainting.

Robert pressed me. 'Jack… *dae it!*'

New pain and Robert's shouting seemed to return the tinker to consciousness, and he looked at me with piercing bright green eyes.

'Ah, Jack, i-it's you... G-g-glad t-t-to see you well.'

I did not recognise him at first, but the eyes and voice were unmistakeable, yet I could not believe. I shouted for him to speak some more, to confirm my identification.

'Willy?'

Robert, seeing my hesitation, brought his head close to my own, and fired hot breath and spittle against my cheek. 'Kill him ye little turd. Dae it quickly. Kill him.'

I turned to Robert and pleaded, 'But I know this man. He saved me once.'

'Then save him a slow death, and send him quickly tae Hell or tae Heaven.'

I turned once more to look upon Willy and his eyes were closed to me. I hesitated still. My head and heart held my knife back against the restraint of Robert's hand maintaining force on my own, preventing me removing the blade. I could feel the anger of Robert, the pressure. So I yelled to summon up all my adolescent strength to drive home the knife. I screamed hard to quell the restriction in my soul. I shouted loudly to drown out the man's quietus. And I closed my eyes on Willy and pushed hard upwards on the hilt. Tears filled my eyes. My mouth broke into sobs and wails. I sensed his life ebb at the point of my blade. I felt him die.

The screaming in my head only stopped as I opened my eyes. Willy was lifeless and I pulled my blade free of his blood-covered chest.

I vomited.

Tom spoke to recall me back from the horror. The rest of the scene remained lost to me, except the puke by my knees. I remember Tom putting his kindly hand on me, looking mournfully towards his former kinsman saying, 'He'll be with his ancestors now lad, and family lost to him.'

His words sank my head into my hands, to hide the sobs, to hide my shame. But muffled through sodden hands and quivering mouth, I cried, 'I knew this man, he was a kindly soul.'

And Francis in a rare moment of compassion said hard and clear, 'Boy, men are not born bad, but bad becomes of men born in this land.'

But his words did not ease my remorse, nor did Robert's hand joining with Tom's on my shoulder to comfort me. No, nothing could console me against my foul act against a friend, murdered by me. Not even Robert's kind manner returned after a terrible lesson tutored.

'Dinnae mourn fer the dead, it's the livin' needin the grievin'.'

Tom picked up and held me like my father never did, and he softly said, 'Dinnae fret, Jack, it gets easier lad.'

I am sorry to confess… it did.

Chapter VIII

Deep winter was not a time for travel. The icy rain, winter snow and cold of the night made journeys both hazardous and difficult, particularly after the first snows. But in some respects, safety was assured as much of the human hazard was removed. Because, although the raider plied his trade best from October to March, when the land froze, the thief and reiver would tuck themselves in their beds with a bowl of potage and warm ale to keep in the comfort; there were no easy pickings in the snow. Travellers sparse, the stock corralled, and tracks and roads lost in the white. The land was a pure place in the snow, feature blended into feature, man's scars on the land wiped clean under a blanket of perfect colour. Man required shelter and without its walls, its roof and fire, he would perish.

Yet despite the difficulty of travel, I was on the road to Carlisle and, as ever, Bendback was at my side to see me safe. My pony was working hard to pick her way through deep snow, made deeper by a cruel wind that filled the sky and piled white against white, and disguised feature and direction. But my journey was for my pleasure and I knew Will would be making the same efforts to make it my pleasure.

The nature of our meetings had changed since Will's battle

service at *Ancrum Moor*. Although never said, I thought he resented me a little. It would not have been easy for him to fight for the English; in a service honoured under a pledge with the English Warden, under the direction of Sir Thomas Wharton, a man he despised. It would have been unbearable to wear the St George on his jacket, to ride under an English banner. But still he was faithful to me, and even though the Warden and my father no longer sponsored our visits, he would still travel to see me. These meetings were only about brother meeting brother, by our own mandate, free from constraint or report, and Carlisle was our meeting place; it offered cloak and security from prying eyes.

The winter may have quietened the world, but not the alehouses in Carlisle. They were full of poor ale, and their walls heaving with degenerates of all professions and guilds. As I warmed my hands around a bowl of hot potage, I was keen for news from Will, and even though bitter thoughts of abandonment often formed a cloud over my days, I still enquired about my father in the hope he had shared a kinder thought with my brother; thoughts of regret and painful separation.

'How is father?'

'Tired. Wore oot he is. He barks but disnae bite.'

'What ails him?'

'Nothing tae discuss in the ale rooms o' this English city.'

'Please tell me, Will.'

Will's tone was sharp in his reply, 'There is nothing tae report, so dinnae ask, *brother*.'

Will's rebuke hurt, and my grey cloud, well banished as soon as I saw my brother, returned, provoked into storm. 'Six years have passed, Will, and I have received no news of consequence from you. No correspondence from my mother, no word from father.'

'Dinnae complain so much, Jack. Ye're havin' a softer life... be glad of it.'

'Yes, as a hostage.'

'Aye, as a hostage, but dinnae grieve on yer condition. We're all bound by chains of different sorts.'

'Chains... me interned... you with freedom... what *are* your chains, Will?'

'Pains of loss, like us all... Loss of pride, honour and principle.'

My anger abated with the look on Will's face, and the sense of sorrow sung on his words, and my wrath gave way to charity. 'I am saddened you are not how you would want to be.'

'Never mind, eat yer slop, quieten yer tongue. Ye're lookin' gud in yer velvets, Jack. Soft chains ye have. A gentleman's sword tae carry, and diction free from yer source.'

Will looked about him. The drinkers were engaged in their own conversations, and Will was satisfied no one was listening to theirs. 'Is yer hunchback aboot?'

'Bendback stays away from alehouses he is not familiar with. He avoids the ridicule and revilement of strangers.'

'Yer beast has brain enough tae stay in the shadows.'

I chose not to defend Bendback. I was ashamed. I simply nodded in forged agreement.

Distractions grew in the inn, as conversations grew into a heavy tune that drowned out easy discourse, and ale that blurred good thought into dizzied judgement and poor picked words. The effects of the strong ale regressed my mind to times long gone, and I easily returned to the self-pity of an internment, that in truth was long past mourning.

'I thought my freedom was assured when we met at *Banksop Foot,* on that iniquitous *Truce Day,* but it too was a dream lost.'

'Mustn't fret, Jack, aboot opportunities well past. Fate is what it is, accept it and ye'll be happier. Drink mair and ye'll be happier still and remember less.'

'Yes, I suppose you're right. It disappointed me to remain in the keeping of the Warden, but I am content in it. I have learned much.'

'Aye, Jack, the Devil has changed ye… Ye dinnae sound like ye were. Ye dress like a popinjay, but I see quite the fightin' man, wi' skill no doubt.'

'Yes, the bow still escapes my artistry, but I am good with a pistol, better with the sword.'

'I suppose ye'll be lodging at the expense of the Warden tonight?'

'With weather too bad for travelling, I'll be lodging at the castle with Bendback. The castle kitchen with its fire if I'm lucky, the stables if I'm not.'

'Aye times have changed, I can remember ye would rather sleep with yer pigs than lodge wi' the English by choice.'

Even through my fading sobriety, I knew Will's displeasure with his enemy would drown our conversation. I knew of no Borderer born, no one more nationalistic than Will. I knew of no man who had found a greater feud with another nation, rather than with a neighbour, with deep rooted grudge and quarrel to consume one's hatred. But I knew of no Borderer that I respected or loved more than Will. I favoured our fellowship, but not our disagreement, so from that point in the evening, I drank more and spoke less. The morning came quicker that way. Fortunately I had a goodly guardian to carry me safely to my bed, and fearsome enough to ensure my place in front of the fire was assured.

*[**Truce Day**; a story under its own title.]*

൭൦ൈ

As the years marched on, thoughts of home faded. My life became my own and I accepted it as my fate. Perversely, I was to recall in later life that I was fortunate to be held hostage, safe in another's keeping. Safe, because I was free from my family name and the responsibility that it held. For Border names always came with discord. And discord forever erupted into bloody feud. Instead it was the Tutor who became much more family to me, as he mentored and schooled me well. My ambitions no longer dwelled on my father's estates, but a wider realm of travel and greater fortune. Desire growing day by day to seek the extended world and what sensory treasures it could offer. Even my counterfeit name was mine by my own choice, and I did not think much on my past identity. My real name abandoned, as I had been by my real parents. Yes, I was John Brownfield, or Jack. No other name would do.

I was not an ugly boy. The Frenchy's oily tuition had provided me with charm to employ upon the girls I fancied. A few were accommodating, and with ale and cider to coerce my prey, I was able to loose my lusts freely and capably.

Robert made a fair trooper out of me. Fighting was a skill learned, but not the only one, as I did not exclude anything that would inform me better. The edges were knocked from me and polish applied. My accent was killed, my stride improved and my appearance was more of an English gentleman than a Borderer. But I still wore border armour well, and much of the condition and spirit of border folk remained within my soul.

Reports from the Tutor, Robert and the Captain's own priest were favourable, and even the Captain seemed to slightly soften his aversion towards me. At the age of fourteen, I had become more a trusted trooper in the Captain's employ rather than, to most at least, an unwelcome hostage. However the Captain's newfound approval was not without limits. He did not care for my attentions towards Eleanor, his eldest daughter. Her maturing charms were not lost on me, and respectful association during our lessons had grown into close attachment.

Eleanor and I enjoyed the land. We would ride the hills and walk the woods in secret around the Captain's home, under the safe keeping of the Tutor, who hid our private meetings from the Captain's eyes. Our friendship grew into fondling, but innocent love it was, honest and true. I reserved the rut for the village lasses and my love for Eleanor.

To be with Eleanor more I had to endure the company of her younger sisters, Edith and Mary. Their childish and priggish manner irritated me, and their games were only to be endured for the sake of a chance moment with Eleanor.

After tuition, the girls' nurse and the Tutor would allow dancing, 'to exercise the body and teach me better manners.' I would act the noble courtier, a foolish picture perhaps in poise and charm. The Captain's wife would participate, very adept at the dance and knowledgeable about those performed at Court; dances such as the *volta, pavane*, and *galliard*. In good weather the practice would be on the lawns outside the hall walls, accompanied by one of the Traquere's stewards, an able musician skilled on the rebec, lute, flute and viol. But more often by the Tutor with his flawed singing voice. Mistress Traquere would lead the dance and her children and I would match her steps. This day though, the Captain's wife beckoned me to stand aside her, to take her hand softly, and looking ahead to our audience—the trees, she asked me to lead. And as we commenced a gentle *pavane*, her discourse punctuated the deliberation of the dance, low spoken and flowing, so as to allow proper count and concealment from all but me.

'*And one . . .* You dance badly, Master Brownfield . . . *and two.*'

'Poor at the dance I am . . . *and three——four——five . . .* I admit it. But I seem poorer . . . *and one . . .* only because my teacher . . . *and two… is so accomplished… and three—four—five.'*

'A gentleman knows how to dance… *and one…* Your northern jig… *and two…* will not impress a lady… *and three—four—five.'*

'I fear the Tutor today… *and one…* marks time badly… *and two…* He is no musician… *and three—four—five.'*

Mistress Traquere looked to the singing tutor, his face showing his own belief that he sounded sweet. His eyes and ears closed to the truth—the crows sang a more melodious tune.

The lady frowned. 'Yes, he hums a poor tune, and taps an awkward beat.' She lost her step—missed a skip—cussed politely, then counted her self back into the dance, continuing with more mocking words to accompany her steps.

'*One and two and three…* Perhaps he too… *and one…* is suited to the northern jig… *and two.'*

'You do not like our jig… *and three—four—five…* Mistress Traquere?'

'It is well suited… *and one…* to this coarse land… *and two*, but not my girls.'

'But the jig… *and three—four—five…* is a heady dance… *and one…* and much more invigorating… *and two…* than this soft dirge… *and three—four—five.'*

'Yes, Master Brownfield… *and one…* a jig will spin a girls head… *and two…* But art and craft… *and three—four—five…* are devoid from its footwork.'

'But surely a bold step… *and one…* is better than a dandy one… *and two.'*

'Certainly, if it be dressed… *and three—four—five…* in a rich slipper, or is powerfully placed.'

The Tutor's singing had eroded my appreciation of the music. It irritated me, and although my aplomb in the dance remained, arm and body, foot and head moving light and sure, I knew of the game. Hueçon and the Tutor had instructed me of the ladies who talk indirectly, who fence with their words, feint and parry. But enough—my nature was born in the Marches, direct speaking a virtue. Time to end the game.

'I fear your veiled message is a clumsy one, Mistress Traquere.'

I waited for the retort, maintaining my poise and position in the dance. I waited for offence to be taken and action to be taken against me. Nothing came, and I broke my gaze from ahead to look upon the Captain's wife.

Mistress Traquere smiled, 'I am impressed you have the wit to discern, but saddened you have not the grace for the courtly dance.'

'I must respect your observation madam, but time will tell if I can step the pavane in the same company as my teacher.'

ଧୋଡ଼

For all I enjoyed new teachings and the commune of peoples new and familiar, it was the nature of the land fashioned by God that was my credo, more so than the word of God as taught by the priests and other godly men. The land of my confinement was different from my homeland. Much of my moor was absent and the marsh not so prevalent. The forest surrounding the guardhouse, stretched from the sea to the mountains. Much was assigned to the hunting grounds of the King, and protected as such, some to the landowners and nobles who bought and sold the timber as a commodity to increase their wealth. Some areas were cleared for arable land, for grazing, for homestead and for better defence. There were also the secret places for those who sought the forest out as their home; woods people, who lived out their lives by the grace of God and His issue of nature's wealth.

But for all of it, the forest was an enchanted place, a place to disappear, a place to be able to find solitude for oneself away from inquisitive eyes. Yes, the forest was always a part of my life in confinement; it was the backdrop to the tragic and comedic plays of my interned youth, its acts and scenes shaded by its greatness.

෨෬

The Captain's coach had been at rest at the guardhouse for over an hour, perhaps more. The horses needed resting and the passengers too, as the journey had been none too kind from the coast. The Captain's wife and her three daughters were out and about the coach, stretching their limbs, battered by the misery of rapid coach travel on poor roads—rapid, because it was the safest pace to travel; the roads increasingly full of beggars, tinkers and thieves; products of an increasingly tormented land.

I was glad of the chance to fuss around the Captain's daughters, one more than the others, for Eleanor's unexpected presence at my quarters delighted me, and I took whatever opportunity was given to ingratiate myself in her particular blue eyes. The Captain's wife seem to enjoy my flattery of her daughter, and I thought my clumsy attempts at being a polished gentleman had perhaps convinced her I was a worthy suitor. I say clumsy, but my modesty in such matters is misplaced, because the Tutor and Hueçon had taught me well, and I shined out from the other boys of age, brighter than even the boys of better breeding.

But in the advancement of love, events not within one's control can often be a greater ally than the teachings of a grandiloquent Frenchman, or an affable tutor.

I was deep in conversation with Eleanor, when the activity around us alerted me to events beyond the simple resting of a coach and its horses. Eleanor could see my mild alarm.

'What's the matter, Jack?'

'There's something wrong.'

Robert approached, hurried and concerned. 'My apologies... but have ye seen Mary?'

'No, not since we alighted the coach,' replied Eleanor, running her hand through her robin red hair, set free from her linen coif, reluctantly worn whilst travelling.

Robert looked to the increasing activity around him. I was worried.

'What's up Robert, have we lost Mary?'

'Aye lad... it seems so.'

Robert was about the assignment in a moment, directing the men around him and the coach driver to the task. He sent them to check the paths into the surrounding trees and directed Francis to guard the ladies.

'Jack, take tae the trees tae the north, search the trail tae *Bewaldeth*. Look well lad, the forest will darken in a few hours... nae place fer a young lass.'

I offered no reply, but before I could set my travel to the trees, I felt a hand on my arm and turned to see Eleanor.

Her eyes pressed her words home. 'Find her Jack—I beg you.'

I ran through the forest. I took the trail suggested by Robert and found nothing. The evening sun through the trees cast confusion before my eyes, but no alien creature could I see in that wild place, no bright hues in a palette of greens. I kept running and shouting, until I could run or shout no more, until cramp stabbed my guts, and a fierce pain filled my chest and stole my breath.

I shut my eyes. I took a long inhalation and drew in the moist breath of the forest. I opened my eyes. I looked to the trees and my fancy asked them for a direction. I then thought on Mary, a girl in skirts walking.

She could not have come so far.

I looked back along my path and thought again on the redoubtable Mary and ran back to look for other paths; paths that I might take if I was her. Paths that showed promise of ways to more enchanted places. I ran some way back before I came upon a deer track, a path through the bracken. I thought again on Mary.

Would she have walked through such a difficult track?

But then I looked on through the track, through the trees, to the sun shining a pool of its warm glow on an old oak tree, showing strange in the harsh shadows of the late evening sun.

Yes, I would travel this route to see the tree, the old man of the forest. I would journey awkward to touch his bark cloak and visit his seat amongst the hidden places of this ancient wood.

And so I ran to meet him.

There was a clearing of sorts. It was a place one might rest awhile. But no one answered my call. No sign of Mary was there. But the ground was disturbed. Something had been this way this day, *a hog, a deer, a poacher.* I was not a skilled tracker. I could not tell. I walked on past the oak tree, so queer in the dappled light, onto the track that lay behind it. I called again, but no one responded. Even the forest animals lay quiet.

After a while the track diminished, and I was lost to know where to go. Mindful I was, that even I, so familiar with the forest ways, was not secure against losing my bearings. But I wanted to find Mary. I needed to find Mary more than I wanted Mary to be found. Selfish thoughts, but I wanted to find her for myself, to be a hero in Eleanor's eyes.

I rested, knowing she could not have entered so deeply into the forest without an easy track to follow. Then again I shut my eyes and thought myself as Mary. So strong in character was she. Not a girl born for the land, but certainly one gifted of sight into the beauty of it. She had irritated me often, but it was her childish ways that made her so. But as the years had travelled, she had left her priggish, childish temper behind. A much more determined girl she had become, handsome and bold.

I opened my eyes then saw a way. There was a track, clear to me now, and a sight of blue beyond the trees. I travelled it quickly and found myself in a clearing.

Bluebells.

It would have been a place to stay—a fine place to lie and look up through the gaps in the trees to watch the sky retreat into night. On any day that is, but not today. I scanned the edges of the clearing to look for other tracks, and then a colour. Green. Not a green of the forest, but a green of a clothier's making.

She was bundled on the ground, not moving, and I bent down to see her. She was quiet, but not sleeping. It was not until I moved her, to free her from the earth, that I saw the monstrous iron around her leg. A mantrap had caught her. An ancient mantrap I thought, laid perhaps many years ago to catch the poacher working the King's forest. There were many laid, and many found innocently. At times, the men of the Watch would find a poor soul caught, often too far-gone to aid. Many were crippled; those not freed would die slow, their rot to add to the forest floor.

Inspection of the mantrap revealed its age had lessened its power, and a past fallen branch within its jaws had broken its bite on Mary's leg. These things coupled with the thick layers of skirts had saved Mary from a wound. Perhaps the leg was broken.

I did not want to leave her. To leave and return would mean night would be on us. So I searched for a stout branch and worked on the trap's jaws, until I could brace it and free the leg. I prayed she would not wake. Prayed she would not feel pain as I manipulated her leg in the trap. But fortune kept her unconscious, and I was glad that God's spirit within the forest had calmed her pain by her faint, and directed me to her aid.

I carried Mary through the dusk and to safety. She bore no weight. My arms did not tire, and as I rejoined the crowd near the guardhouse, through the cheers and thanks for a young girl found, I missed the gaze of the girl in my arms, studying me with different eyes. I missed it, because I was too busy taking in the admiration and joy of Eleanor. Even her mother's smiles were not only for her daughter restored, but also for me—her rescuer returned.

∞CB

The spring turned to summer and it was a good day. Helped greatly by continual favourable weather and a welcome state of good humour. Mary still lay in her bed, with a leg yet to heal, but her health was assured. Mistress Traquere had provided her a small black and white dog to aid her recovery, to which she formed a great attachment. Mary fitted the dog with a stiff white collar fashioned for it, which caused its given name of *Pip* to be changed to *Ruff*, matching as it did its new collar and the only word it possessed in its canine vocabulary. I know these things because I was finally accepted as a visitor into the Traquere's house to visit Mary at her insistence, and Eleanor by her design.

My relationship and tolerated acceptance within the Traquere household had rendered my detention moot and it had fallen almost completely away from my conscience, and life maintained a better sense of regularity.

More days were good rather than bad, and it was on a good day, not to be spoilt by the impending Sunday services, that the Captain's priest approached me. I thought he intended to block my early exit from the Church lobby, and thus my regular escape into the surrounding trees and hills.

'John, Mistress Traquere would have you sit with her in church today.'

'Me, why?'

'She does not confide her reasoning to me, only her requests.'

'But what about Captain Traquere?'

'The Captain is on the road to Lancaster.'

The church was grander than the nearby dwellings it served and fuller than its proportions allowed. I made my way down the aisle to the Traquere's pews, past Eleanor and her sisters sitting with their nurse and the Tutor in attendance. I could sense their eyes upon me, but I only caught Eleanor's and the Tutor's stares as I came to sit in the space usually occupied by the Captain.

The parish priest delivered the services with expected pietistic rhetoric. His act neither a crowd pleaser nor a holy revelation, full of constant glances towards the Traquere's priest for approval during the service. The service felt long, by both my detention and my discomfort at been seated with Mistress Traquere. All eyes seem to fall on us, and heads would bow to ears, as whispered gossip traced the sermon.

After the service, Mistress Traquere refused to dismiss me, instead suggesting we walk awhile.

'John, what do you know of love?'

'I am sorry, Mistress Traquere… I do not understand?'

'Love, John. It is the vigour that burns in every woman.'

Her discourse surprised me and I blushed. I could not hide it. I could only search for a modest reply. 'I… I suspect it burns in men too.'

'Only in some, John,' Mistress Traquere brought her right hand up, palm flat. 'On one hand, men lust,' then her left hand was raised similar. 'And on the other, women love. It is the natural order of life. Lust burns for a moment. It is expunged by the release of a man's seed,' and as she said this she closed her right hand tight, 'But love burns brightly... it is encouraged in a woman's soul,' and she raised her left palm to the sun, as if releasing a bird to the sky.

I was embarrassed. I fought my embarrassment. I hated my embarrassment. I thought I was a better man to be caught sheepish, and so I found confidence and I curtsied deeply and courteously.

'I bow to your knowledge, madam.'

Her smile grew into a grin, which peaked in a short restrained laugh. 'You play the gentleman well, John. I can see why my girls think you a prince instead of the snot my husband believes you to be.'

'It is a pity Captain Traquere has such a poor regard for one he is not familiar with.'

'Perhaps so... perhaps so. I am aware that you and Eleanor are sweethearts. My husband knows it and he would have you flogged if he could. I do not share this rude notion. But what I need you to know, John... is that I approve only to a degree.'

'And what is the degree to which you approve, Mistress Traquere?'

'It is proper for a young girl to richly love, and essential for a young lady to marry richly. I believe you are fine fodder for the fantasy of love, but not a fitting choice for marriage. Eleanor will marry far better than John Brownfield. You will never lie with her.'

'I do not know what to say, madam. Modesty ties my tongue. I cannot reason with a cruelty that sponsors love and denies moral union because of it.'

'You have grown, John. No longer the malapert Scot. Nevertheless you will remain Eleanor's fancy, and no more. You will not ruin her. There will be no moral or immoral union. Think otherwise and your future may be...'

She did not finish her sentence, and I was glad of it. Instead she stopped and turned to join the following carriage, and I was left alone with fresh enmity towards Lady Traquere, and a clarity surrounding Eleanor's feelings for me, and a deeper understanding of my love for Eleanor.

Chapter IX

'Wash yer face, Jack. Get yerself clean and put on yer best clothes. Ye're tae see the Captain.'

I could not help but question Robert, as I rubbed water on my face and rinsed from the large leather bowl, a communal vessel to wash and even piss into when the urine pots were full.

'What's afoot, Robert?'

'I've saddled yer horse. Leave yer weapons and hold yer tongue. I don't have any answers.'

There was stress in Robert's voice—I felt it, and it worried me. I dressed quickly, Robert's urgency dictated it, and I was in my saddle soon enough. We were stationed on the west road, so it took us over two hours to reach the Captain's home, even at a good trot, over the spring clad hills and through fresh green woods. Robert's accompanying silence was not encouraging.

When we arrived at the Captain's gatehouse, noise and activity was all around us, and in the courtyard the Captain's coach was hitched and baggage tied about it for a journey—a long journey. Fretted servants with parcels and bags were running in and out of buildings adding their loads to the coach, and six troopers mounted their nags to wheel out of the courtyard to pass us as we entered. The last trooper was Tom Kemp and I caught him as he passed.

'Tom, what's the packing about, is the Captain on the move?'

'I'm na at liberty to tell ya, Jack. Orders.'

Tom wore no easy smile on his face and I feared more. Six years in the Captain's charge and I had never been called into his presence. My wits debated a few theories; all concluding in the English were finally at full tilt at Scotland and this part of the Marches was at the centre of it. I supposed the Captain was withdrawing his family from danger and I was in the reckoning. I thought this episode would be either fair or foul—there would be no middle ground. It felt more foul than fair.

We dismounted our horses and passed the reins to one of the hurried servants and entered the tower, climbing the whitewashed newel stair. We crossed the great hall to the Captain's private quarters and bedchamber. Robert knocked, and without invitation opened it to enter. I followed.

The steel point of the bolt was on me. The Captain's latch, a small crossbow, was levelled at my chest, and then it was raised to my face. The end I thought would come had finally arrived, and I resolved to meet it bravely, without plea or self-protection. I kept my eyes open and shoulders square to meet my fate. I lost sense of Robert in the room, perhaps my saviour. But my focus on the bolt and the horror of it tearing my face broke my nerve and I forced my eyes closed, and a prayer to enter my mind.

WOOOOOOSH… THWACK.

The sound of the bolt striking the wall to my left opened my eyes, and I turned to it, to see a small collection of crossbow bolts sticking out of a large oak board, about the size of a man. In the centre of a circular pattern of scars and bolts, was a silver coin affixed by a nail. The Captain was across the other side of the room, resting reclined against the edge of a large oak table, examining the crossbow in his right hand.

'Robert favours the latch. I favour the pistol, because powder has the power. But one must be able with all weaponry.'

Captain Traquere twisted his body to select another bolt from a pewter platter and he charged the latch, took further aim at the target and then lowered the weapon.

'Robert tells me you are proficient with weapons. No doubt due to his tuition. Even though I strictly forbade it.' The Captain threw a disdainful look over his shoulder at Robert, standing to attention. Robert bowed his head in contrition, hiding a grin I thought.

The Captain continued, 'Let me see your skill. Here try your aim,' and he held out the loaded crossbow.

I crossed the room to take the weapon from the Captain, and feeling the weight and balance of the weapon in my hand, I turned to face the target. My nerve had not recovered and my heart pounded, so I let my arm drop down. I took and held a deep breath. I counted in my mind, using shepherd's count, its rhythmic tone easing my tension; *yan, tyan, tethera, methera, pimp, sethera, lethera, hovera, dovera, dik*. I visualised the bolt hitting the coin. Then in a smooth curve I raised the weapon to the target and let loose the bolt.

The target was missed by a margin, but not so much to cause me embarrassment.

'Fair,' said the Captain.

'It pulls badly sir. Could I try again?' I replied.

'Certainly, help yourself, *crossbowman*.' The Captain held the pewter platter out, inviting me to take another bolt.

I charged the weapon again, reclaimed my position and repeated the drill. This time the bolt clipped the coin to cut it at the edge, and I tried not to smile.

'Well done,' said the Captain dryly as he stood up from his rest and walked to the target. He traced the coin with his finger and stared hard into the silver disc. Robert remained stolid near the door.

'Reports from my tutor, my priest and even my wife reveal you to be an able student. If you were my own son, I would no doubt send you to university to become a man of value. But you are not my son. I am not your father. How do you say if I send you home instead?'

I placed down the crossbow carefully on the table and stood to attention with eyes ahead as if I was addressing my commander. 'I would say, thank you Captain Traquere. I would say too, that I have come to call this place home.'

'Ah... you ingratiate well. You may even go far,' said the Captain as he moved to face me, to study me carefully, his hands brushing my clothes and pinching the fine fabric of my suit, a gift from Hueçon.

'I have two minds on you. The first is governed by my dislike of you and who you are... *Scot*. The second is born of a pragmatic mind. You are here and have caused me little inconvenience, with the exception, of course, in matters concerning my eldest daughter, who you court without my permission. But I am convinced by my wife that your attentions are honourable, if unrealistic.'

My calm restored was again disrupted, and his move was unexpected. The draw of his dagger was swift and the blade beneath my chin immediate.

'Have you been honourable? Or do you ride her, *Scot*? Do you hump her as you do those unchaste village lasses, whose fathers bother me for recompense for virtues stolen?'

I held my head back. The knife forced it there. My words struggled to clear my mouth, constricted by the point of the blade hard under my chin.

'Your daughter's virtue is intact, sir… I… *I swear it!*'

The Captain sneered. 'My wife vouches for your word. Be grateful for it, sir.'

Captain Traquere's dagger was returned to its scabbard and my breath back to my body, and I was surprised to think of Lady Traquere as my saviour. The Captain returned to a man without malice, his words calm and even friendly. But I thought again. I knew sarcasm when it was presented.

'Good news, John Brownfield, you are to be sent back to your family under a new pledge. You can even lose your counterfeit name and I will not even charge you for its hire.'

Even though I had waited for this day, its announcement left me wanting. 'I will keep Brownfield if you permit. It suits me.'

'Then you shall have it. Have it as a parting gift. Wear it well, John Brownfield. Bring honour to it, for it is a name that has not lived its ancestry in much noted esteem.' The Captain broke his oratory to walk to the other side of the room to take a rolled document from a large oak cupboard. 'A new agreement has been reached between the Warden and your father. You are to return to your home and a connection maintained between our two factions. You are to marry my daughter.'

My eyes widened and joy filled me, more so because marriage to Eleanor was contrary to the Traquere's choosing. I could not believe it, but I rejoiced in it. 'Sir, you make me very happy.'

'I understand you will be a man of means. I am informed that on your father's death you will take an inheritance in coin rather than in land.'

'Yes sir, it was always my father's wish that his estates are succeeded to the older brother rather than be split between children as is lawful expectation.'

'He is a wise man to keep his family's land holdings intact. Land is a ready supply of men, and the sweat of men beget a man's wealth.'

My mind, however, was not on my father's land or even on my return home. It was on Eleanor, and a love soon to be completed.

'I will be a good husband to Eleanor, sir. You can be assured of my aspiration in this endeavour.'

'I am sure you will be a good provider. So it is agreed.' The Captain's voice had a kinder tone, and I thought he must be pleased with the match. He walked back to the oak cupboard to close its door, left ajar when he removed the paper, an act innocuous in itself. He faced the cupboard door, his back to me and he continued, 'You see you are to be my son after all. A son-in-law.'

'Does Eleanor know of this news?' I asked.

'She does.'

'With your permission sir, can I see her?'

Captain Traquere waited, to string out my anticipation. He turned and smiled before he spoke again. 'Erm… to see her will be quite difficult, as today she leaves for our estates in Hampshire, never to return.'

'Sorry sir, I am lost in my understanding. How are we to marry if she leaves?'

'You misunderstand, *Scot*. You are to marry Mary.'

My esteemed lady. It placed a great burden of sorrow on your servant and those who wish your estimable son well, to be robbed of your honoured presence on the day of the union between your son John, and Mary of the House of Traquere this XV (15th) day of July in the year of our Lord, MDXLIX (1549) and XVI (16th) year of your son. Your treasured son and his bride was as beautiful sight to be seen in the whole domain. Villagers and nobles from the realm of Traquere were present, and your other son, William, did acquit himself well as groom's man. All was marked by proper celebration and charity on those beggars and all the poor that entered Captain Traquere's charge that day. In lieu of dowry, I understand it is Captain Traquere's sincerest wish that myself and a number of the Captain's goodly guard accompany your son and his bride back to the comfort of your home, as their retinue, to help his honoured daughter and son-in-law settle amongst your kind hospitality. I will look forward with great joy to meeting you.

Your humble servant, Edward Hendon, Tutor to the House of Traquere, MDXLIX (1549)

Chapter X

The day we were to depart, to return to my birth home, was a day bathed in sunlight. Summer 1549, six and half years after my internment began. All were present outside the Traquere's home, including the Traquere household, many of the Captain's troop, and those peoples from nearby who wished well of the wedding party in their travels to a new home. All were there except Eleanor and Mary.

'Where is she, Walter?' Anne Traquere was walking back and forth nervously, constantly stopping to rap a folded fan against Captain Traquere's chest. 'Where is she?'

'She will be here, Anne. She protests that's all.'

I watched the Captain's wife. She was a woman not happy. Her distress was not simply for a missing daughter, but for a lost daughter, because the Captain and his good lady were moving to Hampshire. They had sold their lands and estates in the north and were moving to their estates in the south, probably never to see Mary again. The Tutor had told me of their plans, of the Captain's deepened contempt of the Warden and his deputy, which had grown to such a degree, that to move from the area was the only recourse available to him—to seek freedom of service from the

Warden and some kind of peace from that war which raged within his soul. Especially the war he waged with Sir Thomas Wharton.

Many of the Captain's standing troop were to stay and seek employ elsewhere, their families not wishing to be uprooted, and some even elected to travel north with Mary and I, to become our retinue. But it was simply not for pay they travelled with us, but for true kinship. I knew this because some would not be so warmly welcomed in another realm hostile to their birth names. But my father promised them employ and sanctuary under my command, and homes in which to dwell. The Tutor, also, was to travel with us, sent by Mary's mother to watch over her daughter's wellbeing and report regularly on her condition in an internment, masquerading as marriage.

We waited, and as we waited, Captain Traquere walked over to me, and looked me up-and-down slowly and smirked. 'Still in your wedding suit I see. You look like a French fop. I take it Hueçon still benefits you?'

'He stays in touch to further my education, Traquere.'

The Captain was taken aback by my reply, and exclaimed, 'Ah you do not use my title. I sense a new boldness.'

'I am free of your charge, and I suspect… if I ask it…my men will cut you down gladly.' I looked to *my men*, searching their faces for a sense of their newfound loyalty. 'Yes, if I order it so… I think it would be done.'

'The little worm has turned, and you have one of mine as a hostage to ensure I doth my cap to you.' The Captain looked about him, searching, 'But you only have a hostage, if your hostage appears.'

Traquere looked to the ground, kicking his heels in the fine powder of the dry earth. Then he kicked dust over my shoes, brushing the sole of his boot over my toe. He grinned at the dirty smudge he made on the clean pale leather. 'Your shoes are dirty, sir. You'd better ask your fancy, Hueçon, for a new pair.'

I looked at my marked shoes, but held my anger. I thought on his words, his vile assertions, taking greater offence that I would deem Mary a hostage. I held my anger deeper still, behind gritted teeth and a steel closed mind. Mary was at best an unwelcome wife, at worse a burden to be borne, but a hostage, *never*. An agreement not of our making bound us together, and I suspected we both would honour that agreement, but she would be welcome to leave at any time she chose. All I really cared about was that Eleanor was lost to me, and the thought of it made me feel wretched.

I looked straight into the Captain's eyes. 'Hostage against what, Traquere? You have nothing I want in return for her safe keeping.'

The Captain broke my stare and softened his manner considerably. 'The Warden wanted continuance in his *special* relationship with your father. But I leave his charge and break the bond, so he has nothing. But despite my sorry demeanour, I am not without generosity, and I will give you something, John Brownfield. Something from my heart… *advice*.

The only way a man can act true to himself is to leave the domain that suffocates the moral good within him. So I say to you, John Brownfield… *son in law*, leave this land and seek your true self in calmer seas.'

As the Captain turned to walk away, the sound of a horse travelling at the gallop was heard, and into the scene appeared Mary, riding side saddle, in plain drab clothes and holding her dog, Ruff, tight into her side. The Captain turned back to me before he reached his position next to his wife, and shouted, his malevolent manner returned, 'Your wife is here in clothes rightly suited for a pig farmer, now all is complete. Go and get out of my sight!'

⁊‡⁋

As we rode, I felt empowered at the sight of the train travelling. My train. My men. My entourage. I could not help but feel a true man, a knight-at-arms, at the head of such a parade. And as I rode, my head held high, I would hold back my horse to let my retinue past so I could see it in all its meagre glory.

All the while I watched Mary on horseback keeping a distance, riding so as not to be part of my procession. But her show of disinterest was overplayed, her horsemanship overdone—done to impress her audience, to shout her anger and her rage, rather than her indifference.

Eventually, she drew her horse next to mine. She wore a manner haughty and cold.

'So what do you expect sire from your gift?'

'My gift?' I replied.

'*Yes sire, my lord, my husband...* your gift. A girl stolen from her future.'

Mary's tone was mocking and I was relieved to hear it so, for she had displayed no sentiment to me since the announcement of our marriage. Indeed even on the day of our wedding she was as hard to read as our Tutor's badly penned digest of the Classics. Yes, I was glad. Mary was displaying her resentment of our union, and I suppose commonality is often the basis of a good relationship, even if rancour was a poor replacement for love. I said nothing in return, but my silence only brought hurt to the surface of Mary's refined display.

'Know you this, Master Brownfield. I cannot be done, sir, as the ewe is done by the ram. I cannot be ridden sir, like a horse at the races. I cannot be...'

I interrupted Mary. 'Pardon me, madam, but I have the gist. Do not worry, I would rather poke a wasps' nest, it would hurt less.'

'Well that's fine, because if it's sweetness you want, it'll be the only honey you will get.'

'I'm not so sure wasps make sweet honey… my little bee,' and as I said this, I raised a hand, dug my spurs into my horse, and galloped ahead to catch Will and Robert riding ahead of the train.

The road was better for the good weather, the horsemen and carriage finding the way easy. Eight of the Captain's troop, assigned as dowry, accompanied us on our journey, and I was comforted to see Tom, Francis, Finn and Bendback riding with the carriage driven by a trooper called Henry Harden. The carriage contained the Tutor and two maids assigned to Mary's attendance. Two more troopers, not familiar to me, made up the horsemen. Both Stephen Howard and James Clarey were well acquainted with Captain Traquere, and thus we thought, were assigned as his spies. Robert rode with Will, deep in parley designed to better friendship, easier because they were both Scottish.

Will was the first to greet me.

'Problems, Jack?'

'No, just the bitter bleating of a bitter bride.'

'And ye, Jack, have ye come tae terms yet?' added Robert.

'How can one come to terms with such an affair? My boyhood was misplaced, now my manhood is to be bruised by a surly curl.'

Will was philosophical. 'Aye, Jack, ye're bruised well enough, but still she is a comely girl, and better brides oft start bitter. Sour becomes sweet.'

For all her youth, Mary was as old as her eldest sister and could be as prickly as her mother. All her good humour, much admired by those who associated with her, had gone. I could not blame her. We had a friendship born out of the forest and freed from a mantrap. We had a common humour and respect. But we had no romantic feelings for each other, I did not lust for her, and I thought she felt likewise. I was sore outside the joy of my release, and my newfound entourage. Sore for missing Eleanor, my love true.

I wore a silver locket around my neck on a bold chain sent to me by Hueçon. Originally, the chain had a pearl and jewelled pendant; a fitting decoration he said, *'for a gentleman with fine attentions on the future.'* But I removed the pendant and exchanged its value for a pair of pistols; weapons to support my own sword and lance, donated by one of Robert's Watch who had elected to remain behind and give up soldiery for woodcraft. The locket was a gift from Eleanor, and it contained a lock of her robin red hair, and I swore to wear the locket always as a badge of loyalty to my love for her.

We had been travelling a long while, past Carlisle and over the border into Scotland, and all the time Mary rode and picked at me. She rebuked the Tutor and her maids when they begged her to ride in the carriage. She would carp as she galloped past to steal ahead, then to the side riding the rises, picking through the trees, then to the rear to circle again. Everything she did was done so as not to be apart of the train and to voice her fury with it.

The day turned hot and the ride was uncomfortable for it. Perspiration soaked clothes, and Mary looked particularly fevered in her heavy wool dress in the heat, picked for its poor show to humiliate me more rather than as a good summer-riding choice.

The Tutor grew tired of the spectacle, and beckoned Will and I over to the carriage.

'I suggest you take Mary and ride a different route, try to converse with her to calm her down. Otherwise she may find herself embarrassed when she reaches our destination. She will not be a welcome sight, an exhausted sodden rag on a sweating horse.'

'How dae ye suggest we entice the vixen tae enter the pack?' asked Will.

The Tutor replied, 'The same way you capture a wild horse.'

We kicked our heels and wheeled our horses away from the carriage, and Will liberated a rope from Finn's nag to form a noose on a slipknot. We then rode at Mary on her next pass, but she saw our intent and spurred her horse from the canter into the gallop, and she flew to the right, up a shallow rise topped with trees.

It was only her horse that allowed Will and I to catch up. A horse well worked by Mary, more tired for it. But trying to put a hand on Mary's reins was a hard task made harder by Will's inept attempts to rope Mary's horse.

The charge through the trees at the top of the hill became dangerous, as the undergrowth became thicker the further we ventured into the wood. There was no easy path, and Mary's horse made distance because we backed off, scared to press Mary into making an error.

It was some time and hard riding before we cleared the wood, onto higher land and open moor. Will and I galloped on and on to catch Mary, leaving our comrades far, far behind.

Mary's horse seemed to find fresh vigour on the fell, and it galloped well, finding the freedom of moor to its liking. But the ground was poor and not fit for the gallop, and Will and I were forced to grit our teeth, and find fresh resolve and greater courage to trust our mounts to find good footing as we chased hard to catch her.

It was clear after a long while that Mary was losing ground, her horse slowing. It was of great relief to Will and I, long fearing the chase would lead to Mary being unhorsed. So we were careful to bring up our nags to flank Mary, so as to slow her horse without peril. Then the worst of it happened and her horse stumbled, and threw Mary hard into the heather.

We recovered Mary from the ground, unharmed by the fall

softened by heather and moss. She was however sweating profusely, deathly pale and not correctly flushed from exertion. Her horse seemed fine at first, just a shoe missing. Then it limped a little.

Will had hardly recovered his breath when he made his assessment. 'Shock, she'll be fine. We'd better get off the moor and find a blacksmith fer her nag.'

Will and I started to walk off the fell leading our tired horses, one limping, one carrying Mary, concerning us with her silence and seeming more poorly than first thought. The day had grown dark, not through the approach of night, but by a threatening sky, heavy with summer storm. Will looked to the sky, concerned at the change in the weather, and fearing a drenching, he checked Mary again.

'She's very sick lad. We need tae get quickly off the fell and find shelter.'

It was a few miles before we reached a settlement, a few houses crowded around a fortified bastle. And in truth, I cannot remember its name, or ever recall asking for it, or being told it. But by the time we reached the first house, Mary was so poorly that she could not sit astride the horse without support from Will.

We knocked at the first door and no answer, the second and third brought a similar response.

'We better try the bastle, lad,' Will's shout was full of concern, and he carefully led Mary on his horse over the rutted path to the stone built bastle house. I was there before Will, leading a lame pony and my own without the weight of a sick rider.

The weather did its worse, and the rain came heavy and hard to drench all those without shelter. Will beckoned me to support Mary while he ran up the stone stairs of the bastle to hammer on its oak door, but again no response came. He then tried to force the stout oak door, but it was firm. He then ran from door to door beating his fist, shouting, begging for entry, but still no response.

The settlement was on a road of sorts, on flat ground that broke sharply beyond the houses to fall off steeply down to a river. There was a tight group of buildings standing by the river's edge, almost obscured by the drop of the land and the trees and shrubs that occupied the falling bank. Will studied the rooftops of the riverside buildings to see beyond them to detect any activity, but there was none. But as I joined him, we both spotted a large stone lean-to structure with an open side; a wood store we thought.

'Shelter, Jack!' Will's shout was jubilant and he feverishly scanned the area for a path down to the buildings. But none was near and the bank too steep to attempt direct decent. I looked down the river to venture an eye to see any way that may be obvious, but the heavy rain obscured good sight. Then Will started to drag all the ponies back to the centre of the settlement again to rejoin the track that ran through the houses. I followed.

The rain did not rest its assault. The whole world and those caught in it were sodden and a sorry sight to be seen. Mary's condition could not be observed, she was wet as the world, and our anxiety for her grew beyond anxiety into a terrible fear.

Will stopped at the bastle, and I was at a loss to understand his motives.

'All tracks lead to the bastle, Jack. So which one leads away to that river shelter?'

There were two paths that ran through the settlement—two that by their lie could feasibly sweep down a longer route to the river.

'Which one would you take to get to the river, Jack?'

In the dark rain, all routes were now becoming feasible as they turned into rivers themselves. All looked the same and I doubted my choice. 'The track to the north is well rutted and worn by traffic.'

Will shouted his reply before I finished stating my choice and he was already leading Mary down the north track. 'Methinks ye pick wisely.'

It was a while before we had confirmation our choice was the right one. There were moments both of us thought of retracing our steps to return to the bastle, to take one of the other routes. But as the track slowly swept down to the river we knew it would lead us to the shelter.

The cover of the stone tiled roof was welcome. There was space in the shelter for all. The store was large, too large for a single dwelling, or even a group of dwellings. It was a wood store, the presence of bark scattered around the empty areas confirmed our conclusions. But for all shelter was obtained, Mary's peril was not abated, because she was wet through and we had no dry coverings to warm the poor girl.

Will had found a well-sharpened axe, its blade buried in a log. He raised it to his face and I knew what he contemplated as he looked back into the rain towards the other buildings, shuttered against the foul weather.

'I'll see if I can get in tae the lodgings, force an entry if I have tae.' Will's voice was full of purpose as he moved towards the open, steeling himself against the heavy rain.

But Will was not able to leave the shelter, because a halberd covered him, monstrous in its size, its blade dripping wet. The halberdier was a dark shadow, not tall but powerful in its form. By its feet was another darkened form; a large dog, offering a low mean growl as a weapon against Will. The halberdier and his dog advanced, and Will was forced to retrace his steps backward, to keep his distance from the halberdier's blade, and the dog's, now bared, teeth and vicious snarling.

'Tinkers, you'd better find yerself another shelter, mine's not for rent,' the halberdier's voice was deep and his delivery direct and confident.

Will dropped the axe and held his hands clear of his sword and dagger to show his compliance. Then he arrested his retreat and approached the halberdier slowly.

'We are in distress, can ye nae see it man?'

'What is your distress to me, tinker?'

Both men had strength of presence, but I could see Will was in no mood for negotiation.

'I'm not fancyin' a fencing lesson wi' yer big blade. So stay yer hound and stand aside and give us shelter, or I'll be cuttin' ye and yer dog, and takin' yer roof as my prize.'

Will's intimidation did nothing and the halberdier stood firm his ground. But he whistled and the snarling quietened, but although stilled, the dog's evil intent towards Will remained evident.

The halberdier spoke again, 'I would advise you to move on, otherwise I'll be separating your head from your body, and *Bouncer* here will be munching on yer sweetmeats.'

The dialogue between the men was travelling only towards violence. I suspected neither would back down, and a bloody fight would not help Mary. So I broke into the exchange, desperate for the halberdier to see Mary and her condition.

'Sir, we have a sick lass. She's fevered and wet. Please take her inside your house. We'll pay well and be no trouble, I promise.'

The halberdier looked on Mary and then me, switching his eyes back and forth. Then although his words were for me, his eyes returned to Will to ensure no skulduggery was planned. 'You're finely dressed for a tinker boy. Unlike your lass and lad here. Your servants I presume?'

Will did not have time to take offence at the halberdier's

presumption, because by the halberdier's side came a woman, holding a blanket over her head against the rain.

'What's the matter, Davy?'

She seemed to hesitate only a moment before she hurried straight past the halberdier and Will to tend to Mary. She cupped her hand on Mary's pallid face and moved it onto Mary's sweated brow.

'This girl's sick. Get her inside the house straight away.'

The halberdier did not protest. The woman firmly instructed Will to carry Mary into her home. She looked past my fine clothes and told me to tend to our horses. The halberdier was told to put down his 'foolish' weapon and bring in wood for a fire. All complied without question. Even the dog was completely under the spell of the woman. It waited on her every command, its mean mood considerably lightened, evidenced by puppy dog eyes and a wagging tail.

I was shown the stabling, empty of livestock except for a few sheltering chickens and a rat or three picking and scratching the ground, all under the disinterested watch of a reclined fat grey cat. That cat glared at me the entire time I removed the bags, saddles and harnessing from the horses. It did not move its feline body only its hateful stare as I wiped each horse down in turn with what loose straw I could find. Its imperious manner lording over me as I feed and watered the horses.

At first I ignored the noise. I thought it simply the rats or hens picking and shuffling amongst the bags removed from the horses. But the noise continued and it drew my attention away from the horses to the bags. I could not see any chickens, so I assumed it was a rat finding its way into the bags to seek out a crumb of biscuit or cheese left from rations long eaten. One of Mary's saddlebags was moving and I thought it a big rat to move the heavy bag, filled with Mary's chattels. So I grabbed a pitchfork hanging from the wall and approached the wriggling bag, worried the rat was feasting on the bag's contents. I was embarrassed by my apprehension, *fear of a rat indeed*. But I summoned the man within me and banished the boy long gone, and carefully loosened the tie strap on the flap of the bag… and slowly edged it back with the tines of the pitchfork.

Suddenly something burst out of the bag, larger than a rat, running. The shock stopped my heart and froze my action.

'Ruff!'

I could not believe it when Mary's little dog ran from the bag, picked up sight of the fat grey cat to send it leaping and climbing to a high beam within the stabling. I ran to pick up the little dog to check his health. He was fine, affectionate and happy to be out of his bag. We had forgotten about Mary's little dog, no doubt rendered unconscious when her horse tumbled on the fell.

It was good to return Ruff to the shelter of the house, away from the rain to find a friendly Bouncer eager to befriend the little dog. I was pleased to find a fire, even in summer, and Will and our host sitting by its fiery face. It was good to take off sodden clothes and wrap in warm blanket, to find my place at the fire too.

I asked Will, 'How's Mary?'

'Davy's gud lady is tending tae her now,' replied Will, still rubbing himself dry by the fire, warming away the chill induced by the rain.

The room was small in size, sparsely furnished with a table, four stools, a bench fronting the fire and a large coffer with its lock broken; its iron fittings torn from their mountings; signs of past robbery, I thought. But although the room was modest, there was a rich smelling bowl of potage and a hot beverage provided for us both; the drink an odd but pleasant tasting concoction of dried herbs.

125

'That's Dotty's favourite mix, she keeps the recipe secret. She's got recipes for everything that ails you, lad,' announced Davy.

'Is she the local wise woman?' asked Will.

'If you mean does she treat the sick, aye she's got a way with her. You were lucky you found us, we're off the track a bit.'

Will released a long sigh. I thought it was a sign that the distress of the day's events had caught him up, and now relief was with him.

'Perhaps Davy… God's hand was at work. Jack and I couldn't raise anybody up the hill, so he sent us down the right path tae visit ye.'

Davy chuckled, 'Are you surprised, lad, with the day so foul and thieves about more and more? The village was twice the size a few years back and my smithy trade was good. But too many burnings, too many lootings have all but murdered the village and killed off my trade.' Davy poked the fire, provoking it into a rich and fiery blaze, 'How do you find yourself here, if not for robbing or ravaging my good lady wife?'

Will smiled at Davy's dry wit, 'We got separated from our wedding party, the lad the groom, the lass his new wife.'

'Bless me, what a way to spend yer wedding night!'

Will looked at me, grinning. 'I suspect it would have bin nae mair comfortable. They are none too fond of the arrangement.'

Davy looked to the fire and his handiwork with the poker. He then smiled at the two dogs sleeping, little Ruff buried in the dark shaggy coat of Bouncer. 'Well at least one of your party has found a fond pairing tonight.'

Davy Allen was a man, middle aged, who wore his grey stained tangle of hair wild, topping off a world worn face. His smile was strong, as strong as his courage, his bravery evident in the wood store as he faced down Will. And as we drank his wife's brew and mopped up his wife's delicious potage with her wholesome bread, his genial manner shone through. He told us of his origins. He learned his metal craft apprenticed at eight years old, but fled the furnace to become a sailor, only to find himself marooned in Scotland when his ship, *Lion,* was captured by the Scottish less than a score of years past. His wife was called Dorothea, and their two young daughters, Meadow and Heather, named after the ground upon which they were thought to have been conceived, were locked in their room, to keep them safe and prevent them from nightly wanderings and regular nocturnal mischievery. Their three other children, all boys, likewise named, Heath, Beck and Tree had passed on, none reaching older than eight years.

After a long while, soothed by Davy's entertaining stories, Dorothea came into the room from another door.

'The girl has a fever, I am not sure yet if it is the sweating sickness. I've made a good fire and wrapped her tight. Boiled plenty of water too for my healing brew, it may break her fever.'

'Will Mary be well, Mistress Allen?'

I could hear distress in my voice, for all I tried to calm it. I was fearful for Mary, as I knew her ailment to be serious.

Dorothea walked over to put her hand kindly on my head, her eyes full of compassion.

'She'll need rest lad. A few days will see her through the worst of it. She will need complete isolation until I know the nature of her malady. Davy and I will sleep with the girls, you two will bed down in here.'

Davy protested, 'The girls' bed is barely big enough for them. I didn't build a new bedroom to share my bed with the children again.' Realising protest was a poor weapon against his wife, he resorted to pleading instead. 'Dotty, what about our cuddling.' But Davy's eyes moved about him and he realised he had unfamiliar company. His face reddened.

Dotty smiled warmly at Davy, her face friendly and her voice full of affection for her husband. 'You'll survive, Davy. It'll be all the sweeter for a few days abstinence.'

∞◯◌

On the third night at the blacksmith's home, Will and I sat outside beneath an unclouded sky. I watched the stars. I tried to count them all as if it would bring Mary to health again. I counted and recounted but I never reached a number.

Will was watching me, I suspect, because he asked, 'Jack, why do you ponder the stars?'

I replied, 'A priest once told me they align to tell us the future, divine messages to the learned and pious. But a wiser priest told me better tales from *Copernicus* and *Nicolas de Cusa*. Theories that the sun is also a star and the centre of the universe, not our earth as taught, and the other stars are simply distant suns.'

I waited for his salute, his homage to my knowledge, but he did not reply and I took my eyes off the stars to look at him. He seemed agitated.

'I sense you do not believe me, brother?'

Will breathed in and removed spittle from his mouth, which he fired with some force onto a nearby rock. The act of discharge seem to calm him and he continued in soft temper. 'It's enough to know they're God's lights tae show the passage of the clouds in the night sky, so we can see the condition of the weather.'

I thought briefly on Will's grounded notion of such a wonder and his mistrust of science. But I thought longer on him—*my brother*. He was different to me, and I thought perhaps I had outgrown him. He seemed to be a man who dwelled in his own thoughts, his typical Borderer equanimity less apparent. A once playful demeanour now more and more clothed in sadness of a form I did not understand.

Suddenly, and without invite, my thoughts turned once again to Mary. And once again, my concern for her overwhelmed me. Dorothea said it was a good thing she suffered. Good, because while she suffered she fought, and while she fought she would stay alive. But two days had passed with Mary suffering and sweating, and I felt hopeless in the shadow of Mary's sickness.

'Do you think Mary will get better?' I asked.

Will replied, 'She's in God's charge now, lad. But I'm afraid ye may be a widower afore ye are a daddy.'

I never thought myself as a father. Until then I never thought myself as a husband. My preoccupation had been with the forfeiture of Eleanor. I had not thought on Mary as one should, as my spouse.

Will spoke, which broke my thoughts again. 'Perhaps, lad, ye would be better off if she passed on.'

As soon as Will said, this I could see regret in his eyes. But he offered no retraction or apology for his assessment. I did not want to reply, for there had been a time before this night that I had been in agreement with Will. I was ashamed of those thoughts and ashamed too that my feelings for Mary were not those I felt for Eleanor, and as the night turned colder and the stars hid from view, I felt the growth of a new sentiment in me; a love of a different kind, and a resolve to be a husband to a wife. I took the silver locket about by neck, and I caressed the cool metal. I looked on it as you would look on a loved one soon to be departed, and I tucked it into my shirt. No more would I wear my love for Eleanor as a badge for all to see.

§◯◊

For two more days Mary was in another world, and fever and sleep were the basis of it. Dorothea nursed her as if she were her own child and with a physician's proficiency. Will and I were grateful for her practiced care, Will referring to her as, *a nun without a habit, an angel without wings.* Will's angel would usher us out of Mary's bedroom and even the house as immediately as we entered, offering a well meant chide against us. We knew her orders were for our own wellbeing, as well as for Mary's.

'Now you lads, keep out of ma house. The last thing the poor girl needs are two fellers breathing all over her.'

We did all she asked. Even Davy would be ejected with the same avidity. But now and again, he would still try to storm his own home armed with feint grumble and grouse, all directed at his wife for her poor attendance to his *needs*.

Each evening after Dorothea had tended Mary, I would steal into her bedroom to sit for a while to watch over her. I would sit close, even though I knew her sickness may be a danger to all those who came into contact with her. Some nights she would be still and calm, and seem to be sleeping as though she was well. But I would still be fearful, for I knew she was sick.

Sometimes, as I sat apart from Mary, I would reach out my arm to her—my hand with fingers stretched in horizontal plane. I would trace my fingers over her fevered body from face to feet. I would pray. I would close my eyes and pray again. I wished her well. I dreamed her better. I imagined I had my Lord's power to heal the sick. I offered God my life for her wellbeing. I wished it and wished it.

∞

The room was a better place for the window shutters removed and a good light filling the dark spaces. Dorothea was busy again clucking about her ward, cleaning and providing what comfort she could in the modestly furnished room. As Will watched the old hen picking at any displaced objects, my eyes were on the occupant of the blacksmith's bed and the patient's pale face. But her smile was rosy enough. Mary's smile said it all; it said the worst was over, her sickness had abated and her life was spared.

Mary spoke in weakened tones, 'How are you, John?'

It was the very nature of Mary to be concerned for others before herself, and I walked to her bed to sit next to her, and I took her hand speaking quietly, 'How am I? You ask that and yet it's you that faced the Reaper and passed him by.'

'It's good to see you, John.'

Mary's face was soft, her cheeks flushed with a colour that had been lost for days. Her hair, chestnut gloss, dark and dishevelled. I picked up a comb from a side table to run it through her tangles, but it snagged and she smiled at my ineptitude in matters of grooming. I was glad to see Mary awake.

'It's good to see you, all smiles and eyes. I have not seen you awake for days.'

Mary's eyes were still heavy and her breathing shallow. 'You look different, John.'

'You look tired, Mary. You still need your rest. We will speak at length in a few days. So rest now and we will travel on when your strength returns.'

⁋⸂⁊

Mary recovered quickly, fortified by the care of her nurse and a groom's newfound affection. And when it came time to leave, we thanked the kindly blacksmith and his wife. We supported our gratitude by a note drawn up for five pounds in settlement of their care, and a promise of endorsement of their services whenever they needed it. The note was never drawn upon, and they never asked for endorsement, and when Will travelled back to the blacksmith's home a few years later to ask them why they had not claimed their reward, he found nothing but a house long ruined.

As for the three—a boy now a man, his newfound wife and his beloved brother, we cemented a bond as we travelled northwards. And when we arrived at our destination, we found family and a lasting comradeship with those commissioned to safeguard us. Marriage to Mary was another story, a one with good intent but little merit on my part. But the story of Will and I, was a tale of a brothers born and beloved. We would hunt. We loved hunting. We loved many things. We found incredible joy and terrible pain, abundance and hardship, all in equal measures. But that was three decades and more past, and a story for another time, and a different chronicle.

[The story of young Jack, Will and Mary continues under the title, *On Solway Sand*.]

PART 2

'the twilight of middle-age'

Chapter XI

'Bless my soul,' said the fat bishop, looking both pleased and comfortable as he sat at Jack's desk. 'It *is* a good tale, Jack… Hostage, tinkers, first-love, Frenchmen, monkeys… *no*… I do it a great injustice. *It is a wonderful tale!*'

'Thank you, Thomas. I am grateful that you find my poor writings and poorer narrative to your liking.'

Jack stood up from the window seat, the stone too hard without a cushion, too cold for his aging backside, and he moved over to the fire to warm out his numbness. He stood over the fire, rocking his heels on the broad oak floorboards, and vigorously rubbed his arse cheeks to bring back feeling, then turned to warm his hands. 'The cold is an enemy I hadn't known till lately. He attacks me even in the midst of summer.'

The bishop did not look up. He was still thumbing through pages already read, and sifting through new pages in other journals to read, but he responded to Jack's gripe nevertheless. 'Yes, I must be honest, I count the age of a man in the number of shirts he wears. My old body requires three these days.'

Jack turned to the bishop, but continued to rub his hands behind his back and warmed his arse over the fire in turn.

'I concur, Thomas. The cold is no friend to old bones. The

blood circulates slowly and forgets to visit hands and feet.'

The bishop shuddered a little and looked to Jack warming himself against the fire, good and large in the grate. 'Be a good man, Jack, and spare a little of your fire for me. I have never known a tower so cold as this one.'

Jack was properly contrite. 'Sorry, Thomas, forgive a poor host.'

Jack moved from the fire, walked across the floor and took a chair across from the bishop. But before he sat, he took a large jug from the table and poured out an ale. The jug only delivered half a beaker and Jack smiled at the thought of a full jug nearly emptied by Thomas, still sober—as a bishop should be. Jack looked at the bishop and smiled again at the man, who had patiently and intently read his journals and listened to his stories. Jack was amazed at Thomas' lucidity and astonished at his capacity for ale, as he watched the big man shifting himself on two generously stuffed and embroidered cushions, easing his discomfort while he rested in a heavily carved oak armchair; the best seat in the room.

The bishop stacked the journals he wasn't reading carefully, and cast a more serious eye towards his host. He saw a tall man, bold in bearing, around fifty years of age, well tanned, as a traveller would be coming from southern climates. Grey stained his dark blond hair and a well-cut beard that sat beneath a thin noble nose. Two scars cut his cheek, not fresh, and from a hard lined face his steel blue eyes sparkled as they caught the reflection of the fire.

'Why do, after all this years of asking, now share your story with me?' asked the bishop.

'I wanted to share with you the story that formed my alias. Why my name is not Brownfield. It is because my name is counterfeit, that my enemies have easily reported falsely of my origins and created fouler beginnings.'

'I already know of your origins. That does not explain why you share your story with *me?*

Jack smiled at the sunny faced bishop, sank his ale and reached to the jug for a refill, and smiled again at the weight of the empty jug. 'I tell you, so that at least one man with the ear of Queen Bess and her counsel, know the truth of my existence.'

'But these journals only confirm you are what you are.'

'And what am I, Thomas?'

'Scottish born.'

'But I have served England.'

The bishop smiled softly. 'You Borderers may flit from Scottish to English sovereigns as you please. You may think of yourselves in terms only of loyalties to kith and kin, neither Scot nor English, but Elizabeth is a ruler in a dangerous world and the Spanish threat grows. She demands loyalty that is born of England's requisites and remains so.'

The bishop looked down to cast a gaze on the stack of leather journals on the desk. He then closed the one he was reading and placed it neatly on top of the others.

The mood between the two men was losing some of its warmth, as the bishop understood the purpose of his old friend's invitation and his hospitality. The smile disappeared from the bishop's eyes and his sunny face became overcast. Jack was dispirited by the bishop's words, but still he waited to listen to the direction of the bishop's commentary.

The bishop put his left hand on the pile of books and looked to Jack. 'I will assume the rest of your journals will reveal a mercenary, one who fights for a price. Jack, I ask you, what sovereign can trust such a subject?'

'A one who has served her.'

'But Jack, you have served other foreign powers with equal zeal. All for money, not as a patriot.'

'I have served only those who fight England's enemies.'

The bishop shook his head. 'Every foreign power is England's enemy, Jack. Politics dictate it so. Just because England winks at the Dutch, it does not invite copulation. Invitations to share a bed do not always beget marriage. Just as arranged marriages rarely beget true love... Besides, I suspect your allegiance to England's causes are those fortuitous sisters; convenience and coincidence, and not the deliberate design of your fealty to sovereigns and their sovereign causes, because I know you have no fealty to princes, *Jack*.'

Jack lowered his eyes to the desk, studying the ring marks and droplets from the jug and beakers. He then gazed deep onto his pile of leather journals and sought a memory less painful to lift his sinking spirit. 'I simply want to plant myself and my men in good ground... and find stone and roof of my own to sit out the winter, and a bed of my own to rest out the nights.'

The bishop shifted his hand from the journals to cover Jack's hand still embracing an empty beaker. His smile returned and the clouds lifted from his face. 'I can understand that. You have been seeking comfort since we met *on Solway Sand* some thirty years past. But you will never find the comfort of home's fire, and you will not find succour in England. Your reputation is well won. Your enemies well placed to see you suffer.'

'Thomas... will you intercede with the Queen for me, as one of her trusted bishops?'

'Ah... I am sorry, Jack. This is the greatest sadness for me. You have wasted your time and your money bringing me here. You have been away too long. I do not provide Queen's counsel any more.'

'Sorry, Thomas, I thought Elizabeth favoured you greatly as a man content to sit off-stage in that tragedy that is the Queen's play. You, who prompts a better line; counsel free from self service and self-ambition.'

The bishop sank a little in his seat and his face relaxed its kindly visage. Jack was sad to see an old friend, one he only knew as a cheery soul, less than he was. The bishop's face recovered after a moment, a smile refreshed on his lips.

'She favours and denies, she befriends and belies.'

Again Jack apologised, 'I am sorry, Thomas. I hear she is a contrary bird.'

'She is more than that. A Queen needs to be ruthless and cruel to wield power in a world of powerful men. Those closest conspire to keep the Queen's interest… and her enmity towards their own enemies.'

'I cannot believe you have enemies, Thomas.'

'No enemies, only creditors and no money. Even the kind and generous gift you give me to journey here, has gone to pay interest.'

Jack's concern for his own problems were joined by new worries; new anxieties regarding a friend he had only known as a man with a good heart, deserving of the good life he had created within his spiritual vocation, and equitably applied good business acumen. Concerns Jack needed to earnestly voice to his friend.

'Are you in any danger, Thomas?'

'No. Dead bishops don't pay, and poor bishops can't pay. My powerful creditors only make me bleed a little. They remove my dioceses, cut my income. They conspire to have my appointments removed… cut me from the Queen's ear.'

'I am sorry to hear it.'

'Do not concern, Jack. I am far too old to have so many responsibilities. Soon enough I will be fitted with wheels to move around, and married to a steward to wipe my arse and put a spoon to my lips.'

'*Never!* You have years of good living ahead.'

'Kind Jack. I am ten years past my time. I ache now to meet

the Lord.'

Jack stood up and returned to the fire, and looked deep within its flames. He hid his face from the bishop to conceal his disappointment, and to lose his thoughts a little. Then he looked above the fire, to its broad oak mantle and panel that straddled the stone above the fire opening. It was a grand affair of oak carving by a skilled craftsman in the art of replicating living form, not naive like the mantles in the poorer homes he had shared, or homes he had visited. This carving was a testament, he thought, to a man who had apprenticed to a great master, a man who provided Church with its fluid sculpture in stone and wood. The mantle was in fact out of place in this poor tower, and Jack pondered on how it found installation in such meagre stone. Jack's hands moved over the carving slowly as he thought on it, only to transfer to a carved wooden stand sitting on the mantle board.

For all the artisan's carving on the mantle was handsome, the delicate carving on the wooden stand that held two swords horizontal in their scabbards was better. Better conceived and better applied, tastefully and perfectly.

The bishop watched Jack as he studied the mantle and the swords upon it, and said, 'They are strange swords, Jack… Oriental?'

'Yes, Thomas, property once owned by a warrior of the Japans.'

The bishop asked, 'How did you acquire them?'

Jack drew the larger of the two swords from its black lacquered scabbard and presented it to the bishop for his inspection.

'The warrior gifted them to me before he slit his own belly and disembowelled himself.'

The bishop studied the fine blade and shook his head in disbelief at hearing about such a barbaric act. 'I have heard of this strange ritual… But why did he pass his swords on to you?'

'I saved his life once.'

'Oh I see,' said the bishop, holding the blade out to Jack for him to take back.

Jack took the blade from the bishop and returned it smartly back into its scabbard. 'No you don't see. After I saved his life, he tried to kill me. I then saved his wife and child, and again he tried to kill me. Then I saved his master, and he was ashamed that… *a white devil*, as he called me… had preserved his master's life, when he could not. And so he killed himself and bequeathed me his swords, recognising me as… as he put it… *the most worthy of warriors to receive his soul.*'

The bishop's eyes were wide with curiosity, excitement even, and he picked a journal out of the stack and flicked feverishly through its pages. 'Is the whole story within these journals?'

'Yes,' replied Jack.

'Then can I read it?'

Jack put one hand on the stack of books and the other retrieved the journal from the bishop's searching fingers. 'At another time, Thomas.'

The bishop, countering Jack's sadness, lifted his own voice and opened his hands in gesture. 'Jack, why not release your journals? Make your story common knowledge. Become a celebrity even… The *populus* love a good tale to send their children to their beds and their own ills into reverie.'

Jack looked deep into the bishop's eyes and shook his head. 'No, my journals will only be released on my death, if at all.'

'Then I cannot help you, but I will try.'

The bishop stood up, disappointed to be denied further examination of Jack's journals and walked to the fire to seek a comfort from his stiffness. Before further words could be said between the men, a pretty blonde serving girl, knocking at the door and entering without invite, interrupted them. She was carrying another jug of ale, which she set down on the table, and as she gathered up the empty jug, she passed a look to Jack unnoticed by the bishop. Jack nodded at the girl and poured out two beakers. He picked them up and walked to the fire and handed the fullest one to the bishop.

'Thank you, Thomas. Will you stay and enjoy my hospitality?'

The bishop took the ale. 'Certainly. With ale as good as this, I will take your offer. Besides, my bones still need a few rest days before I journey back.'

'Then I will make your stay as comfortable as I can. If I can in a borrowed tower.'

The bishop looked about the room as if his eyes could see through the walls to the remainder of the tower. 'Then this castle is not yours?'

'No, Thomas. I have no property, only gold.'

The bishop bowed his head. 'Then I thank you for your gold, your ale, and rejoice this poor tower is not your home.'

'We will dine tonight, Thomas.'

'I will look forward to it, but forgive my assistant. He is newly appointed, old and dry… and self-important. I hasten to say… he was not my choice.'

୨୦୧୪

The excellent roasted birds and boar were consumed with much wine and brandy, and the evening continued to go well as Jack exchanged more stories with the bishop and his dry assistant; a priest of forty or so years. Although Jack had spent the night recounting his troubles to the corpulent old man, the bishop's positive disposition and sympathetic accord had put Jack in a far better mood than he had been of late, and he was pleased the household was, for once, filled with better humour. It was only the presence of the bishop's assistant that made Jack feel a little disquieted, and as Jack studied the man, he could not help but observe he was a godly creation of the complete antithesis of the fat opulent bishop.

As the night wore on, Jack found himself increasingly in a deeper haze of wine and spirit, and mentally disadvantaged against the bishop and the priest; the former who, against all odds and all consumption, had an uncanny sober demeanour, and the latter, who had displayed near total abstinence, sipping a single fill the whole evening, to still leave a nearly full cup. But even through his stupor, Jack could not help but notice the priest's eye lingering over the serving girl as she cleared the bones and leftovers from the table, and refilled the men's finely etched Venetian glasses with ruby wine from a large leather jug; a *blackjack*.

Jack, not wanting to miss an opportunity to tease and test the stolid priest, fought back the murk of insobriety and declared, 'Priest, you admire our Kate?'

The priest embarrassed to be caught leering at womanly flesh, recovered more confident composure, and with a sneer and a short uncomfortable laugh, countered, 'Yes, she is a fine looking girl, she must be a continuous carnal temptation to you?'

Jack, who had been unable to address the haughty raw boned man respectfully by his proper title all evening, answered in mocking politeness, '*Father Freke*, we have had the pleasure of your company, but little in contribution of your intellect, observation or even opinion. Little remains of this night and your gracious company. May I, in the interests of characterisation, test you?'

The bishop, intrigued by Jack's game, pressed the priest to participate. 'Freke, you should indulge our generous host and do as Master Brownfield requests.'

Jack, supported by the endorsement of the bishop, raised

himself from his chair and beckoned Kate to his side. The girl walked over to Jack, her face down, and her manner careful and restrained. But beneath the restraint was a girl unhappy with being included in Jack's game. Her eyes told Jack. But Jack was too lost from sober reason to receive her covert signal.

Jack put his arm about Kate and waved his other loosely in the direction of the priest. 'Father Freke, you look at this girl and beyond her obvious bodily charms what do you see? Tell me about her.'

The priest formed a supercilious smirk, and for the first time that evening displayed some enthusiasm for the proceedings.

'Because you bring your maid to my attention, you expect me to describe her as a poor illiterate servant and locally born. So I will say she is not of servant class, but a displaced person of noble class. This is confirmed by her extraordinary beauty, clear skin and unworked hands; all of this in a province where one cannot tell woman from beast in the field. Her clothes are a little too large for her, revealing her lack of seamstress skill, unheard of amongst women, but especially within the lower classes. I have not heard her speak, that in itself is strange, so perhaps she is not a local girl, and is in fact, hiding her dialect. So she is neither Scottish, nor English and conceivably Irish, or even a European fugitive.'

A victorious smile formed on Jack's face, as he finished his drink and poured another.

But the priest countered and continued, 'But alas, and perchance you read me, sir, like a sailor reads the stars. I suspect you expected me to conclude her to be the exact opposite of what she appears. So I will outfox you, sir, and declare she is exactly what she appears to be, and that she is in truth a local serving girl of poor parentage and poorer education.'

The bishop roared with delight, 'Splendid, sir, splendid.'

Jack smiled, quaffing his drink in a single gulp. 'You are in deed what I thought you are, priest—an inquisitor. One who remains in the background, observes and records, but for whom I wonder, not the Bishop, methinks.'

The priest felt caught on the line of a better fisherman than he, and fell quiet.

The bishop seeing baleful clouds gathering in the room, interjected diplomatically, 'Now gentleman put your *blades* away. Jack, tell me the truth about this wondrous creature you have in your employ.'

Kate, avoiding hearing Jack's disclosure of her, moved away and walked towards the door, picking up more scraps and dregs as she prepared to leave. But before she left, as she reached the door, she turned. She turned because she knew the bishop and his assistant would not be able to see her. She turned to shake her head at Jack, to prevent him revealing truths best kept hidden. But again Jack did not see her. Drink had taken him and held him from good sense, releasing him into impropriety.

Jack had given Kate a lingering look as she retreated, but alcohol had marred his vision and reduced his clarity. Kate was no more than a blur against the door, and he did not see Kate's signal as he began his slurred reveal. 'That girl, sir… is the daughter of a better man than I. A girl… not of noble birth… but of nobler spirit than I. She lives with me as my ward and not as my servant. She is… the daughter of a fine woman called Catherine Dodd, who died consumed by f…' Jack was lost for a moment, and he steadied his head and refocused his eyes before he continued, 'Who died of consumption some years ago. She serves on us tonight in borrowed clothes, because she pretends to be a servant in this tower, in order to hide her presence here from those who would wish to harm me through scandal. Scandal, because she was once lodged in *Newgate Gaol* for killing fourteen immoral gentlemen who would plot to harm me. Bad men, who threw the accusation, *witch*, fallaciously at our Kate.'

The bishop's expression changed to sombre, but his voice remained ebullient. 'How did she perform murder on so many men?'

Jack continued, 'While they banqueted, she offered them a poisoned pie for their delight. Kate tells me it was a fine pie of autumn berries and field picked herbs.'

The bishop's voice now matched his solemn face. 'Who would think such an angel could commit such sin, and how in God's good realm did you win the release of such a flower from Hell itself. No one walks away from Newgate without a shroud or deformity.'

'I paid a lord's ransom for her release,' replied Jack.

The priest added censure to his voice and interjected, 'And where, sir, did you acquire such a lordly purse?'

Jack hesitated and lowered his eyes and forced clarity into his head. 'From a lord of the East.' Jack then turned his gaze to the priest and without slur or signs of intoxication said, 'So, Father Freke, you know the truth of our Kate. Report that back to your paymasters, who ever they may be.'

Just then Kate came back into the room carrying a large wooden tray covered by a larger white cloth. She put the tray down carefully on the oak table, and with one hand produced a fine long-bladed knife from inside her tightly tied apron, and with her other hand lifted the cloth from the tray. As she did so, Kate looked towards the priest, and with a wry smile and a wink said, 'Anyone for pie?'

ಜಃಂಃ

The next morning at low tide, Kate was on the shore collecting shrimp, small crabs and mussels. Enough she hoped for a good seafood broth to feed the household that evening. She had been a guest at the tower, with Jack and the others, long enough to learn where the best sea gatherings were, and especially where the shrimp heaved amongst the rocks. The tower was a good walk and half from the best of the coast, from the rock and seaweed strewn beach that was her favourite place. A place made all the better for the blue of the tufted vetch smothering the marsh thistle that lived on the path to the shore. She collected under a perfect blue sky, with a light wind that gifted her the scent of the sea. She loved it there. It relaxed her mind against the chores and concerns of life.

After an hour, a tall thin shadow appeared on the horizon, its foot on the beach, its head outlined against the sea. The shadow traced the coastline, and after a while the shadow became a figure, then it became a man. Kate looked towards the round tower, far in the distance, and then all the way round about her, to see if the figure was alone. It was, and she was too.

Kate stood, watching the man making time along the beach at the water's edge, not directly walking towards her, but also not appearing to be walking anywhere else but in her direction. She only relaxed when, after a few minutes, she could make out the clothing and gait of Father Freke.

She thought perhaps he was simply walking on a fine morning, but then she thought again, it was more likely he was coming to talk to her.

After a while the priest did reach her, to walk alongside. He drew out a very fine silk handkerchief, not an article fit for a priest, and ran it over his face wiping the sweat from his brow. The weather was mild and Kate thought him not to be a man of active pursuits. So this was not some idle exercise. She was his motive.

'How are you today, my dear?' said the priest.

'I am fine, Father. Did you sleep well?'

'I slept as well as could be expected on such a poorly constructed mattress.'

Kate's smile hid a grin that suppressed her own secret delight in the priest's discomfort. Jack did not like this man, so she did not like him either.

'I'm sorry to hear that we picked your bed poorly.'

The priest ignored Kate's reply and looked out to sea. 'It is truly beautiful here. I forget how the coast is as Heaven, as the city is as Hell.'

Kate was surprised at the manner of the priest. A different man stood before her than the man of night before. She did not trust this new demeanour.

'Do accept my sincerest apologies if I offended you last night. You are a beautiful girl, and I meant no rudeness. It is the wine you understand, it muddles one's mind, curtails the wits and dulls one's manners.'

Kate continued to pick mussels from the beach, carefully wiping the sand from each one, and placing them in a large reed basket that already weighed heavy with the food collected. She thought on his words and her mistrust deepened.

'I am surprised to hear you say that, Father. I did not see you take a drink all night.'

'Oh yes. Not as much as the others perhaps, but enough to effect the disposition of one's morals.'

Kate knew he was lying, but before she had time to think longer on his fiction, the priest continued.

'I am worried for Captain Brownfield, for his soul. As I fear he is godless and thus condemns himself to Hell, together with all who would call him friend.' Father Freke placed his sweated hand on Kate's arm. 'I hope you are attentive to your prayers, and are

148

regular at Church, my child. I understand Captain Brownfield does not kneel to our Lord. His actions preventing those who associate with him seeking out our Lord's comfort.'

'We service our souls best we can,' replied Kate.

'We can never be too diligent where our souls are concerned. Particularly when we travel from one godless continent to another. What do you say, *my child?*'

Kate remained quiet. She held back her words. She waited to see the direction of the priest's enquiries, and the destination of his discourse.

'Your guardian holds a colour in his face only attained in warmer, sunnier climates. It intrigues me. Where has Captain Brownfield travelled from?'

Kate remained quiet.

'Do you not know? I suppose that is a question for your guardian. I do not intend to pry.'

Kate remained quiet.

'Captain Brownfield paid the bishop considerable monies to attend him in this backwater… much monies… Captain Brownfield's adventures must have paid well. I have seen the oriental swords… Perhaps his profit comes from the Japans? What do you say?'

Kate held a secret smile, one she awarded herself for her perspicacity. The priest's game was up. Kate knew her mistrust of him was well founded, that Jack's suspicions were proper. The priest was indeed a spy, and whoever was directing this dry stick of a man, it probably was not the bishop. Kate was also vexed that the priest had so underestimated her, that he thought some brief false kindness, flattery and a pious disposition would woo her to report ill of Jack.

Father Freke grew impatient with Kate's silence, and thought again to attack the armour of her soul.

'Child, I see by your actions of ignorance, you hold hostility towards me, a man of God, a man to be respected and answered when he asks a question. And I wonder if you have proper faith and Christian belief, or perhaps on your travels you have found new heathen gods to worship?'

'Jack believes as I do. We both believe in a Christian God.'

'How can you know God truly if you do not hear the Gospels?' growled the priest.

'We have read the Gospels. We believe in God. We are attended by a priest when we can. We attend Church when we can.'

'*When you can!* I am afraid that is not enough, my child. Your soul will not be assured with such casual devoutness. What is worse, what is distressing, is that I do not even know if you cling to old doctrines.'

'We are what the Queen wants us to be.'

'Ah… but which Queen though. Mary or Elizabeth. Catholic or Protestant?'

Kate's temper was not a kindly place with calm seas and clear skies. It was an ocean prone to sudden squalls and winds of such ferocity, that to be caught in them was to invite any poor sailor that dared them, to be tossed and torn in its wake. Kate was a woman of her own convictions and well read of new ideologies. She was one who believed a sovereign did not have the right to dictate their subjects faith, against the dictate of one's own heart, or the Church's right to generate precept outside the written word of God, which she viewed as absolute and divine.

Her reply to the priest was not guarded, and she regretted it as soon as it left her lips. 'What *we* do not need is to be lectured by a Church, infected by greed, self-interest, politics and deceit, or to be led into strife against our neighbours because of differing doctrines, simply to suit the sway of the Church. Doctrines devised by the vanity of so many learned theologians, and not necessarily directed by God. Was Moses a theologian? I think God speaks to shepherds, not scholars. God is far above the vanity of men and the wicked rule of the Church, over which he must curse its form as it dares to spout piety in his name. What do you say, *priest?*

Father Freke's face showed horror at the girl's presumption and her disrespect.

A mere girl, how dare she chide her better so?

But beneath his horror, within his eyes was the satisfaction of finding a conviction that would perhaps see her and Jack condemned. He did not rebuke the girl. In his mind he was above debate with so lowly a creature. So he simply closed his eyes and crossed himself.

'I will pray for your soul.'

Kate calmed, as squalls do. 'I will pray for yours also.'

The priest smiled, like an adder who had paralysed its prey and now waited at its leisure to consume its prize. But he thought to temper his inquisition with kinder discourse, and sympathetic words.

'Oh my child, such a deficient attitude to one's betters will lead you and your keeper to moral ruination and certainly to Hell. I only speak so, because of fondness, and do not wish to cause you and your guardian discomfort. I only worry about your soul. You see, I once knew a Kate, and she was very dear to me.'

Kate dismissed the priest's kindly words, thinking only ill of him. 'Was she your lover?' she said disdainfully.

Father Freke was held by Kate's harshness, searching for an invention to repudiate her accusation. But he was unable to lie about a precious memory interred within his soul. Scored deep by a hundred days of flagellation; his scourge cutting his remorse deep into his flesh, for him to feel and for some to see.

'Child, I am the word of God, and my word will condemn your keeper. I will, with deep regret, be required to report this further.'

Kate turned her back to the priest, and returned to her task, to scour the rocks and weed for bounty. The priest, hoping his comment would nettle Kate into compliance, into pleading and harmful disclosure, was disappointed to see her ignore his threat, and heeded her ignorance as one of dismissal. So he turned to walk away.

But Kate, still searching the floor, spoke again. 'Father Freke, my words are poorly formed and badly delivered, but I suspect you will twist them into poorer ones, treacherously asserted… but I do not worry, because you will never make your report.'

The priest looked at Kate and said no more. He simply retreated back along the beach towards the tower.

⍹⍦⍹

After Father Freke had returned to the tower, Kate's last words haunted him into the evening.

What did she mean? Did she mean to poison me? Would Jack Brownfield cut my throat in the night? Should I tell the bishop? But the bishop is Brownfield's friend, and he would dismiss any charges laid against him. No, accusation must be made in the proper place, to the proper people, at the proper time.

The priest was unhappy that he had not found out more about Brownfield's movements, or the source of his coin. But in his machinations, he planned to steal and make a present of Brownfield's journals to his patron, who at the very least would be pleased with confirmation of Brownfield's whereabouts. His paymaster would see further foul rumour cast at John Brownfield, and see him further isolated, even accused of treachery and blasphemy.

The priest then thought on Kate, her alluring form corrupting his scheming thought into lustful want. He fantasied with avidity, as Kate's appeal pricked a remembrance of his former lover, lost to him in youth. Lost for reasons of his careless copulation and her resulting condition—an inconvenience to his priestly ambitions within a pious Church.

But as he thought on the rude acts he would commit on Kate, the priest's deep desire and lechery turned to sour intention, as he labelled her in his report as *witch* and *succubus*—Brownfield's demon lover.

However the Priest took no chances that night. He ate no food, drank no liquid. He locked and barricaded his chamber door and retired early to his bed.

ഌ➷ⓒ

The following morning, Jack was shaving when a serving boy came through the door, flustered.

'Terrible news... It's Father Freke… He's passed over in the night... Heart seizure we think. We had a terrible time getting into his room… Barricaded it was.'

By the time Jack had washed and wiped the soap from his face and reached the priest's room, the bishop was examining the cold corpse in its bed. Also present, was the serving boy that had brought Jack the news, Kate, and Jack's devoted retainers—his men-at-arms, Robert and Francis.

After the bishop examined the dead priest, he covered the body with one of the bed's sheets. He then brought his hand to his face, fingers nipping the bridge of his nose, and he wiped the remnant of sleep from his own tired and disturbed eyes, before bringing the reasoning from his tired mind to his lips. 'Looks like his heart surrendered. He was an age… a late night and uncharacteristic exertion yesterday must have weakened it.'

'Uncharacteristic exertion?' enquired Jack.

'A long walk yesterday,' replied the bishop.

'Aye, he was lookin' fer Kate. I directed him tae the beach,' added Robert.

Jack looked to the upturned bench and a misplaced coffer, all used, he thought, to barricade the door. He raised his eyes to Kate.

'Kate.'

'Yes, Jack.'

'What did he want with you?'

'Nothing particular.'

The bishop joined Jack's questioning. 'He must have had something in mind, child. I understand the beach where you collect is not an easy walk from here.'

'Did he not confide his reasons to you, *my Lord?*' replied Kate.

'No, my child, he retired early to write some letters. I did not see him much at all yesterday.'

Kate was clear and calm as she answered. There were no signs of distress in her voice. Nothing to indicate a worry held from the remembrance of yesterday's troubled encounter. 'Then all I can say is he probably wished to spend some time with fairer company.'

'Perhaps. He did seem fond of the sight of pretty flesh,' replied the bishop. 'Still it is a strange affair. He barricaded himself in his room, so he must have possessed fear of something. Stranger still, are his book boxes. They are astray, so I cannot find his letters.'

Jack looked on Kate, her expression revealed nothing. But Francis had his arm around Kate to comfort her against the sight of death. His concern for Kate was admirable, but peculiar. Peculiar for Francis that is, he not particularly known for a tender disposition, or a growing kindliness in his old age. Jack removed his stare from Kate and Francis and addressed the bishop.

'Perhaps he used the excuse of writing letters simply to retire early after his walk. The book boxes in another place. We will find them.'

'And the barricade?' asked the bishop.

Jack replied, 'We are in dangerous lands, Thomas, and the lock on his door was probably rusted,' Jack shook his head, then exclaimed with eyes wide, '*Gads*, I feel like barricading my door sometimes.'

The bishop heard Jack's explanation, but the corpulent man issued no nod or sound of agreement, instead he remained in careful examination of the room. His eyes moved from the strewn furniture forming the broken barricade, to the objects atop the oak chest that stood beside the bed. The candle, in its pewter holder, was completely wasted, the priest's pen present by its side, but no ink well. Then he pulled back the bed sheet, to examine again the dead priest. This time he noticed a slight discolouration on his bottom lip. Ink. The bishop opened the priest's mouth to study the stain more closely, and pulled at the tongue. It too was discoloured. The bishop pondered a moment, creating the last moments of the priest. Father Freke, he thought, did not die in his sleep, as he had not blown out the candle before he retired. But then he supposed, he could have fallen asleep and let the candle burn. But he had written, his pen was there. He had wetted the nib and stained his lip. But where was the ink, the papers? His eyes scanned the room for a chest, or panelling that may hide a secret.

By the fireplace was a large iron wood-box, filled to the top with wood for the fire. Wood was also stacked on the grate, not laid for a fire, just stacked. 'So much wood in summer?' he muttered. He studied the iron wood-box sitting on the oak floor away from the grate, and at the bottom corner there was an ink stain.

The bishop addressed the room, 'Who was at Father Freke's

door first?'

'Me, my Lord,' replied the serving boy. 'I was joined by Katherine, Robert and Francis, who helped me force the door. When we saw the Father dead, Robert went for you, sir, and Katherine sent me to raise the Master.'

The bishop then turned to the bed, prodded and poked the mattress and again looked around the room. He looked at the oak panelling, at the few richly embroidered wall hangings, then he spoke again in a sterner tone. 'Captain Brownfield, I am dismayed and disappointed.'

Jack's face showed concern, but it was nothing to the look on Kate's face. All Jack could do was reply to the bishop. 'Sorry Thomas, how are you troubled?'

'Troubled by you to have me as your guest and treat my comfort so badly, this is a far comfier bed and better room than mine.'

'My apologies, my Lord.'

'Accepted. I need to prepare for my return. Jack, will you tend to poor Father Freke? He is another assistant I have outlived. God rest his lamentable soul.'

The bishop walked to the door, but hesitated to leave. Instead he turned to Kate.

'My dear Kate, if his letters show up, send them on.' The bishop shuddered, 'The summer is warm, but the room is cold… I suggest you warm it up and light the fire. There is plenty tinder in the box… wood… and *paper* perhaps. But, my child, make sure you first remove Father Freke from the heat. He is already beginning to smell fouler than he did in life.'

Chapter XII

Four old men rode the hill; Jack the youngest and Tom the oldest. But old age is one age. There was twenty years between them in fact, and although twenty years between four boys defines men from boys, twenty years between four old men defines nothing but old men. All wore the same age, all were seen the same—*four old men.*

Tom started the ballad as he rode, his nag surefooted on the ridge. Robert, riding alongside, joined in with the response,

> *'My bones ache.'*
> *'Have ye bones tae ache, or are they powder in yer flesh?'*
> *'Nah the bones are there because they ache.'*
> *'Then be glad ye feel the pain in yer head, because if ye didn't ye'd be dead.'*

Jack brought up the rear, grinning at the men's ballad, warmed by their company and their wit. And even if the other three older men viewed Jack still their leader, Jack saw nothing but old friends in front of him, unfortunate to take his lead.

The land was poor around their tower hideout. Marsh covered the low areas near the coast, the soil poor over some considerable area before better land could be found. Only the higher areas had fair pasture, but it led to extensive moor fit only for grazing sheep. This was *Maxwell* territory, Dumfriesshire, but the power and wealth of their reign was not reflected in their land, or the poor peoples that worked it.

Francis groaned in his saddle and announced, 'The moor is to the land as the head is to the body after a heavy night's drinking. Witless and poorly.'

The years had certainly not mellowed Francis. They had not produced a kindlier old man. He was what he always was, and worse still—a sour soul.

'It's nae so bad,' replied Robert. 'There's poorer land we've seen. At least it's green.'

'The question is, are we to call this green our home?' countered Tom.

'Nah, the question is, why are we ridin' this green, it been so hostile?' replied Robert.

'Well are we stayin', Jack?' asked Tom.

Jack had avoided sharing with the men since the bishop left. He had suppressed a heavy heart from his friends. But the question was asked and all three men were looking to him for an answer.

'Seems I'm not welcome on this island.'

Robert was the first to reply, 'Then we should go tae a better island.'

Robert's response lifted Jack a little. 'I am afraid we will find no sanctuary in England or Scotland. Henri Hueçon has done his job well. I am seen as a traitor, and you by association, traitors too.'

Robert shook his head. 'I told ye when ye were a lad that you should watch yerself with that Frenchy.'

'Yes, Robert, I recall your concerns. I will say again what I have said time and time before. Henri only seeks my demise or my contrition. You will fare better without me at your head. You do not walk away from the *Black Merchants Guild* without consequence.'

Tom replied, 'Ye were always ower dramatic… Ye should have been on the stage, perhaps dressed like a lass.' Tom as ever made light of a seriousness, and Jack felt his hair tingle as if Tom's fingers were amongst it.

Francis then spoke, 'I take it the old bishop couldn't speak on our behalf?'

'No… I suspect Henri's hand is at the throat of anyone that can help,' replied Jack.

Francis shrugged his shoulders and raised his eyebrows. 'Then as soon as our location is known, there will be no hiding here.' Francis shook his head. 'An old man should be spending his last years by the fire, and no riding cold hills in heavy steel and chafed by leather long past its wearing. We'll need to go further north, I suspect, where it's colder and wetter, or over the seas where it's hotter. Where my sorry steel will make me sweat even more, to chafe my skin even worse.' Francis shook his head again. 'Jeopardy is not a good game for old men. I'll pray for the day when I'll be able to close both my eyes when I sleep. When my company is only women to warm my flesh and feed me fine.'

Robert, nettled by the bleating, shouted for Francis to hear, 'I can make ye close yer eyes today, ye sad sour man, that is if my blade disnae shatter on yer brittle auld bones.'

Robert's retort was lost on Francis. He was still caught in his own world of woe and distrust, and he looked around for the hidden eyes he felt upon him, and he muttered low for only himself and his horse to hear. 'Kate's wicked brew was for nothing I suspect… One less spy for Hueçon perhaps, but I suspect the Frenchy watches us even now.'

The men rode a while more, maintaining a steady course on

the ridge with the sea on their right hand, Dumfriesshire on their left. As they rode, Jack recalled times before he lived life as a hunted stag. Before he was chased place to place by a man long practiced in the stalk; pushing him on from his safe places, wearing him down, prolonging the kill because the kill was not the pleasure of the hunt, but to seek his surrender, and for him to bow down exhausted, to invite death by the hunter because death is all that was left to give. The woes of Jack were heavy. He looked on to his three old comrades and his sadness grew deeper. He knew that not even escape within the Marches; a bad land of disorder, could protect them for long. Then out of deepness of thought, came a lighter thought, and Jack drifted into reverie. And as Jack drifted into times past, and remembered other rides like this one; taken for a ride's sake and nothing else, he recalled Eleanor to his side, and they rode once more the hill and valley, bareback and free.

Eventually a village came into view; a few houses only, all with smoke; a blacksmith, sounding out anvil tunes; some enclosures free from stock; and more importantly, no towers.

'I need a drink,' announced Tom, 'There's bound to be an inn or drinking parlour down yon village.'

Robert nodded. 'Aye, time tae take drink and rest my arse. This saddle must be new, it needs mair breakin' in.'

'I suspect it's your bony arse that's broken,' replied Francis, turning to Jack to say, 'Is it wise to show ourselves, *Captain?* We who hide. Strangers will be noticed, and any welcome will be shallow.'

Debate followed, and solution was sought by a show of hands; three to one, and Francis grumbled all the way to the village.

There was no inn, but a house showed a sign that it served ale and beer. The four men entered and ordered drinks, and because of their better attire, the housekeeper ensured her poor ale was better served, and her feigned hospitality better delivered. Francis was the first to notice the attention of another four men, sitting in the corner of the large room; a byre converted into a drinking parlour. It was not hard. The parlour was far from busy.

As the drinks were consumed, Francis belaboured his concerns. Tom and Robert cracked on, and Jack had left the parlour to relieve himself. However on his return, he was stopped by one of the seated watchers, by a question.

'Whit's yer name, auld man?'

The men were fighters not farmers; their wrapped weapons under the table announced it. *Swords and bows,* thought Jack. No steel about them, but reinforced leather jacks about their upper bodies and steel caps by their sides.

Jack responded, 'What is it to you, *friend?*'

'Friendly interest in strangers in such fine attire,' replied the spokesman of the four, wearing a disparaging smile.

'Well, friend. We're strangers wishing to remain so,' replied Jack.

'Ye carry nae local dialect, so I'm figurin' ye must be an English gentleman? Are ye an outlander? A poor soul who has lost his way? A stranger tae oor land, its rules 'n' customs?' The spokesman looked to his comrades and grinned. 'Ye must be, otherwise why would ye be drinkin' in my presence, without payin' me proper respect?' The spokesman paused, waiting for Jack's response. None came.

'Lost yer tongue, Englishman?'

Jack's anger, quicker to provoke in his maturity, was apparent. 'I'm no gentleman, and if you prefer dialect; *cush mun*, I'm nee Englishman, but a canny Borderer man, who divvent want t'clart aboot wi' a load o' feckless *cuddys.*'

The man's smile disappeared from his face at the insult. 'D'ya wan' a clout, *stranger?*'

Jack rested his anger and smiled, heedful of Francis' protests. He surrendered to the fact that his veiled presence in Dumfriesshire would be better served without public shows of petty brawling. So behind Jack's relaxed smile was a silent shepherds' count, calming thoughts fronted by a friendly voice. 'And why, sir, would you want to fight me? How about I pay for another round of drinks for you and your friends. Make it two, in lieu of my ignorance to your local customs and, of course… *your importance.*'

'Nah, it's too late, I'm afraid I'm wantin' mair than ale tae satisfy my hurtin' honour. My ale here is free, and I'm findin' yer hollow words prick my pride sore.'

'And sir, what would mend your pride?'

'Well I like yer breeches. I've never seen fairer clothin' fer the legs,' and pointing to each of Jack's seated colleagues in turn, he said, 'And his fine jack, his bonny cap, and his boots.'

'Ah, I see, spoils of war,' replied Jack.

'We are four, ye are four, seems fair.'

Jack looked the four men up and down. 'Not so fair, you don't seem to have anything we're needing.'

The man took the insult, jumped up and sent his stool clattering to the wall. He barked, 'Outside, auld man. This *cuddy* is aboot tae kick yer arse.'

'Swords, fists?' asked Jack.

'Fists I think. Wouldn't want tae cut them breeches.'

The noise in the inn all but disappeared for a moment, until the sound of footsteps travelling over the stone floor, aided by a walking stick, broke the silent tension.

'Ah, the other auld man approaches,' said the now standing spokesman, addressing his still seated colleagues.

Tom made his way to the table, aided as he did in older age

with his stick, Knocker. Except Knocker this day was upside down, on his fat bulbous head. Tom's progress was slow as he put feeling back into stiffened legs, but accompanied all the way with a warm and confident smile.

'What's the matter, Captain, these lads cussin' ya?' enquired Tom.

'No, Tom, they're proposing a fight. We are just deciding terms.'

The spokesman's face changed; cocky it was no longer, concerned it was. He looked to his ale-mates for direction, because he had thought better of a tussle with these four old men. Jack's easy manner, joined with Tom's easier demeanour, had unnerved him. His ale-mates were anxious too, none more than the one nearest to Tom. He shifted on his seat, and his eyes darted from his leader to Jack. His leader's intimidation had failed. The man knew Jack was inviting the fight, and suddenly the shifty man did not see four old men, only four seasoned soldiers. He rose rapidly, and started to draw his dagger, but Tom's action was swifter. *Knocker* made hard contact with the man's head at the end of Tom's violent swing. Jack acted too, and seeing the remaining three men's attention on Tom's action, he launched himself at the table, tipping it over so it separated men from men—men from their bundled weapons. Jack lunged at the spokesman, his fist swung heavy into the man's face, the impetus knocking him off his feet, to fall hard on the floor.

The others, seated, did not move, because Francis held them under cocked and pointed pistols; hidden pistols produced from under his own bundled cloak.

It was Francis that ushered the two men outside, dragging their colleagues under pistol's point.

It was Jack who raised his thanks with Tom. 'Must you always intercede with regards to inn fights, Tom?'

'Aye, it's a habit, hard to break.'

But Jack did not reply, because a change in the horizon had caught his attention. In the far distance, a group of horsemen appeared riding steady.

Ten or twelve, it was difficult to reckon—fresh trouble? Jack thought.

'I reckon we've walked into a wilder place than the wild place from which we have just walked,' said Tom, as he brought Knocker strong against one of the detained men's genitals. The poor man screamed, and doubled up collapsing to the ground clutching his crotch.

The other man still standing, quickly offered words to save him from a similar beating. 'They're oor kin... We were meetin' them here prior tae a raid.'

Francis looked on, and spat on the two unconscious men heaped together on the ground. 'He lies. All here are a stranger to the truth. All born with a lie on their mother's lips to whom their true father may be.'

Jack was not so sure, and he proffered, 'Even so. So many men on horseback are not good news. There could be truth in it. Better ride, and ride hard.'

The man's plea to save his balls from a beating from Tom's friend Knocker was heeded. His genitals were saved from pain, however his skull was not, and four old men took to horse to leave the four younger men on the road, either insensible or in pain.

The four managed to keep a distance between their pursuers, their own nags better rested, better ridden. It was twelve or fifteen miles from their tower, and although they galloped to it, they all were unhappy at the thought of revealing their hideout location to *reivers*, unknown in terms of family, connection, or purpose.

The ride was hard, and Francis, the better and swiftest

horseman due to his meagre build, led the group all the way. All the time their pursuers did not relent, they came on strong and swift.

After two or three miles, it was clear no ground had been gained from the reivers, and Francis steered the fleeing riders to a hill, hoping to find better ground and cover from which to shake off their pursuers.

It was with difficulty that they cleared the crest of the hill, to view once more the coast, their progress slowed by the climb, allowing the reivers to close—merely a pistol shot away. But it was not the sight of the approaching reivers behind that drew the old men's attention, but another sight of horsemen to the fore, hidden on the other side of the hill—*three hundred horsemen.*

The four riders halted briefly, to study the troop at the foot of the hill—their delay a delight to the chasing group, their cheers and hoots ringing in the four's ears. But still no pistol discharge.

The four, spurred on by the closing shouts, galloped on down towards the host below.

Robert was first to draw his sword. He screamed, *'At em lads!'*

Jack, Tom and Francis joined Robert in his war cry, and drew their swords, waving steel at the gross line of horsemen.

As the four men galloped down the hill, the three hundred spurred their nags and drew their swords to meet them, with deafening cry. Soon the sound of the three hundred drowned out the noise of the four.

At their point of closure, and as the pursuing reivers cleared the ridge to see again their quarry, Jack, Robert, Tom and Francis wheeled their nags to join the three hundred in the charge back up the hill to meet their pursuers.

Those reivers ran well that day, but with tired nags they were soon caught by the gross host, and butchered—every one of them.

ඟ✕ඬ

By dusk, Jack had reached the round tower ahead of his troop, and he gathered Robert, Tom, Francis, and the sergeant-at-arms who had led the three hundred horse against the reivers.

'Return to *Ayre*, and this time stay your position,' ordered Jack, addressing the young sergeant. 'We need to be circumspect without a banner to fight under, or a friendly sponsor to pay our salary. The Maxwells will not be pleased to have us trampling their ground.' Jack threw a commanding look towards Tom. 'A steadier hand will go with you—to ensure you heed your instructions.'

The young sergeant-at-arms dipped his head in a shallow bow to display regret. 'I apologise, Captain, but I was unhappy to have so much distance between us, so I brought half the troop.'

'I appreciate your good thoughts, but kind thoughts do not make good tactics,' replied Jack.

'Has your lady arrived yet, sir?'

'No. Not yet, sergeant.'

Robert ran his nag around to bark orders at men, and then returned to Jack. 'I'm afraid today's skirmish will unsettle oor hosts. We'll soon find oor welcome diminished, and we'll be needin' tae go. Better be foreign mercenaries in a foreign land, than findin' ourselves scrappin' with the Maxwell's. So where do we travel, Jack?'

'First we wait,' replied Jack, 'More visitors to welcome. Then to Antwerp, to deal with the *Frenchy*—scores to settle—gold to collect. Then perhaps to the Americas for more gold and land to settle.'

[The score is settled under the title, *A Man of Antwerp*.]

Chapter XIII

Jack had turned the anteroom to the hall into his office and quarters. It was a place to write and to be alone. It was, for a while at least, a place to escape his responsibilities, and it was as comfortable as he could make it, with what belongings he was allowed to have in his fugitive life, and the best of what the tower could provide in the way of a bed and limited furnishings. Jack spent many hours there writing and waiting, whilst his men stood guard. And as they waited, a few visitors more came while they lodged, and Robert feared them all, for Jack had not disclosed their purpose to him, and because of this, he could see nothing but danger.

The danger this day formed itself into the shape of twelve armed horsemen riding into the tower compound accompanying a coach.

'I'm here to see Jack Brownfield.'

Robert recognized their leader, but hid his familiarity under a dour countenance. 'Who calls on him?'

The lead rider dismounted, clearing his mouth with a lusty mucous bullet that barely missed Robert's left boot. 'Tell him Jed Maxwell comes a calling.'

Robert raised his vexed eyes from the shiny spittle to a thin sharp face that wore a thick black moustache, which in turn topped a sneer. Robert knew of the man, a senior within the Maxwells and well related to the headsman of that clan, but with aspirations to enhance his own reputation even at the expense of his kin and family's name. Robert looked past Jed to survey the riders, all fighters without doubt, and then he looked about himself for the support of his own men and only Francis was around to be seen. Robert could only hope that others were about and hidden from view, but even so, the numbers still were not in his favour. The danger was seen and considered. Actions were considered and dismissed. Resistance was dismissed and compliance accepted.

'I'll show ye up. Yer men can stay here,' announced Robert.

Jed Maxwell had followed Robert's eyes as he weighed up the riders and he knew what Robert was contemplating.

'Dinnae worry lad. If I was comin' tae take yer leader, I'd be bringin' mair men.'

Robert led the Maxwell to Jack's quarters and showed him in, but as he closed the door behind him he left his ear at the door.

'How do ye find the accommodation?'

'Modest.'

'I'm sorry we had no palaces tae offer.'

'Yet the fee you take for this tower would pay for a palace.'

'Sanctuary has a heavy purse, Jack Brownfield, or should I address ye proper by yer clan name?'

'My proper address is John Brownfield, my clan name long forgotten.'

'Perhaps by ye, but many have longer memories. If ye were not payin' such a bonny price, we'd be handin' ye over tae yer enemies fer a fee.'

'I suspect your family would not do my enemies such a

favour.'

'Perhaps so, *Brownfield*, but your presence in our care can become a worry tae my family, if yer boys have a mind tae trample our land. We may have to reconsider our bargain—our fee.'

'Then I will tighten the leash on my men, and bear the draughts through this pile of sorry stone without further complaint.'

Jed Maxwell looked around Jack's room. He looked at the walls with meagre decoration and floors with poor coverings, thinking of the tower's history; an inheritance held by the Maxwells in abeyance, whilst dispute between female issue of the Cairns name, long moved on, fought their battle for rightful ownership. 'Aye, it's a sad house for its loneliness.'

'What may I ask is the purpose of your visit? Is it simply to issue a warning? I suspect it is not simply good hosting.'

Jed Maxwell walked to the door of the anteroom, clicked up the latch and pulled open the door. 'I have a guest for ye. A lady Eleanor Howard. We intercepted her coach traveling from Carlisle. Stay here. I'll send the lady up. I would not like my men to see ye. Some have Armstrong kin, and thus have long outstanding scores to settle,' Maxwell smiled, 'and I would not like their steel to deprive my family of yer gold.'

Jack's face lit up with the news. *She comes to see me.* He had feared she would not respond to his invitation, business of the heart unfinished. He thought the journey too dangerous for her, but her presence here confirmed a love lost was not forgotten.

But as he waited, disquietude waited with him. He could not disregard his nettling companion. He could not send it away. And for all he hoped she would come, and wished reunion, he grew nervous at the very thought of it, and now the moment had come for meeting; he wished he never sponsored it.

Again he thought he would not be worthy of Eleanor's effort.

For to travel from the safety of the South to the menace the North was task indeed, and a task that only love would sponsor, *why else would she come?* But for all this reason, he now doubted her motives and grew fearful of the outcome.

His anxiety rattled a dozen questions around his mind.

He did not know how he would be with her? How would she be with him? Would courtesy mask her feelings, or would her feelings have disappeared so many years ago?

Jack paced, and paced some more. His march up and down the oak panelled anteroom was punctuated with sharp punches of his fist against the wall.

Violence to clear his mind perhaps? No, it was violence to clear his heart of feelings—feelings that may betray him.

Eleanor, now widowed, had been married for a very long time, and to a man not sympathetic to Jack, or Jack's cause.

Would she be sympathetic to him, or would she view him as one would treat a noble enemy, with only cold courtesy?

The door opened and Eleanor came in. Jack's nervousness did betray him and he could not speak. No courtesy from him. No address. No smile.

She was as he remembered. Age had not dulled his view of her. Time had not marred his thought of her. She was what she always was, what she had always been—his first love.

'Do you not greet me sir, as one should greet an old friend?'

Her voice was the music of a time not forgotten. It had not diminished in his heart. The sound of it brought back a boy—a boy without the scars of years of cruel existence, of violence and hardship.

He found sounds to offer back, his heart provided them. 'It is beyond the realms of my dreams to see you once more, my lady.'

'Sir you address me well, like a gentleman. Not like my

stripling Scot.'

Her words were warm and her smile warmer still. She had not disregarded him. Time had not worn down her resolve to love him for eternity. Jack's heart lifted itself from fear. It soared into the clouds. He walked forward and instead of kneeling to take her hand to kiss it like a gentleman, he took her and kissed her like a man who had been parted from his lover for a very, very long time.

ഇൗരു

The days after that meeting, and the days before she left him to return to her home in Bristol, were the happiest he could remember. Happiest, because his days up to now had been harsh enough make him forget what happiness was. These new days were without the discomforts of life. They contained no facade of cordiality, no discretion. No secrecy was issued to hide their love from the disapproval of parents, the prying of their servants and the censure of their secretaries, or indeed from any in the world who would deem their coupling improper.

On the last day of their reunion they walked along the coast that fronted the tower. A coast long and wide, with a path firm and fine. They chose it to be alone, but they were not alone for Robert, concerned for their safety, kept a loyal distant sentinel. Robert ensured there was no intrusion into their world so they could speak privately. Their words hidden from a society that would offer them harm and possibly harm to come. They walked in quiet commune, too frightened to ask what the years had done to each other; what sufferings and miseries had eroded their spirit, but at a point along the coast; where the sea, path and hill came together in perfect communion; where the sight of all God's glory was too much to hold back a praise of its form, Eleanor spoke.

'Did you ever find your perfect place?'

Jack smiled at Eleanor's remembrance of a long past dream. 'No, but there is always tomorrow, so hope for it exists.'

Eleanor was caught by the beauty of the Solway sea, the land and mountain in the distance, the sand underfoot and the green all around. 'Is this not a perfect place?'

'It is a fine place in a good, but harsh land. My life now seeks calm and its perfection.'

'And how has your life been, Jack, whilst searching for your perfect place?'

'I suppose it has been how it was meant to be. How God planned it. He has kept me alive for some purpose greater than myself, and believe me that has been no easy task.'

Jack brought out a locket from under his shirt and showed it to Eleanor. 'I have your locket. I keep it always. It has been taken from me many times, but I always retrieve it.'

Eleanor smiled and put her hand on the locket and returned it into Jack's shirt. 'I am glad God watches over you.'

Jack held Eleanor's hand against his chest, as she released the locket. 'I am glad you watch over me too.'

Eleanor paused her discourse and her walk. She stood, eyes away from Jack towards the sea, in quiet, sad acceptance, and her understanding of their reality was on her lips. 'I sense I will not see you again.'

'I sense it too. I am lodged here for good reason. Too many enemies, including those with a royal and not so forgiving ear. It appears I cannot offer a soft life here for those I love. I can only bring misfortune.'

'Where will you go?'

'Far away. Far enough that I'm forgotten by those who wish me dead or worse.'

'Is there such a place?'

Jack thought on Eleanor's question a little, and without conviction answered, 'The Americas… *perhaps*.'

Eleanor filled her senses with the sea and thought on Jack and her life. She did not wish him gone from her, nor did she care greatly for her life as it had been. She turned from the sea and looked desperately into Jack's eyes and clung to his hand. Squeezing it hard she pleaded, 'I will go with you. Let me go with you. Robert has told me all that befalls you. All that makes you fear for your kindred… but that does not matter to me. Give an old woman some adventure before she dies… some danger to put a smile back on sorrowed lips… please, *I beg you*.'

Jack held Eleanor's hand tightly and his feelings for her erupted in his voice, 'For all that I love you, *old woman*, I cannot take you.'

Eleanor pleaded again, this time a tear fell from her eye to wet her lips, 'Take me with you. Do not lose me. We are free. Do not put our love in chains.'

Jack could not believe it—a woman; a chance to change his life, to find comfort waiting for him each day. A love he thought lost—returned. It was not to be. It could not be. For Jack's life would not allow it. A shared life could mean her death. He would have to walk away.

Eleanor looked deeper into Jack's eyes, and he closed down his soul so she could not see the hurt dwelling within him. Jack could only see her smile, so soft. Her face framed so beautifully in the cool light of the morning. Eleanor's free hand came to greet Jack's face, to cup, to touch his cheek. It came to display her affection for him, and his face bowed and fell into her hand. Jack closed his eyes. And the hurt within him rose up and, free from his restraint, escaped into the warmth of her palm—and she knew his pain.

Eleanor talked softly now, no urgency in her voice. It only rang with calm and compassion. 'You will leave me?'

'I have to leave.'

'You think by leaving me you will save me from your troubles?'

'To stay with me, may bring death to you.'

'My Jack. My love. Do you think I stay alive if you leave me?'

'Death is close for me, Eleanor. I have escaped it so many times. I have lost many friends. I do not want to lose any more. If you go with me, I may lose your life and I could not bear it.'

Eleanor pulled harshly away from Jack, wiping the tear from her face. Anger colouring her words, 'Then why do you summon me to you, simply to send me away?'

Jack said nothing. He had no words to comfort her.

Eleanor's fury abated and she replaced it with a feigned soft laugh, composure and less desperate words. 'Forgive an old and tired woman her childish desires.' She took a deep breath to remove the remainder of distress in her voice and continued, 'I suspect your friends provide you respite from death. I suspect they love you more than you know.'

Jack looked to Robert in the distance and nodded. 'I know of their love, it has been demonstrated a hundred times, in sacrifice and loyalty.' Jack's attention returned to Eleanor and he said, 'I love you, Eleanor. I will tread more confidently if I know you are safe.'

'Then I will go and be safe, and I will mourn your parting from me as I did all those years ago.'

Jack smiled and took Eleanor's hand, and they walked a while longer on the rocky path into a deep blue day.

∾∾

The next morning was cold and grey. The horses were complaining in the courtyard. Jack checked everything meticulously. He inspected the horses' harnessing, the wheels and bearings, the horses' hooves, the coach for its comfort and the coach driver for his fitness to pilot the carriage.

'Take care of the coach, Francis. A pretty hire this will have cost, and a prettier cargo it does carry. Pistols loaded?'

Disdain shaped Francis' mouth. 'Ask if I've remembered to put my boots on, why don't you. I ask you, *captain*, what's the point of an empty pistol?' Francis' mouth found pleasure in his remembrance that his skill with pistols was far better than Jack's, and he found a cloaked insult to throw. 'Mind you, *captain*, some would find a pistol a better bludgeon tool, or as a missile to throw. That way, they would better see their target hit.'

Jack stared at Francis with raised eyebrow, and Francis thought better of his jibe. He thought it better to impress with his diligence, rather than nettle a man already grieving for the loss of his woman. 'For this sorry land, I've brought two more pistols, tucked into my blanket.'

Francis plucked out two fine wheel lock dags from the folds of his blanket and presented them to his captain. Jack examined the pistols closely.

'I recognise these pistols. Father Freke had a box of pistols just like these. Fine pieces.'

Francis, not knowing Jack had prior knowledge of their ownership and thus their theft, retrieved the weapons quickly from Jack's inquisitive examination.

'Aye, Jack, not right for a god-man of the Queen's cloth to carry such fine pistols.'

'The Queen's cloth. Do you suspect he was Elizabeth's man?'

'Perhaps not. The gold in his purse was Dutch, so perhaps he is sent by way of another preened imperious feminal prince.'

Francis then looked about him as if a hundred eyes were on him and he simply winked, not at Jack, but at his accomplice, Kate, who stood beyond them near the coach.

Jack dropped his interrogation of Francis and turned his attention to Kate and the condition of the morning air. 'Kate, fetch more blankets, it will be cold today.'

Kate, wrapped well against the early morning cold, ran into the hall to fetch more blankets as he requested, and Jack moved his scrutiny to beyond the coach, to Robert and the four riders with him. All the horses kicked and fussed against the icy air and Francis and the other riders worked hard to keep their will in check.

'Stay with her, Robert, keep her safe. I beg you.'

Robert bowed forward on a great grey mare, a prize from their recent encounter with the reivers, smiled and placed a leather-gloved hand onto Jack's shoulder. 'Fear not, Jack. I will ensure she returns safely. But what of ye? Will ye be safe?'

'I will wait here until you return. There are men still with me to assure my safety, Maxwell patronage, and besides, I have my chronicles and writings to keep me busy.'

Jack's response did not appease Robert's concern, because he knew his safety could not be assured. 'Can ye trust these Maxwells?'

'We have their amity, well paid for, and I have their word. That will suffice.'

'Aye, we've paid a healthy fee fer their hospitality, and fer a healthier fee they'd see ye harmed just as easily.'

'Do you not have faith in a pledge between Borderers, Robert?'

'Honour and repute has its price, Jack.'

Robert's concern remained undiluted, but he smiled nevertheless. Robert's smile always warmed Jack, and he felt easier for having him protect Eleanor. Robert turned his head and looking towards the house announced Eleanor's appearance in the courtyard.

'Eleanor comes. Jack, it's time fer ye tae say goodbye.'

Eleanor was too beautiful for the morning. The morning was too grey, the air too damp, too cold. She clothed her nobility in an ermine trimmed cloak of fine crimson velvet. The wide hood framed her face, soft in the mist, her eyes wetted by her tears.

'Captain John Brownfield, my soul weeps that I will never see you again.'

Jack amused by Eleanor's use of his proper name and title, replied, 'I have no soul to weep my love, you have taken it. But it is in good keeping, I suspect… I may reclaim it one day. I could never say never… it's too absolute.'

Eleanor smiled and she boarded the coach. She took one of the blankets placed by Kate from the seat next to her and wrapped it around her against the cold. Jack mounted the footplate and leaned through the coach window.

'I'm sorry it's so cold, Eleanor. God forsakes the Marches. He does nothing but breathe cold air onto us and the poor people here.'

Eleanor, still smiling, replied, 'They are not poor, Jack, they have spirit and God knows it. They have their own nobility and God knows it. My sister, Mary, your long departed wife said all of this.'

Jack thought of Mary and bowed his eyes reverently. 'You have an unerring sense of your sister. She, like you, always could see into the hearts of people. She had a very fine temper, equable and compassionate. A good woman, and I loved her in my poor and deficient way.'

Eleanor put her hand softly on Jack's hand to console him and said, 'We never talked of Mary. I did not wish to talk of past sadness for you during a time of joy for myself. Did you ever exact justice for her death?'

Jack looked upon Eleanor and sorrow distorted his smile. 'Mary is with God. Yes, I sent her murderer to Hell.' With this truth, Jack's eyes lowered and he continued, 'I will join him there one day.'

Eleanor once again smiled at Jack, repealing his self-condemnation. 'You will be with God. I feel this to be true. You are too hard on yourself, my fine Borderer.'

Eleanor had raised Jack's spirit, and with his shoulders squared, he jumped from the coach, ran and slapped the lead horse, shouting, 'In that case, Eleanor, I better make more suitable my time on Earth before I meet him.'

The riders were caught out by Jack's quick action, and Robert, sensing Jack's reason for the deed, responded by spurring the men and coach driver on to take Eleanor quickly from Jack's discomfort.

Jack watched the coach hurry away. Eleanor did not turn around to look at Jack. She did not yell out a parting. She simply closed her eyes and mouthed a whisper.

When the coach was gone—when the last rider paled from view—when it was clear it would not return, Jack walked from his solitary stand to the hall, where Kate waited in the lighted doorway furnished with solace and a blanket to wrap around Jack's shoulders against the cold. Jack's smile thanked Kate for her kind intentions, but his right hand checked her against her offer of comfort. He walked passed her to climb the stair to the hall, to find a chair and the fire burning well under the mantle. He sat undisturbed, and began to remember things long past.

After a long while, he entered his quarters and took up a quill in hand, but the paper remained blank. Another long while passed into the morning and paper was still without ink, until he finally penned a thought...

There are times when it is advantageous to forget an episode of life. When past events bring one to such fierce melancholy, that the very existence of God's divinity is questioned. These times are best forgotten. Allegories and accounts are best left hidden from the page, or from the mouths of poets. One's sorrows are not for others to recount for the amusement of the inn, or to be reported to one's enemies as intelligences against him. Perhaps these times are for only God to know and for God to judge.

PART 3

'the scars of youth'

Chapter XIV

Six brown riders formed a line on the road from Carlisle. Not seven or eight, or even the twenty that travelled that road sixty and six months ago, on their way to France in service of their Queen, from their homes in the Scottish West Border. Twenty riders that would return as six; the six that would mourn the death of the fourteen; the fourteen who died of pox and bloody wounds these past ten months.

Heads of horses and men were low, their passage laboured. The first rider stopped to allow the second to catch up, and lowering a dirt worn woollen scarf from a dirt worn sullen face, spoke to the second in gruff low tones.

'I think another seven hours, lad.'

The second man stretched high in his saddle, shaking off the weary bonds that had kept him rigid since Dover. His face touched the sky as he breathed in deeply.

'Scottish air, Robert. A sweeter smell I have not had under my nose these long past months… *You can almost taste it.*'

Jack was six foot tall, lean and aged beyond his years; twenty five years of life, which showed as forty on his face. A red beard shone beneath blond hair bleached by salt and sun. His face bore no scars and carried a thin nose that gave it a noble bearing. Eyes of steel blue peered out from under bonnet and over scarf to scan horizon, hill and tree to find familiarity in his surroundings. He sighed deeply as he adjusted his body in the saddle.

'Robert, the hills seem smaller and the land less green.'

Robert contemplated Jack's observation before he answered, 'Aye, the land is not as kind a sight as I hoped.'

Both men had come far across the sea from France as mercenaries, paid fighters in a foreign war. Made richer by the share of fees uncollected by their comrades, made poorer by the absence of their comradeship.

Six brown riders gathered together on the road from Carlisle. Brown leather and dented steel under brown woollen cloaks. Heads under rusted iron helmets. All were seven hours from home, all were glad to be near journey's end.

ဆၢ

Fourteen days on the road from Dover had changed the hues of the greens, dulled by the season. Russet and brown, heather and dying fern spread around their way. The topography of the land was now a remote natural barrier of stark and rounded summits atop meandering steep sided valleys. It was wild and rugged, sparse of population, poor of refuge. The peoples spoke with different dialect, but their common protestation and enquiries regarding the riders presence in their midst was discernable, it was full of mistrust. But employing their familiarity of its bewildering landscape, the six riders could pass undetected from one kingdom to another. And so they travelled the high places away from towers and the watch of sentinel posts; eyes against reiver incursion and foreign invasion.

The border crossing long made, they descended towards the populated places. On the approach to Langholm, a modest town, nestling within four hills and the River Esk, it was time to say a goodbye to half their number, as Francis Bell, Henry Crosser and Tom Kemp left to find their wives or women; long left, long neglected and either sore to see them, or glad. But each of the men had a fat purse, so Jack suspected a warmer welcome. Robert was not so sure though, as Tom's wife had long chided him for moving his family ten years back, from, as she put it, 'their soft and downy nest in Cumberland to a hornets' nest in Liddesdale.' However the relocation was less of a hardship for Tom, who had quickly found a warm and accommodating widow in Langholm to soften the loss of his Cumberland home. The parting of husband and wife sixty-seven months ago was none too pleasant, as wife was less than fond of a husband leaving her and four children with no relatives close by for comfort, in order to fight overseas. But the angry parting with his wife was sweetened by a comfortable month between the thighs of his widow. Thus Robert and Jack debated to whom Tom would be returning to that night.

'Methinks Tom will want to see his children,' offered Jack.

'Perhaps, I've seen his bonny bairns, they're as sweet as honey.'

'So it's his wife then, it's decided,' said Jack.

Robert looked towards the direction of Tom's wife and widow in turn, and with careful re-consideration said, 'Castration or caress, chide or charm. What would you be preferin' Jack?'

'A thump or a hump? Mmmm, difficult,' grinned Jack.

Both men smiled and continued on, comforted to know Tom would be back with them when all his reunions and pleasures were indulged.

The remaining three, Jack, Robert and Finn, rode on into the town, larger than last they saw it. And they thought perhaps it was an indication of some degree of new prosperity, some measure of improvement in a land long impaired by the hands of its own peoples and Royal ambition.

The populous was out and milling in the streets, a market was on, and the town was excited. A group of children ran about the riders shouting cheerfully, unsettling their nags. They were hitting and pushing a filled and top-tied bag around the earth with sticks. The bag jumped and shook, cried and hissed as it skittered over the ground.

'Sounds like a cat in a bag,' announced Finn.

'By the noise of it, sounds like two or three,' replied Jack.

'Aye, two or three mousers that would be better employed protectin' the grain,' added Robert disapprovingly.

To see la'al bairns playin' warms me heart,' added Jack sarcastically, mimicking the absent Tom, but failing to exactly capture the big-hearted Cumbrian's droll observation, and vernacular delivery.

'Little divils more like,' countered Finn, looking about him as he steadied his nervous mount.

There was a larger crowd further on; a concentration beyond the market. As the riders picked their way through the busy throng they could see a gallows where the buildings were spaced further apart to open up the street. The crowd, with eyes on the gallows, was seen to part, and the steel heads of three halberds were seen moving through the opening. Eventually, the three blades grew men as they climbed the scaffold. Between them was a man, in hose and gown, hands tied and head low. One of the halberds, under direction from a well-suited gentleman, tore the gown from the poor man's back and put the noose around his neck, whilst a priest looked on. As the riders passed in single file, the crowd's excitement rose as the rope was tightened around the wretched man's neck. Striped and gaol dirty, he met applause from his audience with his involuntary urination, and a tumultuous mocking salute as he was lifted off the scaffold floor by the hangman, to wriggle and kick; his choking quietened beneath the persisting cheers of the crowd. Cheers soon turned to jeers as two rag-clad women ran onto the scaffolding, to each grasp the man's flaying legs, pulling down hard so as to bring his agony to a merciful end.

Finn, sharing the assembly's pleasure, reviewed the grisly scene and hastened his pony to meet Robert ahead of him, and against the noise of the crowd leaned into Robert's ear, whispering, '*Hangers-on.* His kin, methinks.'

Robert turned to witness the spectacle and was in time to see a woman and girl being grabbed and pulled off the scaffold by three grey liveried soldiers.

'Aye kin, or lasses want'n part of the killin'. Who knows, who cares?'

Finn pulled back his horse, his amusement at the cruel spectacle arrested by Robert's doleful carriage. They passed through the remainder of the town without incident. No one seemed to notice the armed riders, or if they did, they seemed not to care.

∞∝

Close to journey's end, when Robert felt his protection of Jack was complete, Finn and Robert parted from Jack. No wives to be reunited with, they took their purses to Edinburgh to find women and better ale to spend it on. Before they left, promises were made to return to Jack before the worst of winter, to return to duties. Jack knew they would return, although little reason existed to maintain their service to him, except the bond the men had with Jack. Closer than kin they were, dedicated to their death.

Jack thus found himself on the road alone, travelling the last few quiet miles towards his father's tower, and to his home. He took this last rare moment of solitude to think about what was to come and what had passed into history. He pushed a hand deep into his shirt to pull out a folded piece of paper, much soiled by a long term of campaigning. He unfolded the dirty paper to read its contents, to remind him of that which was in fact well known to him. But the act of unfolding the sorry piece of script and reading it line by line was his atonement for the lives lost in the folly of his foreign adventure. The script was a muster roll, the names of his men, those goodly and deficient souls he took to war. Many names were struck off, but they would be forever etched in his memory. As he read the list he felt the pain of loss, but his sorrow, long ago seeded and much grown by the death of his comrades and a bloody term of fighting, was naught in comparison to the dread he felt riding on the road to the tower, to a wife long unloved and a father long disregarded.

The Muster Role under John Brownfield, assigned troop captain

Robert Hardie ~ Lanarkshire

Thomas Kemp ~ Cumberland

~~Ned Little {known as Tup Heid}~~ ~ Dumfriesshire ~ Died of fever, France

~~James Nixon~~ ~ Liddesdale ~ Killed, France

~~Henry Musgrave {known as Bendback Bob}~~ ~ Cumberland ~ Killed, France

~~Edmund Turner~~ ~ Liddesdale ~ Died of fever, France

~~James Clarey~~ ~ Cumberland ~ Killed, France

~~Thomas Irvine {known as Pinchback}~~ ~Annandale ~ Killed, France

~~Stephen Howard~~ ~ Carlisle ~ Wounded, Calais, died at sea

Henry Crosser {known as Digger Jack} ~ Liddesdale

Richard Hunter {known as Thumper} ~ Liddesdale ~ Deserted, France

Francis Bell ~ Cumberland

~~Henry Gilchrist {known as Windy Gilly}~~ ~Annandale ~ Died, fever, France

~~Robert Black {known as Slack o'Jack}~~ ~Annandale ~ Killed, France

~~Edward Irvine~~ ~Annandale ~ Killed, France

Finn McCuul ~ Carlow, Ireland

Henry Harden ~ Cumberland ~ Missing, France

~~Stephen Moffat~~ ~ Dumfrieshire ~ Died of fever, France

~~Henry Nixon~~ ~Annandale ~ Wounded, France, died at sea.

The last hill cleared, the tower house was in sight. Sited well, defensible against skirmish and raid, but too small to throw off serious assault, it stood amidst several stone built outbuildings, stables, storehouses and dwellings that housed family, followers and servants. The settlement was substantial against others similar, enjoying a long history of a family who had served King and Queen for three hundred years. Jack's home was amongst the cluster of buildings, modest in size, but better appointed than many homes in the Marches. Rooms enough for a new family, but empty through failure of Jack and Mary to produce a living child, a great sorrow to them both, but Mary more so. The house had been much improved by Jack's father, providing a fitting shelter for a returning son and his new bride. No expense had been spared to better the comfort of a house once occupied by Thomas and his wife—Thomas, who was lost at Solway Moss some sixteen years past. The house remained empty after Thomas' widow died a few years after her husband. Some said she had a weak heart, others said her heart broke with the loss of Thomas, who was a considerate and wise husband.

The much larger four-storey rectangular tower house had been much improved over the years, with addition of a large four-storey wing to accommodate growing status and increasing family, a larger enclosing barmkin wall to protect new housing, a grand hall, gatehouse and bigger stores.

As Jack approached he was soon recognised by the men and women in the field, tending stock. But their nods bore no smile for a man previously well liked by his father's peoples. He received similar guarded greeting as he reached the gatehouse. The armed men at the gate simply nodded and stood aside. Acknowledgement, as Jack dismounted and handed over the reins of his nag, but no real greeting.

At the fore-stair, the stone steps leading to the first floor external entrance to the tower, Edward, his father's steward greeted him.

'It's gud tae see ya, Master Jack, ye've bin away too lang.'

'Good to see you, Edward… I hope your lady wife keeps well.'

Edward looked furtively about him as if Jack's mention of his wife was for her benefit, so she must be close. But she was nowhere to be seen.

'Er… aye, she keeps well. If ye want tae go up t'hall, I'll fetch the family.'

Edward said no more, and as he scurried off, Jack thought him curiously relieved to be away from his company.

Jack climbed the stairs, still puzzled by his subdued reception and walked through the open door, and as he did, he ran his gloved hand slowly over the stout timbers to evoke a child's memory, and then he pushed aside the thought with the *yett*, an inner iron grated door.

Access to the upper floors was by a narrow winding staircase, a newel stair with its risers built clockwise to advantage the defender against any attacker's right-handed swordplay. The scars on the wall as he climbed the stairs, reminded him of the endless sword practice with his brothers, and how his father would bind his right hand to his side for weeks at a time to force an even handed skill with his left hand, and thus advantage him in fighting. He was thankful for his early tutoring, although at the time he hated his father's cruelty in his delivery of it.

On the first floor was the great hall. It was well appointed and more spacious than the remainder of the tower house. The fireplace bore a large crackling fire, testament to his father's age and lessening resistance to the cold, and as he walked over to warm his backside over the intense orange flames, he forced out a long breath filled with inquietude that had been constricting his body ever since he had entered his father's house. On further inspection of the lintel above the fire, the painted frieze of hunters and dogs pursuing their prey; stags and wolves together, it seemed less colourful than Jack remembered, and as he looked about the room, at the wood cladding and the tapestries, the painted walls and the stout oak furniture, the room appeared less grand. He remembered how it was all those years ago before he left for foreign war. He thought on the many times, as he lay on cold sodden fields, or traveled on mud filled ruts the French declared to be roads, how he longed to be lodged in the comfort of this great hall. But this was no longer his home he thought. Comfort was the next bed and hot meal, not the remembering of childhood and the rare moments of repose it brought.

'My son, praise God you are here!'

Jack turned from the fire to see his mother, carrying her age beautifully as always, in a simple grey-blue gown over a grey-blue dress, modest as befitting her age, but ornate enough to mark her rank.

'How are you, Mother?'

'*How am I? How am I?* Approach me my lad and kiss me.'

Jack was careful to preserve propriety and took ten dutiful steps towards his mother and affectionately kissed her softly on her lips. He could see her eyes sparkling with tears and Jack's correctness was disarmed. He could no longer maintain proper protocol and he embraced her warmly. After a few moments lost in tender reunion, Jack retreated from his embrace.

'I am sorry I took my time to return. War has no schedule and we were delayed.'

Jack's mother looked on him with affection, her hands sweeping up and down his arms as if to invite further embrace, but Jack's eyes were about the room behind her to look for further presence.

'Where's Mary. Where's Will?'

His mother pulled away to hide a sorrow that she could not bear to reveal to Jack. She hid her face, and fresh tears appeared.

'Oh my dear Jack. I am so sorry.'

Concern stained Jack's voice. 'Sorry for what, Mother?' Jack put his hands on his mother's shoulders to turn her to face him. 'Tell me, mother, why do you declare regret?'

'Mary is dead.'

Jack stopped. Everything in Jack's world stopped for a moment—his thoughts, his breath, his understanding. All suspended for a moment and then another, and then another.

'Mary is dead, my son. Killed over a month ago during a raid.'

His mother's words slowly became real and their message clear and hard. His mind suddenly filled with a hundred questions, and he struggled to find the ones that would find magic to undo the terrible news his mother had delivered. Then he asked her, 'At whose hands and how?'

'She was caught during a raid. They found her in a church… to the south. She was strangled.'

His mother's answer did not bring clarity, or ease to Jack's fevered thought, just more questions and further disbelief.

'Raid… who were raiding… which church?'

His mother wiped her tears and answered, 'We thought she was travelling with her maid to see Will. It seems instead she travelled south. She been goin' south quite a bit over the last year with her tutor. We don't know why.'

Jack's helpless thoughts became directed onto a target he could see in his mind, and he steered his grief away from Mary and into enmity towards the Tutor. His tutor. His friend.

'Where is he?' Jack demanded.

'If you mean the Tutor, he left soon after Mary was killed. Mary's maid is missing too.'

Jack's thoughts remained on the Tutor, a friend lost when Jack suspected his relationship with his wife, Mary, was more than it should be. However a man entering the room at pace broke Jack's brooding, his steel clattering against door and frame.

Will was smiling, voice raised above all the grief in the room.

'Jack, my brother, lost nae mair in the world, returned tae us.'

Will brushed straight past his mother to embrace Jack, warmth and energy radiating from his hug. The welcome however for Jack was inappropriate against such terrible news and he respectfully pushed Will away.

Will was still smiling as he spoke. 'What's the matter brother? Nae affection fer me?'

'Sorry Will. Mother's told me of Mary.'

Will's smile retreated, his eyes fell and he turned away to hide his face from all in the room. A deep inhalation and exhalation marked the rise and fall of his shoulders and he turned to face Jack again. Jack was calmer now, shock had receded slightly, but the questions had not.

'Will, who was raiding. Who killed Mary?'

Will took his time to reply. He searched out his words and delivered them calmly. 'Armstrongs, we think, but it also could be any of the families from across the border; the Storeys, or even the Grahams. Mary must have sought sanctuary in the church, but those godless bastards must have found her.'

'Was she violated?' asked Jack.

'No, she was spared that. Bless the mercy of God,' answered Will, his eyes falling deeper.

Jack let out a breath filled with contempt. 'God has no mercy. I have seen no mercy from God these past years, only his neglect.'

Jack's mother rebuked him, 'Please Jack, I feel yer pain, but we all are in the hands of God, including you.'

Will's calm suddenly evaporated and he moved feverishly

around the room, nervous and angry.

'Din'na fret, Jack, we don't know fer sure who did the raidin' yet, but we will find oot, and we'll apply justice, Border fashion.' Will's agitation was extreme, his eyes wild as he continued, 'Aye, and string em all up.' All attention was on Will's sudden disquiet. Then he stopped at the fire and he gripped the mantle to calm himself, looking deep into the flame speaking softly. 'Aye, we'll get the reet ones soon enough.'

Jack directed an unanswered question at Will. 'Where's the Tutor?'

But Will was lost in the flames of the fire, and his mother started to answer.

Then Will turned quickly to interrupt. 'With regards tae the Tutor. With Mary gone, the dog had nae mistress. He announced he was goin' tae Newcastle.'

'Was he with her when she died?'

'We din'na know fer sure, Jack. All we know is Mary kept him close… she'd been goin' tae Carlisle 'n' Cockermouth wi' him.'

'Where's her maid, have you spoken to her?' asked Jack.

'Nah, she's missin',' replied Will.

'Missing or killed?'

'We've found nae body. She's probably run off with the Tutor. He was fair fond of the ladies.'

Jack thought on Will's theory and dismissed it. He knew the Tutor's relationship with women, and a maid would not be his fancy. But Jack dismissed thought regarding the Tutor, and his hurt returned to Mary. And he reflected on a woman he had left uncaring, but now missed profoundly.

Will mistook Jack's contemplation of Mary, for thoughts still on the Tutor. 'I am sorry, Jack. I know he was the reason ye left.'

Will's words brought back selfish hurt to Jack, to a man more betrayed by a wife than a husband bereaved of a wife. Jack's face showed a new sadness and such despair that fresh tears found his mother, watching the grief on her son's face. Jack gripped himself to find strength against new debilitation, and forced out a confession.

'She loved him, I suspect. She had secrets from me but not from him. I thought he was my friend. I was a fool to think that.'

Jack's mother interrupted to defend Mary. 'Jack, I'm sure Mary was a faithful wife to ye. It was not in her nature otherwise. Hard it sometimes was… here away from her family.'

But Will interrupted. 'Kind words will nae deflect the truth o' the matter. When we have discharged oor duty here, we'll catch up with the Tutor in Newcastle. And if he's moved on, we'll track him doon. Thar'll be nae foul English city, or fortress, that'll keep us from him. We'll have the truth from him… or his balls in a bowl.'

Chapter XV

Two days had passed, and Jack lived in a world of contrast—grief and guilt in equal amount. He experienced the distress of a fine woman murdered, and his shame of her abandonment—a wife without his protection. He thought on the goodness in Mary he would never see again. He rebuked himself for the ill he thought of the Tutor, his friend. Two days he rattled and raged in his mind. Berating himself for his selfishness and his doubt. Cursing himself for his self-serving retreat overseas into war—into the foreign world he always craved, and his suspicion of a man he loved like a brother, like his own brother, Will.

❧❧

On the third day, three riders arrived at the tower—one with news. The one, the Headman of the family, was Jack's father.

'Armstrongs!'

The call was loud; clear for all to hear, and all went outside to meet it. All came from about to see him, to hear news from the Headman, old and grey, but still strong and bold, or so it seemed. The Headman was in fact a man far less than he was. He had been a vigorous man. He had done great service, but now he was old and weakened by his years of loyal employ, and by his sorrow at the state of his home and his peoples; impoverished by constant raids by Borderers. Yet it was still said that he executed his mantle dutifully, and all within his protection had the protection he could give, and his ear when they needed it.

Jack was in the courtyard. Everyone was in the courtyard, and Will was the first to respond to the old man's news.

'Are ye sure, father?'

'Aye… the reports are true. Armstrongs were on the raid the night Mary died, thievin' an reivin'. It was them alreet.'

Jack stepped back. His father's news was heard. He retreated from his father's sight, not wanting to attract his attention. But a voice shouted him back—his father's voice.

'Ah, I see another son. A son without a wife.'

Jack stared at his father, and remained silent.

His father, still mounted, called again to Jack, 'What no greeting for yer daddy. *No gifts?*'

'Greetings, *Father*,' announced Jack, as he pushed through the small crowd.

'Aye, my son. Armstrongs took yer wife's life. Ye are a little late tae save her.'

Jack stood, refusing to be humiliated by the old man's public chide. He stood and looked, and felt nothing.

But his father did not stop, and another blow was landed. More cruel words. 'Have ye brought back any men tae avenge her, or have ye lost them too?'

'I've brought back men. Fewer than I took. But the ones I return with, are ten times the men I took, in matters of spirit and skill.'

Jack's father sneered, 'Still wi' the fine words, tainted wi' the English. Ye have not lost ye pride my boy.'

'I am my own man—*no one's boy.*'

Jack's words annoyed the old man, and his nag became twitchy, picking up on his rider's vexation, forcing the old man to dismount to calm him. He handed the reins to another, and turned to walk closer to Jack, so that the words that passed between them were hidden from the gathering.

'A man does not leave his lands or kin without protection.'

Jack countered, 'A general does not taunt his captain in front of his troops, in order to bolster his own importance.'

'Ye think yerself a captain?'

'More than I think of you as a father.'

'D'ye think ye can take me boy… beat yer daddy?'

'It would only take a single stroke, old man.'

'Perhaps so, I can see a warrior in yer eyes. A look new tae me… Aye perhaps so… Perhaps ye are a man.'

☙❧

On the fourth day, Margaret, Jack's mother, was at her needlework, and she was waiting. She had witnessed the brittle encounter in the courtyard between her beloved husband and her beloved son. She watched the men's meeting and saw no embrace, no fitting welcome between a man and his boy. So she waited to raise her issues with her husband. She had long learned that there were moments to criticise a husband, long vexed by circumstances surrounding a son. His temper needed to be cool, and his nettlesome discomfort with his old age needed to be softened by warm ale and warmer fire.

Needlework was a distracting pursuit for a lady with a few servants to endure the mundane chores and toils of life. But she was old enough to have known the hardship of life; of childbirth and loss; and the suffering of distress in a land where no peace had truly existed in a dozen life-times. Where unrest, robbery and murder were a normality justified by men of pride, and endured by women of patience. Where women did the careful sewing, and the men did the futile killing.

She preferred her favourite chair for her woman craft, but although the light in the hall was poor, the light at the window was strong, so she sat on the cushioned window seat and bore the chill of the stone, while her husband enjoyed the fire, sitting at his desk, writing.

Margaret did not raise her eyes from her work as she spoke to her husband. 'I heard tell of your conversation with Jack yesterday. You should not chide the boy so.'

Jack's father continued to write, only moving his eyes from the paper he was writing on, to another piece paper he was using as reference for his composition. 'The lad can take it. He's big enough now.'

'Mary's death was not his fault.'

'I know lass, but he should have bin here, and no galavantin' around France, fighting wars not of his concern.'

'He had his reasons, James. You blame the boy for things long past his doin'. None of our woes are his doin', yet you pick at a boy you should be embracin'.'

The Headman did not answer his wife. He knew she was right, but he was his father's son, and Jack was his son in turn. All shared the same virtues; all shared the same sin—*pride.* The Headman waited for his wife to press again for him to show some further contrition, and perhaps a promise of kinder resolve in his dealings with his son. But nothing more came, and he knew his wife had said her peace. She needed to say no more, because she had put kinder thought in his mind. The Headman knew the lad had done little wrong. The years spent as hostage were not his fault. The woes visiting him, as he did the English Warden's bidding were not Jack's doing. Still, Jack's presence always nettled the Headman, his sight a reminder of dire battles fought against his own kin under the English flag; actions taken abhorrent to him; all done to save his son from Wharton's well-practiced threat to hang Jack, if the pledge was broken. Therefore it was easy for the Headman to condemn Jack for leaving his dutiful place within his own family, for leaving his wife, Mary, at home without a husband. Mary who, despite her birthright, the Headman had come to love like the true daughter he never had.

Suddenly a tap of a hand on his shoulder interrupted his thoughts, and he looked up to see Edward, his steward. The Headman, as ever, was amazed by his steward's stealth, and glad he never gave him reason to put a knife in his hand and hatred in his heart. But more amazing than his stealth, was his appearance in front of the Headman. His appearance meant he had a matter of importance to be dealt with. A matter, that is, important to the connubial hands that held tight his leash.

Edward was a good man, but poor in clothes. He had served Jack's father well for thirty years, as keeper of his tower and administrator of his affairs. But his pay was his wife's, and she was his master in *all matters*. Thus his service to Jack's father was by her permission. Edward was ever there when she commanded and never there when his duties demanded.

'Auld Sam waits on ye sir, in the anteroom,' announced Edward.

'Thank thee, Edward. How's yer lady wife?'

'In fine fettle, sir.'

Jack's father eyed his steward and the clothes... no... rags he wore. 'I see the money I pay ye isn't wasted. Keepin' yer new suit for Church are we?'

Edward shuffled his feet, and thumbed his poor jacket, threadbare and patched. He was at a loss how to answer his master's sarcasm, so he used the truth. 'Nae sir, new clothes were bought.'

'And how does yer wife like her new dress?'

Edward was about to respond, when Jack's father rose from his desk and gestured an upright hand to halt Edward speaking, and he excused himself from his wife, busying her hands at her needlework.

In the anteroom was a man dressed in worn cloth, dirty boots and cap. He was known to the Headman, and was well liked by him too. Will stood with Sam, and both were waiting. Both nodded their heads to the senior man, and waited on his invite to speak.

'What troubles you, Sam?'

'Reivin', Sir, that's the trouble. I had twenty coos, all good milkers. All gone by way of thievin' Armstrongs. Last week I lost ma plough horses to raidin' Kerrs, and when I left to visit my ma this morning, I had a healthy number of ewes and a good tup, reived again by Grahams.'

'What's left, Sam?'

'Me wife and bairns, with little tae eat.'

The Headman searched for some little consolation. 'Well at least ye were left them safe.'

But Sam simply shook his head. 'A wish they took them instead of the tup. It was a valuable beast, worth twice whole herd put together.'

'Well at least ye have yer roof?'

'Aye, still standin', but fer how long?'

Will, standing impatiently, addressed his father, 'Da, we need tae bolster oor defence. Have oor men ready tae counter the raids. Bloody some noses and cut some throats, tae send a message hard and clear tae those thinkin' were a soft lass tae be violated when they take a fancy.'

The Headman was hesitant. He had no response to Will, and Will pressed his father again for advice. 'What d'ya suggest, *Da?*

'We'll raise a report. Take it further.'

Will was unhappy with his father's suggestion. Making reports and endless complaints to the local Scottish Wardens, was, in Will's view, a waste of time. Law enforcement was meagre, and remonstration had little effect against lawless men with profit in their sights, and laws to disregard. 'No, *Da*, we need tae press all able men into a standing guard. Post them around ready tae counter-strike the raids.'

Sam butted in, 'Will ye be watchin' my land. I hope so. Because I've little will tae work it. It gives me nowt but grief. A pondering shared by many a neighbour.'

Will answered, 'Sorry, Sam, we dinnae want tae scare'em off. No, we want them tae raid, so we can cut and kill them legal.'

The Headman argued against Will's proposal. 'I say we make proper report before takin' up arms.'

But Will shouted down his father. 'No, *Da*... The time for writin' 'n' talkin' has long gone. It's time for huntin' 'n' killin'... Doin' not ditherin'... time tae find yer guts!'

'No, son. Ye'll bide yerself, and dae what I say.'

Will spat out his words. 'Headman ye're no longer steel, but grass fer our enemy's coos tae feed on.'

'Hold yer tongue, lad!' shouted the Headman.

'Ye ken the truth of it. The Armstrongs know it. All yer enemies know it. Your kith and kin know it too.'

Will did not wait for a reply, or to be dismissed, he simply swallowed his rage, turned, and ushered Sam roughly out of the room.

Jack was in the courtyard, as Will marched out. He could see his brother was angry and not for talking, but he stopped him nevertheless.

'What's the matter, Will?'

'Nowt a dram of courage could'nae fix. Except the old man's flask is dry.'

'He troubles you?'

'He does nowt but sit on his arse and write letters, while his sword rusts.'

Will pulled away, and Jack had to walk fast to keep up with him, to stay close enough for his words to be heard without shouting. 'Where are you going, Will?'

'Tae set a trap fer the Armstrongs. Tae stop their reivin'... and procure justice fer yer dead wife.'

'Then I will come with you,' said Jack.

Will stopped and turned back to Jack. His word firm and hard, *'No.'*

Jack was caught surprised by Will's refusal and said again, this time insistence replacing request. 'Then I will come with you.'

Will spat on the ground and growled, 'Stay here and change the old man's piss pot.' Then he calmed suddenly, and put a kinder hand on Jack's shoulder. 'Besides, you've few men, and they're all absent.'

Chapter XVI

News came in by way of a rider. One of the sentries, concealed on a point of access into Will's charge, did his job well and alerted Will to the raid. Bad news at any other time, shaped better by the timing of it. The sentry reported that the Armstrongs were on the snatch again. Their arrogance had proclaimed it. They had announced their intentions to plunder as a courtesy on entering another man's land, thus in perverse fashion they had maintained the tradition of legalising their reiving. But their confidence was their weakness. They were confident in numbers, having such a large clan, but Will had more men to hand that night. And, foolish of all, they had abandoned surprise… and Will intended to make them pay.

Will was well ready. His men had been at arms for five nights for this reason. He intended to pursue and persecute the thieves, to kill them all. He would not leave their thieving to a foul and faint judicial system. He would catch and kill, and if necessary murder every one of them.

He picked out thirty men he knew were the swiftest to ride on ahead. His plan was to cut off the retiring Armstrong raiding party; ambush them at the very point at which they entered his watch.

Loaded with spoils and stolen beasts, their return home via the paths and hill-ways would be slowed by the night. He knew a fast ride would steal a mile or two before the Armstrongs reached the valley exit and open land that could not offer ambush, only battle. A pitched fight in the open heath beyond was not what Will desired. He needed all his men. He did not intend to lose any if he could help it. After all, in the overall reckoning, he was still outnumbered five to one.

The local Armstrong clan had strength in numbers, and as it is with all conflict, it is often numbers more than skill that wins the day. This was very true of the Armstrongs. It was said not one of their women, from the age of fourteen to forty, was without child. The many in dispute, and the countless in disfavour with the Armstrongs, would lament at the news of another Armstrong brat born. Birthed into perpetual feud with their neighbour—more to fuel the lawless fire that kept the Marches burning with a white-hot self-destructive flame.

'All Armstrong women are tae be seen wi' a brat in their bellies, one at the teat, one in their arms, and two wee bairns tuggin' at their skirts. Whilst their whelps are oot thievin' 'n' reivin', 'ravishin' 'n' marryin' afore their age, to beget mair boy bairns—more Armstrong brats.'

Will's father cursed the Armstrongs more than any other Borderer name. Their reiving was often the most painful and carried with it the most fatalities. To him, there were two kinds of bastards, the poor unfortunates born without a father to hand, and the greater unfortunates born to Armstrong men.

'Bastards born. Born to steal and bear more bastards.'

Will ordered up the remaining men. He called his right hand to his side, Tam Wyatt, to give the order. 'Wait a while, and then follow the raiders at a pace. Be careful not tae persuade them that an expeditious retreat is necessary.' Then he took his nag's reins from a boy, and mounted, turning to his men bestride their horses.

'Make sure we announce oor chase. Carry a flamin' turf aloft lads. Signify the legality of oor pursuit… oor *Hot Trod.*'

Three hours exceptionally hard riding, parallel to the only manageable course of the Armstrongs, found him ahead of the raiders, in a place where the track was flanked by thick gorse that offered good cover and a few exits for counterattack. He set ten muskets high on the sides of the valley, with good vantage and in range of the path; ten he concealed in the gorse around the track; ten were positioned hidden at the head of the path to block the Armstrongs' progress. Orders were given to all the men and they concealed themselves and waited.

Within the hour, two riders entered Will's position, scanning their environment, keeping steady pace and reconnaissance. Will knew the scouts would have no dogs; the *slew hounds* would be with the stolen stock to keep it in check. Will also knew that the scouts would be looking ahead for clear passage, and not expecting ambush so far along the track. Any retaliation to their raid would likely be from garrison men, riding hard on their tail, not from men sitting and sneaking on trails far from the trouble.

Will was greatly relieved that adherences to his instructions were well observed. The Armstrong riders passed through his trap unmolested, gaining pace once they cleared the thicket. Watched by ten men concealed at the head of the trap. Watched until the men rode out of view; mindful they would be back when the fray alerted them.

After a while the raiding party came along the path; four riders to the front followed by between ten and fourteen riders, ushering stolen cattle with stolen horses running amongst them. A further dozen or so brought up the rear; their true numbers hidden by the failing moonlight, receding behind a newly clouded night sky. Will was worried that the party was larger than his intelligences had reported, and strung out too far. His trap may not contain them all, and his own men following may be too far behind to bring the attack to the rear. He looked again to the trap—at the gorse constricting the path, and he reasoned that it would funnel the column tightly together making men and beasts bunch up, and his ambush in fact would be effective in reducing their numbers without the support of his absent men.

Will's men were good. They waited as the whole column entered the killing zone. They kept their positions and they maintained their silence. Will was correct, the gorse did well, and indeed pushed the men and cows together—squeezing them into an easy target for bow and inaccurate matchlock musket.

The men waited, and waited.

Will let out the shout, *'In them boys. Let them have it!'*

Matchlock and bow were all let loose from behind the gorse. Six of the raiders fell from their horses. Musket fire from the valley sides, trained on the mass of men and beasts, brought no death only panic, and the cattle slew into the mounted men, rearing their horses and unseating two more. The men hiding in the gorse, let loose more arrows. A few more had even managed to recharge their firearms to join the volleys of arrow to the front and side of the column. And within a few minutes, half the Armstrong number had been removed from their nags by projectile, or by stampeding beast. The remaining desperately tried to steady their mounts to bring return fire onto the gorse, but some reckoned differently, and thinking the situation hopeless peeled off to the rear of the column, to retreat down the trail they had just travelled. But the fleeing riders were halted by the Armstrong rearguard, much larger than Will had first thought.

A few riders at the head of the column, free from the confusion of the huddle of beasts, had been able to make contact with their ambushers. But Will's men, who laid down their ranged weapons to leave their cover, working in twos to tackle the riders, outnumbered them. Will's men worked well, one with halberd to fell the rider from his horse, and the second with sword to slash at the fallen rider before he could recover. However other Armstrong riders from the rear, clearing the cows, saw their comrades fall, and rode hard at Will's men to unsettle them. Will's men now found themselves outnumbered, and their defence lacking as they continued to bloody fallen Armstrong riders, as they themselves became victim to mounted Armstrong lances.

The Armstrong rearguard had formed up to counter the ambush. There were fifty at least. Not a number in Will's favour, as the Armstrongs, wise to the possibility of counter to their raid that night, had feigned smaller numbers to bring on an attack deliberately.

The Armstrong rearguard then split to encircle their ambushers' position.

Will, meantime, was working well, moving around his men's positions to rally and direct. But in doing so, he exposed himself to attack, and found himself without the support of his men, and hidden by thick gorse, he found himself surrounded by three dismounted Armstrong blades.

Will did not hesitate, and he ran at the nearest Armstrong to slash at the man, only to be met by a parry. He ran through the man to turn and face his attackers, his position bettered by having three opponents in front of him, rather than surrounding him. The three came on, and Will readied himself for attack. He did not call for aid. His pride dictated he was not outnumbered, simply inconvenienced. As the men advanced, Will again threw himself in close so he could trust at the first opponent, and use him to deflect any blows from the others, but one of the men had space to stab at his side with sword. Will felt the pain of contact with the point of the blade. But his steel reinforced leather jack had done its job and the blade failed to cut through to the skin. Will countered the blade and pushed it aside, and stepped back to strike again at the first opponent. He ran at his man, screaming murder, only to run into pain and darkness, as a blow from the rear hit hard his neck under the rim of his helmet, sending him crashing to the earth.

Chapter XVII

The morning was bitter and thick white hoarfrost covered the land. Jack wiped condensation from the leaded glass and peered out onto the courtyard below. No one could be seen, and Jack strained his gaze to look beyond the window's offer to see if anyone was about in the wider world. But the world was empty.

He held his watch, even though serious voices from over his shoulder tried to distract him from the outside scene, but his gaze maintained its vigil, hoping once more his brother would appear into his view. But the voices in the room behind him were growing. The sounds of Jack's father and the seniors of his family, all huddled around the room's large oak table. The men and women's sober voices grew in Jack's head, until he could no longer ignore them, but despite all the chatter in the room, his attention was firm on his father's counsel. Jack stood alone at his post and listened. His father's voice was calm and assured.

'Then it is agreed. We will send oor protest tae the Armstrongs and settle the request fer ransom.'

Jack frowned and turned from the window, to approach the table. 'Have we not paid enough?'

His father closed his eyes in the futile hope it would block out Jack's words. But his words had been spoken and his dissent had to be rebuked. He looked at Jack, and with vitriol in his voice said, 'What have ye really paid, *boy*?'

Jack ignored the scold and continued, 'They raid and raid, and we should not pay and pay.'

'It will be as I have said. The Armstrongs are powerful. They take and we must pay. I have not the men tae bring fight tae their door.'

Jack knew his own reasoning would not find favour with his father, worn down by his own reality of life in this hostile territory, so he turned and walked away towards the exit leaving his words at the table. 'Then I will take the fight. I have men enough to take Will back, and perhaps take a hostage or two as future persuasion to keep the Armstrong foxes from our hens.'

His father raised his voice to catch the retreating Jack. 'You are foolish… *boy*. The Armstrongs will take ye too, and I will have twice the ransom tae pay.'

The chide reached Jack before he reached the door and he countered, 'If I am caught, save your money and buy some courage. It seems the Armstrongs have stolen yours.'

Nothing more was said, but by the time Jack had entered the courtyard he regretted his words. The cold reinforced the regret, and Robert, with horse in hand, appearing beside him did not ease his contrition.

'What tae dae, Jack?'

Jack looked at Robert and he clamped his hand onto Robert's broad shoulder. 'Armstrongs to do, Robert… to kill. A brother to rescue. Pride to restore. Madness it all is.'

'Aye, it is, Jack. But it puts breath in us, it does.'

Jack looked on to see Tom, Francis and Finn at hand, all returned from their wives and their spending in Edinburgh. All but one, Henry Crosser, and he asked, 'Where's Henry?'

Francis replied, 'He's not coming back. His wife won't let him.'

Jack laughed. 'Good to see you all, your money spent, bairns and wives petted. Ready for work?'

All the group said, 'Aye,' and Tom added, 'I'll be glad o' the rest.'

❧❦☙

Two days picking slowly and quietly across the land had brought Jack, Robert, Tom, Francis and Finn to a safe camp within striking distance of one of the Armstrong towers. It was well reported by allied friends and family in the heart of the Armstrong lands that Will was being held at this tower, site of a substantial Armstrong garrison. Finn had found good vantage over the tower, and held hidden sentinel and covert reconnaissance for three nights before he could return with the information that the men needed.

When Finn returned to camp, he found the rest of the men seated on the ground, taking what comfort they could in a cold camp without fire.

Finn gave his report, 'I think your brother's being kept in a storehouse within the curtain walls. I see two men enter the store and change every four hours or so. There are far too many guards for us to tackle, and I have no idea how they watch Will within the store.'

Tom raised his concerns. 'We are too few, Jack.'

'If we were more, we would not have got this far undetected.' Jack then asked Finn, 'How do they patrol?'

'Two walk the perimeter.'

'With torches?' asked Jack.

'No. There are braziers on the walls and at the gate to warm the watch, but no torches are about with the men as they circuit the walls.'

Jack pondered a moment to consider the facts, pulling his

cloak tighter about his shoulders against the cold. 'Then the wall watch cannot have good sight of the patrol.' Jack looked at Finn. 'Do the watch confirm?'

Finn replied, 'Yes, they call out '*All's well, Armstrongs*', as they pass the wall guard.'

'And as they pass the gate watch?' asked Jack.

'They stop at the brazier to warm their backsides for a wee while.'

Jack focused his mind and continued his interrogation of Finn, 'Is the gate overlooked by the wall guard?'

'No,' replied Finn.

Jack stood up, letting his cloak drop to the ground, and thought for a time before he revealed his plan. 'We take the patrol. Take their place. Approach the gate. Take the gate watch. I go into the storehouse alone to tackle Will's guards. I hope to get the guards before they know it. Perhaps even if they are alarmed they will not kill Will, or raise the alarm if they see only one man.'

'A risky strategy for you, Jack. You inside alone with all them Armstrongs close by,' offered Francis.

'Risky, yes, but it is the best plan I can think of.' Jack chewed his mouth, as if his words were sour, badly issued, and his plan badly devised. 'Finn. Tom. You take the patrol's place and make sure you get the call right. Is there a good place you can take them?'

Finn confirmed, 'I can think of a few wee shadowy places to bump the patrol.'

'You'll have to take the gate guard quickly. Approaching them will be tricky without raising the alarm.'

Finn again had an answer, 'I have a bonny idea on that.'

'Good. The rest of us will get as close to the gate as we can. The trees will give us cover. We will help Tom and Finn when they strike, and then Robert and Francis can take the place of the gate guard. Remember Robert, keep the fire low and your faces out of the light.'

'If we awake the whole watch, we'll have twenty or thirty men at our throats,' added Francis.

'More like fifty. The Armstrongs are keeping a strong force at hand. Methinks they expects a reprisal,' countered Finn.

Tom looked up at the condition of the sky. 'The day's still overcast. It'll snuff the moon's light.'

Jack looked on to catch any more comments from his men. None came. 'Then it's settled, we go tonight. The longer we camp here, the greater chance of discovery. Get some rest till the night deadens the world. We'll need all our strength to run hard back here for the horses, and then ride harder to get out of this alive.'

∞∞

The night was dark. As dark as it could be, and a good gusty wind had joined the night to cover the noise of the men's movement as they crept within striking distance of the tower's walls. Jack gestured to Tom and Finn to go forward, whispering, 'Careful boys. Let us avoid brutal requital and do this without any killing.'

Finn's backward smile at Jack offered him little reassurance as the pair melted into the dark. Jack, Robert and Francis moved carefully around the perimeter of trees that surrounded the tower, until they could see the gatehouse and its guard. Their hidden position was a fair distance from the gate, and even in the darkness, impossible to approach without early challenge from the gatehouse guard, and at best, difficult to approach unseen under the noses of the wall guard, snug about the rampart brazier. The men watched as the patrol appeared out of the darkness, approached the gatehouse, stopped and exchanged a few words. It was less than a minute before they rejoined their circuit of the

215

perimeter wall. Shortly after, a shout was heard, '*All's well, Armstrongs.*'

The scene replayed. But on the third pass, one of the patrolling guards was to be seen supporting his comrade, folded as if wounded, helping him to the security of the stronghold.

Jack could hear, over the wind's blow in the trees, a muffled cry from the wounded guard, '*Help me.*'

The two standing at the gatehouse brazier ran to assist the men, but before they could reach the troubled guards, the wounded man threw his cloak over the head of one of the gatehouse men and set about him with a club. The other patrolling guard did the same, but the flash of steel could be clearly seen in the light of the brazier's fire.

Before Jack and the remaining men could reach the gate, Tom and Finn had retrieved the stolen cloaks from their first victims and were retracing their quarry's steps around the wall.

'*All's well, Armstrongs.*'

Francis and Robert made sure the gate guard were no further threat, and took their cloaks and caps to replace their own. They threw dirt on the fire to turn its fiery glow into a blackened whirlpool of smoke in the wind, to hide their faces and form, and Jack, with his shield and sword in hand, approached the storehouse and entered without challenge.

It was a surprise to find Will so easily, him locked within one of the storerooms. A bigger surprise to find the tower's ale stock lodged in the same cell and Will sober.

'Well, Jack, again I have tae thank thee fer freeing me from a dungeon.'

'Where's your guard and why are you sober?'

'The guards disappear from time tae time. I'm sober because I'm telt the price fer each gobful of ale was one of ma fingers. I considered drinking a barrel o' ale tae end my sorry life.'

'Sounds like you may be drunk after all, brother.'

Keys were found on a nearby stool and Jack opened the door. Will was free and both men were heading down the corridor towards the storehouse door.

'Hey, who goes there!'

Jack turned to face the shout, and two men stood in the narrow corridor behind, one with axe and one with sword.

'Go, Will. Francis and Robert stand guard at the gate.'

But Will stood his ground. 'Nah, I'll stand wi' ye.'

Jack barked at Will, 'You've no weapons, and no use to me without them. *Go!'*

Will ran, and Jack turned to the men. His steel-blue eyes darted from the passage of flight to the one of bloody assault. *Run away or stand and fight*, his mind took only a moment to choose, and with gritted teeth he forced the fear from his lungs. He tensed hard his muscle and sinew, filling his whole being with his God of War, as he drew sword and shield to lead his way to his enemy. He was on them in a desperate cry of hatred from his mouth as he pushed his sword and shield upwards at the axe arm of his first opponent, and pushed harder his knee into his groin, running through the man to unbalance his stance. Distracted by pain, his target stepped off his mark and Jack quickly recovered his pass on his enemy, bringing down his sword hard to cleave the back of his man's shoulder and neck. The gaping wound gushed blood as his adversary dropped axe to desperately stem the flow of life from his body.

Bloodied, the first fell, and the second ran forward shouting death, but Jack's shield was there to receive his blow and he countered with a trust to the second man's face, destroying flesh and feature. The man's screams became muffled as his hands reached up to cover the horror of his wound, as he too fell to the floor on knee in an anguish of torment and suffering. Jack then drew back to hack at the first man again, as he tried to recover and retrieve his axe, this time felling the man hard to the floor, quivering in pain and death.

Jack stood back, breathing in for the first time since his attack began, desperately filling breath into his lungs and he contemplated the scene. He moved forward to finish them off, but hesitated.

'There will be two less Armstrong rats to nibble at our neighbours' stores tonight,' he seethed, and thinking of his poor wife, he sheathed his sword to let them suffer longer in agony and their desperate quietus. Instead he moved over the bloody mess of flesh and bone and spat on them, to mark his prey and show disdain for their parentage and their skills as warriors, and with still cold eyes, he moved back towards the light of escape.

₞)ℙ

Three hours had passed since Jack and the others rejoined their horses. They left Tom to keep covert watch on the Armstrongs; to survey their actions in pursuit, while they rode hard to reach an isolated fell, to later rendezvous with Tom. The men knew that the moonless night and deteriorating weather would make tracking and rapid pursuit difficult, and the fell was well away from any likely escape routes.

At the fell, and dismounted, Jack gathered and debriefed breathless men. The ride was hard, and good providence rather than good horsemanship had saved their nags from injury on the poor ground of the high fell. Providence, because good horsemen would not be riding untried routes, so unknown, so rapid, and in such poor light.

'Well, lads,' announced Jack, 'Did we do this without killing?'

Finn was the first to report, 'Sorry, Jack… ma knife slipped.'

Robert, the second, 'Tom's took a nasty knockin'… Cracked heads under Tom's stick rarely heal.'

Jack responded to the reports with the sad acceptance that deaths were inevitable, especially with Finn to the fore. 'Well it matters nought. I took two.'

As Jack stood amongst the men, he lamented further—this time over the failure to kill more Armstrong men. 'There will be thirty, or forty looking for us when daylight comes.'

ဆ၇ၐ

A rider came into camp an hour or two later. Jack was glad to see Tom safe, and Tom was relieved to find the others, particularly in poor light and worsening winter weather.

'It's a durty night. Ma nag could hardly find his way proper.'

Jack was quick to hand Tom a drink of brandy from a pewter flask, 'Glad you found us. How goes it, Tom?'

'Are they following us?' interrupted Francis.

'Give me time to catch ma breath, and the brandy to loosen ma tongue. I've had a hard ride to reach ye,' gasped Tom. He drained the flask, holding it high and sucking out the last drops, before he spoke again. 'They took some time to rally, about an hour-n-half, but they're out searchin' now, but not followin'. There's no moon and the weathers bad, so they're not ridin' hard. They've split up, lookin' to head us off further down the road, I suspect.'

Robert nodded, 'Aye, they'll nae be able tae pick up oor tracks in this dark, and they'll be aboot coverin' routes fit fer horses tae the east and south.'

Francis broke in, 'What do we do, Jack?'

Jack was clear. 'There'll be no rest for us tonight. We need to lose the horses. Come better light, the Armstrongs will track

219

horses easy with the ground this soft.' Jack pondered a few strategies in his head, the men holding their tongues and breath while he considered the best plan. 'Francis, take the horses, weigh them down and lead them north. Take them as far north as you can. Come back by safer routes. If you have to lose the horses, do so. The rest of us will go over the fells on foot.'

Will was the only one to speak up to counter Jack's direction. 'It's a long walk. I hope the weather's kind fer foot. Best we stay on the horses and outrun the bastards.'

'The foul weather will be our greatest ally,' replied Jack, 'I suspect the Armstrongs be a little less fervent in your immediate recovery, Will, if they get a good soaking for their troubles.'

But Will shook his head. 'We killed men, they'll be wantin' recompense fer that. They will be fired up tae take some blood… a little wet will nae trouble them.'

Jack disagreed. 'Blood they can take another day, no doubt sweetened with some stolen cattle. They may come for you, they may come for me, but we'll take that day when it comes.'

Tom broke in, 'Before we go, I have a gift for ye, Jack.'

'A gift?'

'An Armstrong man foolish enough to come on me in the dark. Tied up and unconscious on my packhorse. He found *Knocker* waiting—he niver sleeps. The Armstrong cut me though.'

It was then that Jack noticed the dark wet patch on Tom's arm, not mud or rain, but blood.

'Did he cut you bad?'

'Nah, only a lick, lad. Nowt that ma good wife can't put reet.' Tom clutched his arm and Jack knew his pain was bigger than he professed, but smaller than his Cumbrian pride would admit to. 'I thought you might want to question him about Mary.'

Jack thought on the opportunity presented by Tom, and Robert butted in. 'We've nae time tae wake and question him, and if we are tae lose the horses we can't take him wi' us.'

Finn walked between Jack and Robert, with a proposal. 'Leave him to me, give me a little while and I'll have him waking and singing like a nightingale, sweet and true.'

Jack knew what this meant and moral apprehension held him from immediate agreement. But time was against them and Jack wanted to know about Mary's death. So he reluctantly gave the order. 'Go to it, Finn, make it quick and as kind as you can.'

Finn licked a finger and held it up to check the wind's direction. 'I'll take him downwind. It'll soften his screaming in yer ears.'

The men waited, and their uneasy rest was punctuated with periodic muffled screams. Jack was unhappy. Robert's face shared Jack's misgivings about torture being committed under order. Both men knew torture. They had been within its grasp themselves. Both had felt its evil abuse of body and mind.

It was a little while longer than Finn had intended, before he returned bloodied and smiling. 'Aye my lads. It were Armstrongs right enough. The dear boy admitted it.'

Robert stepped in, 'And how far did ye go, afore ye obtained his admission?'

Finn's smile changed to a smirk. 'I must be true to you. There was quite a bit of him cut off, and lined up before his eyes, before he squealed. I suppose he could have been lying to me. It would be a terrible thing for him to fib… Nothing worse than a lie. But he's past fibbing now he is.'

Robert scowled, unhappy a prisoner had met a much fouler end than a mere killing under his watch. 'Better mark his body then, so his kin can find him.'

But Finn shook his head. 'I think it better they never find him. His ma would grieve badly at the sight of him. What's left of him that is.'

Robert sighed. 'Where did you leave him?'

'In a fissure in the moor, with a dead sheep covering his carcass and his stink. He'll be well rotted afore they find him.'

'You were lucky to find a dead sheep close by,' said Francis.

'Not luck, there was a stray. I led her to the fissure.'

Tom shook his head. 'Seems yer knife has been busy.'

Jack looked onto the direction of the dead Armstrong man. He shook his head and thought of words to say, but held his tongue and simply beckoned the men to move off. All the men stayed silent as they prepared to travel. Francis with the horses, weighed down with what rocks they could find on the fell. Weight to feign horses laden with men and iron, leaving deeper tracks to fool their pursuers. Tom, Finn, Will and Jack on foot to walk their way out of danger, across open fell, hill and valley. Wet and dark their passage would be, dangerous routes to take. Finding their way by their noses, for no stars showed a way, no deft nags to carry them safely. They kept away from path and track, from easy way and soft incline. They climbed and scrambled, and all the time the sky poured wet on them until no part of them was dry.

Chapter XVIII

The Headman had cause to worry. One son kidnapped. One son had failed to return from the other son's rescue. Cause to worry indeed. But those concerns were only a handful of seed in a bucket of grain, because outside his tower were sixty Armstrong riders. All come-a-calling. Fully armed. Wearing menace and a mean manner.

One Armstrong stepped his horse forward and called out, 'Ned Armstrong to see the Headman. Scores to settle, or agreement to reach.'

The Headman raised his hands, and sent a signal to his men at the gatehouse to open the outer doors. The men hesitated at first, but the Headman directed them again, with another, more urgent signal.

Ned 'Yaffle' Armstrong gestured to his men to stand their ground and stay mounted. He in turn rode into the courtyard at speed, dismounting before the horse arrested. A display designed to prove vitality existed in an aged body. He was as old as the Headman.

The Headman waited to meet the rider. He hurried Edward and two other servants, as they brought out a table and two chairs from the kitchen block. He sent them back for a blackjack of ale and two pewter goblets. All but the two old men retreated, except Ned's horse, which knew better than to leave his master's side.

Both men took seats across the table. No greetings. No handshakes, or even a nod of acknowledgement. Just quiet regard, as both found comfort in uncomfortable circumstance, in a makeshift court.

Ned commenced the parley. 'It's bin a while since we sat together to drink.'

'Last *Truce Day*, Yaffle,' replied the Headman.

'Aye., that was an affair worth a drink… *Eh?*'

The Headman smiled at the old badger, dressed in green with a bonnet of red; his favoured attire. His clothes and yaffling war cry naming him after a green woodpecker, a comedic byname to mark him out from the forty-four Armstrongs named Ned that ran the Armstrong domain in Liddesdale. But he was no Picidae, more a Corvidae—a carrion crow.

Ned Armstrong pulled free his red bonnet from his head and placed it on the table. He lifted the blackjack single handed to pour an ale. The jug so heavy with liquid, that Edward had struggled to carry it from the brew house.

'Last night your boys cleaved and clouted six of my men. Four of them killed, and one left daft from a knock on his heid. My son is missing too. Your boys are on the fells, I suspect. Walking away in order to escape our search parties.'

'I take it Will's amongst my lads.'

'He is.'

'Then they've done their job well.'

Ned Armstrong laughed and poured himself another ale, drank it all back, running his leather gauntlet across his mouth to clear the spillage from his beard.

Ned was a headman in the Armstrong clan. One of many, because the Armstrong name was spread wide in the Marches, both south on the English side and north with the Scots. They were true Borderers, in the sense they regarded themselves only as Borderers, neither English nor Scottish. They had learned long ago, cross-border marriage, against the laws of the land, was the only way to assure the name survived in strength. Thus Armstrong became foremost amongst the 'Names' of the region, both famous and infamous. Living outside the law. Living on their acts of criminality, because criminality provided the only true profit in a land laid-bare by the pricking of hostile sovereigns and their ambitious agents.

Ned reached into his breastplate to retrieve a paper, which he placed squarely on the table.

'I am here in answer to your grievances.'

'Then, Yaffle, ye agree there are grievances tae answer fer?'

'I will agree only that there is error in your list of complaint.'

'And my *error* is…?'

'The murder of your daughter-in-law. None of my men are admittin' to killin' her.'

'And dae ye believe all yer men?'

'I accept there are bad'uns amongst my lads. Those partial to takin' a lass without her permission. But while they were raidin' that night of the complaint, they were only cuttin' in self defense.'

The Headman, who had not poured himself a drink, took the blackjack considerably lightened by Ned's refills. He sat and looked at Ned's face, old and worn. He looked deep into his eyes to see if a trace of a lie was on his lips. The old Armstrong was a complete depiction of deceit, and the Headman knew the only truths this man would issue would be to his priest and the Almighty. The Headman then poured a drink.

Ned was looking for a reply from the old headman. He was irritated from the lack of response. And as he toyed with the folded paper, he poked the old man to get one.

'I think you overplay the injustices I inflict on your clan. They are no less than the harm inflicted on my family by you and your neighbours.'

The Headman sank his drink and said, 'Aye, we've been none too kind… still honour must be maintained…' then he broke off to think on his words, amused by his own understanding of the term honour and continued, 'Why is it a Borderer takes affront so easily. He only perpetuates his own destruction. English Queen Bess will likely die withoot issue, and Scotland's monarch will likely be England's too… and Royal sponsorship of strife in the Marches will be at an end. Then oor felonies against neighbours will be an embarrassment tae those Royal backers that sponsored it. Border ways of reiving, theft and extortion will nae longer be able tae exist… and we'll pay a far, far bigger toll.'

Ned nodded, 'Aye, my auld daddy would agree wi' you.'

The Headman poured another ale, and drained his goblet. He then stood up saying, 'Ye have pecked at my table, and discussed oor complaint, Yaffle. Can we have a respite from retaliation?'

'Aye, I suspect your boys have my lad. Return him safely, and there will be no further reckonin'. And as an act of good faith, I have a gift—one of your lads… We picked him up travelin' north wi' your boys' nags. We return him safe. Mind you return my boy in the same condition.'

∞∞

Jack and the others had spent two nights on the fell, travelling away from their intended destination. Routes designed to take them away from Armstrong patrols and search parties. Arduous travel on foot with Tom all the time carrying a wound far worse than he declared. The winter season was rarely considerate to travellers on the fell, but unlike the first night, the weather had been far calmer but colder. The sky remained grey and no sun shone on them as they walked and rested little.

'Black hills, black sky. It's like walking tae my tomb,' declared Will.

'We're all walkin' tae oor tombs, lad. It's just it takes some of us longer tae get there,' added Robert, feeling the fatigue of the march, him more suited to the saddle than the hike in matters of long travel.

Ahead was another hill to climb and Finn was sent forward to scout the top, while Robert helped Tom ascend, weaker now with blood loss. Will was with Jack, making hard going of the heather as they climbed the hill, an ascent more difficult than it first appeared.

'You know, brother, I used tae love huntin'. I used tae love the chase.' Will looked behind. 'I'm none too fond of being chased though… it lacks pleasant thrill.'

Jack was feeling the cold, and tired of the travel. He regretted sending the horses away, and wiping his running nose and rubbing his eyes sore with lack of sleep, he replied, 'Yes, I think the only thing getting caught this chase is a chill.'

But Will was deaf to Jack's discomfort and continued to share his thoughts. 'I used tae love many things. The light of a cloudless day. The retreat of the sun at the end of it.'

Will's head was high to the sky. His travel seemed to be less difficult than the other men's effort. All other men accept for Finn, who being a former Kern and well matched to the fells on foot, made light work of scouting ahead and making hill top faster than the others.

Will continued, 'Ye know, Jack, I found joy in all of it. But all joy has drained away.'

Jack grimaced and pushed hand on knee, and pushed knee on rock and heather, to help him mount the steep hill.

'So profound, brother… what took… what took your joy?'

Will turned to Jack and responded with a sigh and a delivery of drunken words. 'The loss of the lights—that steer our life—towards a better fate.'

Jack was breathless now, his legs hurting and his back too, laden with shield and sword, pistols and pack. He was in no mood for fanciful thought. 'You… talk in poems… Will. It is… not like you.'

'It's just I'm thinkin' on Thomas, our brother. If he were atop this hill, we would run tae embrace him. If Thomas Wharton, the English devil, were atop I'd be runnin' tae embrace him too… with my bare hands around his throat!' Will broke his disclosure and looked on to Jack and the reality around him. 'Never mind me lad… look t'yer self. What's the root of yer melancholia, my brother?'

Jack answered, gasps and heavy breathing punctuating his words. 'Life when I was boy promised so much… it offered delight… but instead, delivered desertion, without deliverance.'

'Aye lad, I'm sorry fer that. Are ye still bitter about yer internment?'

'Not so much… only the path… to which it has brought me.'

Will by now was feeling the labour of the climb and wanting the summit. 'Aye, this path is certainly a hard un.'

Finally all the men reached the top of the hill to meet up with Finn, who was carefully studying the distant peaks. Tom, Robert, Will and Jack collapsed on the ground, too exhausted to question Finn, to tired to care what reconnaissance he had carried out.

Finn smiled at the tired men and returned to his watch, and as he studied, he saw a trace of smoke rising beyond the farthest peak about mile away, perhaps more. He was satisfied he had found someone else resting, maybe Armstrongs, and Finn alerted Jack and the others to the presence of the smoke and the probable camp fire that was its source.

Robert moved to sit alongside Finn, to share his observation of the wisp of smoke.

'Could be a fire still burnin', its makers long travelled on,' proposed Robert.

But Finn disagreed. 'No, I can smell meat still cooking. I'll need to have a look... Stay here and rest.'

Finn looked at the topography between him and the peak beyond, and reckoned it would take an hour's rapid travel to reach the top overlooking the valley issuing smoke. It took him two.

ॐ

As he moved against the rocks, Finn was careful not to show his outline against the horizon. He moved carefully to find good vantage and he spied down on his quarry.

'Three,' he confirmed to himself quietly, 'Beef cooking too.'

The beasts were in the wrong place to be anything but stolen beef. But there was only three reivers watching them. Finn was surprised they had cut a cow out for slaughter for only three mouths, the beast being better value alive than meat for only three. He contemplated they may be split from a larger group, holding the herd and waiting for more to join them from other raids.

Finn scanned the campsite and saw no ranged weapons amongst the men, but he thought there might be pistol or two hidden from view. The three men had positioned their camp well, but badly for Finn and his comrades, because he knew to go around them safely would be hazardous and involve a long hard detour. There was also the risk that the three men would break camp and possibly discover his group on the fell, or worse still, other reivers may join the three and bolster their numbers. But in his foremost reasoning; the very driver that steered Finn's action towards assaulting the camp as a matter of haste, was the beef cooking well and smelling fine in his nose; a nose above a mouth not tasting roasted meat for several days.

He weighed up the thought of a direct challenge, but thought again. The amount of ground he would need to cover was large, and the likelihood of being spotted great. Strong possibility therefore of either being evaded by the men, or met by a stronger challenge without the benefit of surprise. Finn looked down the mountain as far as his eyes could see. Not certain at first, he concentrated on an alien hue in the russet and grey landscape— *blue.*

Auld Nick was fond of his blue breeches.

Finn descended without his weapons, open and without stealth, singing aloud an Irish ballad, taught to him by his father as they ploughed the fields of Carlow for whoever could pay. The three reivers in the valley floor quickly rallied, and two produced hidden bows from under blankets and covers used to keep them dry against the damp. They covered Finn as he climbed down. They pointed arrow at him as he picked through the rocks, hopping and running the descent and making light with his merry tune. Finn was in their camp soon enough, still singing.

Blue Breeches spoke first, because he recognised the tune and the man behind it.

'Ye lose yerself in the mountains. A place free from men, yet around every sorry rock there's an Irishman lurkin'. Dae yer kind nae like yer own green island so much, fer ye to inhabit oors so readily… Finn McCuul?' Blue Breeches relaxed his guard and sheathed his sword. 'Ma men were declarin' ye to be a goat, nae a man, so ye're lucky ye did'nae find yerself over the fire as more meat for oor bellies… How's ye doin', *goat-man?*'

Finn arrested his singing and replied, 'I'm fine Nick. Ye're a little away from yer patch, ma handsome lad.'

'I am a wee too popular south of the border. The price on ma heid was getting heavy. Thought I'd lose myself in the hills and see what I could find.' Auld Nick looked about him and the beasts grazing off grass. 'Ya niver knows what ye can find in the hills.'

Blue Breeches, called friendly by kith and kin as Auld Nick, was once a border headman with a modest family, turned ambitious raider with a hunger for bigger profit, to later turn tinker as his ill-considered thieving brought ruination on his family. Now it seems he was a fugitive without a realm of his own, much like Finn.

Finn nodded and smiled at Auld Nick. 'Aye, Nick, you were always prolific when it comes to borrowing beef… and other men's women.'

Auld Nick scanned the horizon to look out for others that may be travelling with Finn and asked, 'Are you alone, Finn?'

'Aye, I lost ma horse a wee bit ago, weapons too. Saw your smoke and thought you might share a little beef with me.'

'Can you pay?' asked one of the bowmen.

Finn untied his leather purse from about his belt, opening it and turning it upside down. Nothing fell from it. He smiled with his action and added, 'It's an unfortunate state my purse is in. No gold. No silver.'

'Then why should we share our beef,' demanded a bowman.

'Because I want to join you. Truth is, I was running with another band, but they were cut up bad in their last raid. And finding myself being alone in the world, I was looking for new friends.'

Despite Finn's words, Auld Nick maintained vigil on the horizon looking for any trouble Finn might have brought his way. 'I'm a little confused, Finn. I thought ye were a trooper in gainful employ around these parts, nae a thief at all.'

Finn was caught, but he kept smiling and maintained his demeanour. But he knew Auld Nick was wily. In Nick's business he could not afford the luxury of trust, especially towards mad Irishmen.

'How did you find us, Finn? Were you lookin' fer us?'

'No, my bonny lad… I easy saw your smoke… too much damp wood… too much fat on the fire. Your blue breeches were like a flag announcing your presence in this fine, fine landscape.'

Auld Nick looked down to his legs, rubbing the slashed and padded bright blue velvet hose.

'Aye, I cut em off a rich merchant. Made his wife sew em up tae fit me… before I shagged her hard and left her feeling sore.'

'You always had a *kind* regard towards women,' announced Finn, still smiling.

'Now Finn, although it's gud tae catch up… and in truth I'm fair enjoying the crack, but I'm of a mind to have my lads here let loose their arrows, and use ye fer target practice, unless ye can persuade me otherwise?'

Finn did not show reaction to the threat, but knew a better strategy was needed.

'I have a proposition, Nick. Ye see I'm lying to you. I have got friends, but like you they're runnin' and hidin'. But they've got gold, and they can pay.'

The two bowmen relaxed their aim at the mention of gold, but their arrows were still strung.

'How many friends?' asked Auld Nick.

'Four,' answered Finn.

'I don't like the number, Finn, me with only two. How do I know you won't jump us?'

Finn maintained his smile, but now instead of it hiding his malicious intent from Auld Nick, it held a satisfaction of knowledge. *Auld Nick was a band of three and no more.*

Auld Nick thought he had Finn covered, but he failed to stop Finn edging forward during their discourse, or even keep Finn's hands in view. Finn had removed his helmet, and during their conversation was continually rubbing sweat away from his brow and the back of his neck with both hands.

'Ah be sure, it can raise a fair sweat walking the hills. I tell you what ,Nick. I'll go back and get the gold and…'

Action was immediate, as Finn pulled two steel darts, about six inches long, from behind his neck and launched them simultaneously at the two bowmen, hitting both targets true. Auld Nick grabbed the hilt of his sword, but before he could draw it completely from its scabbard, Finn ran at him and kicked hard into his blue velvet crotch, which took Nick's hand off the hilt as he doubled with pain. Finn then freed Nick's sword from the remainder of its sheath and ran at the bowman who was first to recover from the shock of being hit by Finn's heavy dart. Finn cleaved at the first bowman's shoulder, splitting it, then he ran to the second, but the second bowman had put an arm up to protect himself from Finn's blow. The sword cut into the man's forearm, not severing it completely, but breaking it clean and leaving such a wound to the artery that blood pumped out rich and fluid. Auld Nick had recovered, but without weapons he ran to the first bowman, dead on the ground, to relieve the man's sword, but its release was difficult as it was under the dead weight of the man's body. But it was too late for Auld Nick, as Finn had seen him recover, and he ran to thrust his sword hard, two handed, into Auld Nick's back.

The remaining bowman had no stomach for a fight with such a wound. He tried to stem the blood and clutched his arm. Finn did not even glance back at him. The man's horror was to be heard, and when his cries grew silent, Finn knew there was insufficient blood left in him to give him consciousness, and death would follow.

Auld Nick was not dead as Finn turned him over. He was alive because one cut would never be enough to end Auld Nick's life. Finn looked into the fallen man's eyes, watching them squeeze up with pain, and he heard Nick spit out, 'You Irish bastard!'

Finn crouched down beside the man and thrust the sword into the earth close to Nick's head, and with a calm and measured tone said, 'My friends will enjoy your camp fire. I'll need to build it up though… keep it alive while I fetch them.' Finn laughed, 'Alive… seems ironic.' Then he smiled at Nick like a man who would smile in friendly gesture to an old friend. 'I think I severed your spine, so you'll not be walking, but you've life in your arms. Perhaps you can crawl away… or even pull a bow at me. You'd better think what to do, because if you are here when I return, I'll be cutting you some more.'

ജരു

When Finn and his comrades returned to Auld Nick's camp some hours later, when the gloom of night swallowed the dusk, the fire was still smoldering and Auld Nick was nowhere to be seen.

Robert was the first to comment on Finn's craft, as he and Jack removed the dead reivers to behind a rock.

'Did ya ask em if we could share their camp, or kill em first… and where's the third ye were talkin' about?'

'No, Rab, I conversed nicely, asked them for help I did. But things were getting nasty and with Auld Nick, nasty is all you get. He'll be crawling for now and dying later.'

ജരു

Hours passed into the night, and none of the men seemed keen to seek an end to their day by sleeping. All the slaughtered meat had been cooked, better for the open fire in the cool mountain air, perhaps insufficient to satisfy the group after such hard activity, but welcome none the less, the other beef having long wandered off to find better grass in the mountains.

After talking for a long while for the benefit of Tom, who with his wound freshly dressed, wanted friendly chatter to take his mind away from his pain, all the men laid down against the stoked and well-fuelled fire.

Robert smiled at Jack from his resting, picking fat and sinew from his teeth with a broach pin, and Jack looked for something to say in response.

'Yes, the night is kind, dry, and for a change, not damp.'

Robert grunted and turned his face to the stars. 'Hmm, but without the rain and wind tae keep the Armstrongs in their beds, we better had keep swords at hand and bows strung.'

Jack took Robert's advice and drew his sword and drove it into the ground by his side and grinned. 'Yes, if only it could stick into the Armstrongs so easily.'

But Robert did not smile at Jack's quip, because he had other thoughts to share. 'I can't understand it, Jack.'

'What troubles you?'

'I've said nowt till now, because it was nae my place.'

'Sounds like you are making it your place, my friend.'

'Stranglin' Mary. Stealin' is one thing, even killin' men 'n' boys. But murderin' women while raidin'. It disnae sound like the Armstrongs. The Elliots, aye, but the Armstrongs... It is not their usual reivin' way. It attracts too much bad blood, perpetuates feud. There was no rape attached tae the killin' either. I can understand a wicked man dipping his wick and stranglin' in the heat of the act. But that act against Mary seems fouler.'

'Yes, the matter had crossed my mind. Anger blinds, but logic illuminates. Perhaps we look to the wrong butcher?'

'The wrong butcher, Jack?'

'Yes, perhaps it is another butcher we are needing to find, or to be more precise, *a tutor.*'

'Everyone was quick tae point a finger at the Tutor, but ye seemed more concerned aboot his relationship with Mary. I did not think ye thought of him as Mary's murderer.'

'Perhaps I was in error. I was quick to dismiss it. When we return, Robert, will you travel to Newcastle… to find the Tutor?'

'Sorry lad, I'm no leaving ye and Will while there's threat in the air. I'll send Francis when he returns. He's good at sniffin' oot rats in a sewer. I'll send Tom too, to make sure Francis acts kindly.'

'And I'll send Will to my uncle's house in Hawick, away from my father's tower, at least till we know how much trouble there is.'

Robert turned his head and buried himself under his cloak to sleep. But Jack was not for sleeping, and he found Will on his bed of heather to talk over his plans.

As Jack approached, Will could see the concern on his face and thought him worried about the chase, so he was quick to try to calm his brother's fears.

'Perhaps they don't follow or search, Jack.'

'Perhaps. Still we will need to be more conservative in our actions, we cannot afford a pitched battle with the Armstrongs.'

Will did not offer up any counter discussion to his brother's observation, only a long pause and a sad reflection that deepened his voice and made it unrecognisable to Jack. 'Revenge is a purse that will cost us all dear.'

For all of Will's sadness witnessed by Jack over the years, such deep melancholy he had never heard on his brother's voice before. Jack knew his brother was troubled, but the nature of the land bred troubles in all men and women alike. Easily bred like so many rabbits begetting rabbits. It was the way of life in a land subject to recurrent war. War begets conflict, conflict begets loss, loss begets hardship, and hardship in man gives rise to a troubled soul, *so what of it?* But with Will it was more, and Jack wanted to share the pains of his brother.

'What really troubles you, brother?'

Will looked up as if caught poaching on another man's land, hesitated to find words in reply, and when he found them he spat out a dismissive. 'Ye know, things of concern, but of nae concern tae anyone else, brother.'

Jack found Will's tone in reply, harsh against his own words of concern. 'A man's thoughts may be his own, brother, but a brother's solicitude should be welcomed.'

Will reacted quickly to heal Jack's wound and arousal in his brother's voice. 'Sorry, Jack, I was thinking of episodes tae come… Fear of danger and death cause a man tae think on himself.'

Jack thought on his brother's response. He thought it delivered to divert him from Will's true thoughts, but Jack chose not to follow further in order to seek the truth, but instead to disregard the lie.

Chapter XIX

'None too shabby for Francis, eh Tom?'

Tom looked to the left and to the right, and let his nag pick his own route through the narrow streets, littered with human detritus. 'Na, dinnae like the city. It's a durty place.'

'Don't fret, Tom, we'll no be too long.'

'How are we goin' to find the Tutor in this Sodom?'

'S'pose we'd start on the inns. He might be drinking.'

'Then better for us to find a *laal* guide to the better ale.' Tom scanned the faces lining the busy streets, looking for a likely candidate; one with a sharp eye and a needy disposition, and it took but a moment to find him. Tom halted his nag, leaned over to his right, and gestured to a young lad that was eyeing the two riders up as they passed. 'Hey lad, d'ya know this spot well?'

The boy ran up to the two horsemen, and keenly responded, 'Aye, I'm local.'

'Do ye wan' a half-groat?' Tom asked the lad.

'What ye after… lasses, gamblin', or a clean place to stay?'

'Nah, we're after a man. A scholar with gold in his purse and a fondness for drink in better company.' Tom smiled at the dirty lad, and waited on his consideration.

After a while of contemplation, the lad said, 'A groat.'

Tom looked on Francis. 'Price of petty fact, a pretty price in this foul city.'

Francis gave out a half-meant laugh, which deformed into a strangled guffaw that frightened his horse into whinny, responding to the unfamiliar hoot from his master. The rare sound frightened Tom too, and the horse whinnied again to share Tom's concern.

'Aye, Tom, give the lad a penny instead,' said Francis, recovering his solemnity.

The lad was quick to recover the original offer, and tugged on Tom's bridle. 'Na, half-groat ye said!'

'Allreet, a half-groat, and another penny if we find him afore nightfall,' offered Tom, stroking his injured arm, healing well.

The lad was a good guide. He knew his way about the city, and the better inns and taverns. The alehouses of Newcastle were no better than those in any other city. They held the lesser of men, and the company of women bereft of good moral character. Lasses of age, that for a few coins and a drink or three, would empty your balls in the evening, and leave you with pox in the morning.

Francis and Tom were fortunate, and after not too few establishments, and not too little consumption, had found the Tutor in one of the better inns.

The law and scholarly professions favoured the *Herded Goose*, and although the company was just as poor as one could desire, the wine and brandy were of better heritage, the food better conceived, and all were politely served.

As the pair of troopers approached the Tutor's table, they could see the Tutor was deep in conversation. His confessor was no ordinary ale-mate, his clothes defined him different; they labelled him prosperous and most likely foreign. A bright hue in a drab room. The Tutor saw, through furtive eyes, the familiar troopers approaching. He quickly ushered the tall, flamboyant man away from his table, with a measured hand gesture that sent a clear signal to the foreigner to melt away. Francis' eyes followed the retreat of the foreigner, and lost him as though he were a wisp of smoke in a mist.

'Greetings, Tom. Greetings, Francis.' The Tutor's smile was wide, and his voice lucid and sober.

'It is gud to see ye, Tutor. We have travelled far to find ye,' said Tom, his hands meeting the Tutor's arms in embrace.

'Then have a drink my friends,' proposed the Tutor, as he easily caught the eye of the serving girl. Easy, because she already had her admiring eye on him all evening.

'Two ales for my friends, and bring two more for company.' The Tutor turned his attention off the serving girl, only after a lingering look, admiring her form. Then he shook his head in strange atonement.

'What brings you here, Tom? I thought you none too fond of the city?'

'None too fond reet enough. We're here at the request of Jack, to ask why you left after his wife was killed.'

The smile left the Tutor's face, and his eyes dimmed. 'Aye… poor Mary… Foul business.'

'We've accused the Armstrongs, but they're denyin' murder.' Tom's face showed his words were not his thoughts.

'You think them guilty, Tom? An act befitting their craft?' asked the Tutor.

'Aye, murdering women folk. The ambition of malcontents,' added Francis.

The Tutor screwed his face tight to hold back a truth, and find an answer less revealing. 'Perhaps. I've no doubt they've had their share of murder.'

The serving girl arrived at the table with four cloudy ales, and lingered awhile to catch the eye of her handsome customer. The Tutor raised his eyes to the girl, and with his arm, pulled the girl in tight to his side.

'Ah lads, this is Annie… and if I were a ruder man, I would take her to my room.'

The Tutor's empty boast was caught and countered by Francis, finding the Tutor's lusty show irksome. 'Then why don't you wet your wick. We'll be here when you've finished.'

Seeing his feigned lechery had failed to impress Francis, the Tutor let go of the girl. He had thought to bring good temper to their meeting. But avoidance was no sober strategy, especially when his inquisitors were less than sober themselves, and had travelled far and hard to ask questions—*questions perhaps too difficult to answer.*

'Why do you seek me out for questions, if you already blame the Armstrongs?'

'Captain Jack's not clear why you left,' answered Francis.

'There was no reason for me to stay. I was there only for Mary.'

Francis was less than cordial with the Tutor, it was not his nature to be otherwise, and he barked, 'Will tells a different story… One where you ran off with her maid. Now the truth from you, or do you require some… *encouragement?*'

Francis meant business, and the Tutor knew Francis was mean enough to deal out violence without much provocation. The Tutor took a deep breath, and rested his mind. He waited awhile before responding, and the two troopers waited on him to respond.

'I came in search of Catherine, the maid who left after the murder. And like you came to ask me, I came to ask her why she ran away.'

'And did you find the lass?' asked Francis.

'Yes… and I think you should take her back with you, to see your Captain. Although I have debated hard, whether John should meet her… But you are here, and she is safe in my room… Make sure you are kind to her.'

⁂

It took Francis and Tom two days to travel back with the girl, and Robert brought the young maid to Jack's house on the third night; to his bedroom, where he was resting amongst the candlelight and warmth of a room well heated by a fire.

Mary's maid, Catherine, was an attractive girl, short on years and had a manner that belied her menial occupation. She curtsied to Jack, but her humble greeting was not in her eyes. Fear dwelled within those blue eyes, but also a sense beyond fear—a greater spirit.

'This is the girl with a story tae tell, Jack,' announced Robert.

Jack took the girl from Robert, and led the girl deeper into his room to question her.

'Be calm, no one will hurt you… You can go when you tell me what you know.'

Jack did not know Catherine. She had replaced Mary's last maid, Moira, who had been appointed by Jack's mother in lieu of Mary's original two maids and confidantes. Jack remembered well those two poor girls, who easily found retreating back to their birth homes in Southampton, without the promise of work, preferable to the harder toil expected of them in a new household. Two pretty flowers who wilted under the weight of all those unrefined advances by local men, whose idea of chivalry was to wipe their hands and mouths before they snatched a kiss, only to befoul clean linen with dirty hands, and declare their dirty minds.

Jack had long suspected his mother of conspiring in Moira's appointment. A mother who found advantage in placing her own spy in Mary's house, to keep close watch on an English woman with ways and wiles not to a Scottish matriarch's pleasing. And although the girls and Moira were of similar age, they were an age apart, for Moira was a harridan, old by nature. A brittle temper, badly hidden. Jack recalled living with Moira in their service; it was a relationship with two people; a lickspittle and a termagant; just as Jack was revered, Mary was reviled.

Catherine, however, was a different girl, and had an appeal Jack could not define, but she was frightened and Jack tried his best to calm the girl's fears. But her fear of Jack was too great to be diluted by a few kind words and Jack's smile.

After a few moments the girl stammered, 'I kn-know only a little sir.'

Jack repeated his request more softly, 'Tell me the little you know.'

The girl looked at Jack and then at Robert, and then again at Jack without offering further words.

Seeing the girl's reluctance, Robert stepped forward and snapped, 'Tell him lass!'

Jack raised his hand to quell Robert's barking, and sensing the girl's continuing reticence and fear, moved to make light of Robert's unhelpful interjection. 'Forgive Robert, he thinks he marshals his troops, instead of talking to a pretty girl.'

For the first time the girl smiled, and her eyes flashed from cold to warm. It was the cue for her to speak. 'It was the night o' the raid, sir. The night the mistress was killed.'

Jack then further settled Catherine on his bed and with another gesture of his hand ordered Robert away, to further calm the girl.

'I thinks sir…. I knows who killed your wife.'

'What do you mean, Catherine, *you think?*' asked Jack.

'I was with the mistress on that night. We were far away from the raid. She was nowhere near the church where they found her.'

'If the raiders didn't kill Mary… who did?'

'I know nothing for sure, sir.'

Jack moved his hand over the girl's hand, and again offered a smile. But the girl's eyes changed—flashed back to cold and no further words were offered from her lips.

'What do you know?' asked Jack.

But the girl remained quiet. She knew her answers would not maintain Jack's kindness to her. But she also knew silence was a poor strategy in the company of war-men intent on the truth. She did not know what to do.

Jack's concern at the girl's silence changed his manner from kind to cruel, and his voice from soft to shout.

'Tell me!'

The change in Jack's demeanour frightened the girl further, and she, through a veil of tears, sobbed words and gurgles. 'Will was arguing with the mistress.'

'My brother and my wife?' asked Jack.

'Yes,' replied Catherine.

'But Will said he had not seen Mary.'

'He was there… he was there with me,' cried Catherine.

'Will… with you?' Jack was becoming more confused. 'What do you mean, with you?' Jack's face and head dropped heavy with questions that pricked at his brain. 'Was my brother bedding you?'

Catherine wiped the tears from her eyes. 'He said he loved me... I thought he loved me… But he rejected me.'

Jack sat a while holding the girl's hand. He did not press further. He held his tongue and wore a kindly face, eyes deep and searching. And through the fog of tears, she saw the resemblance of Will in Jack's face. She looked at him as though he was her sweetheart. She peered into his eyes—at the sorrow within them.

'She was a lady… your wife. She was always gud to us… made sure we were looked after.'

But Jack was outside the comfort of her words. He was dwelling in an unforgiving febrile confusion. In all his vengeful thought and action, none had confessed to his wife's killing. He had not sought disclosure by admission, only retribution. Now horror of a possible new truth and the obscurity of events dwelled in the same thought. Jack did not doubt the girl's words. *Will had lied. He was with Mary that night, but had he killed her? Why would he lie if he had not done this foul thing? Was he covering for another?* Jack shook his head. He tried to shake out the terrible thoughts of his brother's deeds the girl had planted there. He tried to banish her evil claims.

'Why would you lie, girl? Why would you tell so foul a lie?'

The girl returned to fear at Jack's accusation. 'It's the truth… I swear it.'

'There are few truths from a spurned lass, looking to punish her former lover.'

'I love Will, I would not hurt him… I… I carry his baby.'

The feeling in her words countered Jack's recrimination, and his eyes widened and rested on the girl's belly.

'Catherine, do you think Will killed my wife?'

'I don't know… I don't know… I…don't…' she dropped her head into her hands and sobbed. A muffled repeat coming through her fingers clasped around her face. 'I don't know.'

Jack looked away to Robert, and beckoned him to come and comfort the girl.

'Robert… take care of Catherine.'

'Aye, Jack.'

'And Robert… keep her here… and keep her safe.'

'Where are ye goin', Jack?'

'To see Will.'

෨෬

Jack arrived at his uncle's house in Hawick before dusk. A few servants were about to take and tend to his horse. The stone built house, three storeys, was large amongst the other houses in the town, and inside, the rooms were well furnished, with rich tapestries and exceptional furniture. All its splendour was testament to Jack's grandfather's wealth and foresight to provide a fine family home, big enough to furnish comfortable lodgings for re-establishing his family after its dire losses at the battle of Flodden, forty-eight years earlier. Its rich treasures survived hostile times, protected by secret basements to hide all its wealth in times of war or raid.

Will occupied the house when it pleased him. His uncle often absent to tend to business interests in the South. Will preferred the company of town to the isolation of country, especially when the town provided more enjoyable social pursuits. Cards and gambling were Will's escape, and the dissolute women that live off men with money in their purse, and insobriety to loosen their hold on it.

The servants pointed Jack to Will's location and he soon found him, sitting by a table, a glass in hand and a jug next to him, all with wine.

'It's a grand evenin', Jack, but yer face tells me its nae so good for ye.'

'No, Will. It is a foul evening, made so by fouler news.'

'News, Jack?'

'Yes, Will, news and a question, my brother… Did you murder Mary?'

Will poured wine into a fine Venetian glass and put it to his lips. He hesitated, and drank a large part of its fill, and then poured more from the jug to fill it again. The jug seemed almost empty and Jack supposed his brother had been drinking for some time gone, but he appeared sober.

'It's a strange welcome ye give yer brother.'

'Welcomes are for better times. Did you murder Mary?'

Will sat motionless, contemplating Jack's question.

To Jack, Will seemed at a loss for an answer. He seemed to be a man thinking a strategy, and not a man with denial to the fore, and denial was the only proper response to Jack's question, if the question was a nonsense to ask.

Will finally answered, 'Dae not ask me this, Jack… Dae not.'

'I will ask you again, *brother*. Did you murder Mary?'

'Ye dare accuse me of this foul deed. Why dae ye accuse me?'

'Because I have a witness to your meeting that night. Why would you lie, unless to keep a foul deed hidden.'

'Who is this perjurious witness?' Will let out a breath to force out his injury, and he smiled. 'Who has a better standing than me, brother?'

Will's easy manner settled Jack a little and his brother's smile reassured him that all was fine and the doubts in Jack's mind were simply foolish. But Jack's comfort lasted only a moment, because Will's reaction to the accusation was at odds with reason; his response strange, as if he had expected the charge.

Will enquired again, 'Whose lies dae ye accept over yer blessed brother?'

'Catherine Dodd's… but I think they are truths… not lies,' replied Jack.

Will's face changed, and his easy expression changed in the light of elation. 'Kate. How is she?'

'She is well. Her belly is filled with your child, she tells me.'

'So, that is why the lass bolted. I thought it was because I had rejected her.'

'No, I suspect she ran from fear… Fear perhaps of what you did.'

'Did what brother?'

'Murder Mary.'

'It is a lie!'

'The only lie is yours. Why hide the truth, brother. Even if you did not murder her, you were still with Mary on the night she died, and therefore you know who killed her. Who do you protect?'

Will turned away and stood at the window, his gaze deep into the head of the hilltops, outlined in the darkening sky, and his mind fell deeper into his own dark deeds.

Will's silence provoked Jack to a fierce anger; a boiling rage that he found impossible to contain. *You strangled Mary… you bastard!*

'No, brother.'

But Will's denial was poorly offered, weak and unconvincing. *Why did you kill Mary? Would she not lie with you?'* demanded Jack.

Will turned from the window to face Jack, his words deep and solemn. 'No… I loved Mary. Loved her like a… like a sister. She was precious tae me… It was ye who rejected the lass.'

'Then why did you kill her?'

Will opened his mouth as if to speak. Then he looked away, taking the words with him. He formed fists and gripped hard, his teeth clenching in frustration at the words he wanted to say, but could not. He looked to the floor. Closed his eyes, and he buried the truth deep within him.

Jack looked on a man at odds with himself, and angry at the accusation.

Will slowly raised his head and opened his eyes. 'Jack.' Will's voice deepened further, and a new look accompanied a new voice. Will spoke as another man.

'She was the seed of the Devil. She lived a lie, Jack. She admitted it tae me… She did… She thought she was the spawn of the Devil… The Devil—Thomas Wharton, the English fiend…. So I purified her… with my own bare hands.'

248

Jack's face held shock, his mind filled with disbelief. Who was this in front of him? Will was in another place, another body. He had to be, because the foul soul that issued this poison was not Will.

Will's eyes were wide, but he held himself steady, and with a low measured voice he pushed out an admission through gritted teeth. 'When the delight had gone… I cried… I was wretched… disgusted at my sickenin' act—my gluttony. But in a moment the pleasure had gone too. My need had gone, but Mary in my hands was not. So I squeezed her neck again… hoping a dreg of stinkin' Wharton life was left in her… but alas she was empty. Mary was a fool… perhaps innocent. But she was the daughter of Thomas Wharton—I knew it in my soul. She was there… and I was hungry fer retaliation. One moment of victory in a thousand days of sufferin' n defeat.' Will's eyes closed tight in remembrance of the foul deed. 'Mmm… aye… my mind released oot of darkness into pure pleasure. And after… after I killed her… I strapped her English carcass tae a nag, tae let it lie in a deserted church. A church at the centre of a raid reported tae me that very night.'

Will opened his eyes, and he lunged at Jack to hold him tight, and from his mouth, more fevered words, moist with spittle, hit Jack's face. 'She was a foul lie and I extinguished her flame, her foul Wharton stench.'

Jack, disgusted at his brother's demeanour, broke his grasp and pushed him away, disbelief filling his brain. 'Ramblings you fool. Come to your senses man!'

Will ran to the corner of the room then back to the window.

'Ye're right brother… Sorry, sorry forgive me… Me… Aye, aye I need forgiveness… Aye.'

Will, from his mad ramblings, seemed to gather his composure for a moment, and he straightened himself. But Jack could only stand and watch, appalled. His brother was insane.

Jack did not want to listen any more to Will's madness. His demented words confused him. Truth or lies hidden beneath mock or real insanity he did not know, but what he did know was that Will had murdered Mary. For what true reason, beneath the ranting of an unfamiliar brother, he had not discovered, but he knew further interrogation was pointless, and he turned away to leave.

But as he strode out through the open door and into the darkness of the corridor, a new wave of blind anger assaulted his senses. A violent wave that washed all other reason and consequence from his head. He turned quickly without break in momentum, and at a quickened pace, retraced his steps and re-entered the room to the surprise of his brother. With only a glance at his brother's illuminated form in the candlelight to fix his position, Jack looked beyond to the right and focused his stare on a red curtain hanging on the wall behind his target. Without break in his step; without abatement in the wave of violence washing over him; without word or utterance, Jack drew his sword and with a two handed grasp held the blade high over his right shoulder.

Will, seeing the murderous intent of his brother, reached to his dagger, but the velocity and impetus of the assault was too great.

Without break in his gaze upon the curtain, or hesitation in his progress, Jack moved quickly past his brother, bringing down his sword with all the fire and fuel of his hatred and betrayal, and Will's flesh gave way under the heavy steel blade.

Jack not once looked back at the falling of his brother, nor removed his eyes from the red curtain. He did not need to know if his blow was a killing stroke, nor did he hear the plea of his brother not to strike. Silence befell the room. A brother was dead, and as Jack returned his sword to its scabbard without wiping it, coldness was about him.

But Jack remained in the room, and after a while his hate cooled. He no longer knew or cared why he had reason to kill his brother, but the regret within his heart for his own vengeful action was present and real. He put aside the dead man's odious deed, and looked upon his face and remembered a brother. He looked into his heart, and he cried. He knew what he had done. Fouler deed he had not known. He knelt down with Will and wiping away his own tears, reverently rearranged Will's body, covering it with a blanket, as if God would see his atonement for his fatal action and forgive him.

Jack sat in the room, not moving, his heart sinking to the depth of his grieving soul, and he looked upon Will's body and his head rose to the stars. Hours passed, snuffed light and deeper darkness had covered the room, hiding the still presence of Jack, and Will's body.

When the today had gone and turned into tomorrow, three men entered the room, and following them, from the soft light of the open door, was an old man—*his father*. The escort moved into the room and set down the candles they were carrying at Will's corpse. Jack remained in the shadows where he had been sitting, and kept his presence from his father. He surveyed in silence, his eyes watching the old man's face, restrained and white in the reflection of the candlelight. Jack's father knelt at the side of his dead son and pulled back the blanket away from his head. The suffering on his father's face was clear. The old man looked upon his dead son's face and neither saw, nor cared about the men standing around him, watching his anguish. None that knew him had seen him display such sadness. None thought him capable of such a display of open grief, because no one really knew him—not even Jack.

Jack moved from the shadows, and his father's gaze lifted up from the cold body of Will to his other son, and the old man knew what he had done. His father would not forgive him; his father would not be able to forgive. Two sons were now gone from him. Two sons dead before his own time. Two sons he loved. One taken by the third. Taken without his permission. Plucked from his dreams and aspirations.

The last son now stood before him, his sword offered; a device presented so that his father would understand his son's atonement; a device to end a murderer's life, as is the right of the father seeking retribution for a murdered son.

Instead, Jack's father rose to face him with words. 'I have come direct from Robert. I feared the truth of Will's involvement in Mary's death. I suspected it, but washed it from my mind. I hid his madness, his insane hatred o' the English. He blamed them fer all his woes, Thomas Wharton most of all. I knew Mary thought she was Wharton's bastard… I begged her tae keep it secret.'

Jack could only say, 'I am sorry, father.'

'Dae not call me father, ye are nae my son. Ye are a man, and ye have done what a man must dae tae safeguard honour in himself. I have nae sons now. Take yer blade. It is nae yer life that is forfeit here, it is mine. I have nae longer leisure in my heart, only the torment of two sons dead and now the third lost tae me. Take yer sword, Jack, heir tae nae property o' mine. A man of this world, but not of my estates. No longer a captain of my men. I know not if God goes wi' ye, but ye must now go from my sight.'

Jack looked on his father, heart breaking at the sight of an old man showing older with the pain of loss. But there could be no justification, no plea offered by Jack. He knew his brother's life was, in his father's realm, more important than his own wife—a wife who in reality had meant little to Jack these past years. It was too late for words, too late for conciliation, so long outstanding. So instead, Jack simply bowed his head, acknowledging the seniority and rank of the older man in front of him, turned and walked away.

Chapter XX

Rest welcomed both the men who had travelled a far troubled route. Jack was reunited with the Tutor in the Herded Goose, and Jack's men, with money in hand, had found either a better bed to sleep in, or a bench on which to drink, and some, even a whore or two to offer them more than their wives' Church directed missionary delight. But what the night had given Jack, was time with his friend alone in a private room with good wine and a good fire. Time to be secure, and to put the horror of his actions six weeks back behind him for a while. The Tutor was also pleased to be with Jack, and although he knew he was hiding deeds not for sharing, he still talked of his time since he last saw Jack, three years ago.

'John, they say you killed a Catholic priest.'

'I did, but not because he was a priest.'

'Because he was Catholic?'

'No, because he was an evil bastard who killed innocents.'

The Tutor smiled wryly. 'Are there *innocents* in this world?'

'The newly born are innocents. That bastard French priest burned babies simply because they were born of Protestants.'

'He probably thought it was right to do so, for while children grow up in adversary to one's beliefs, conflict will surely follow. *Ugly born, ugly be*, I have heard said.'

'I have found all faiths to be both beautiful and ugly, for all faiths can move mountains. I have seen it muster thousands to defend its call. And I have seen thousands, defeated, turn away from it to embrace another man's belief, simply to live. I have seen people adhere to their faith's call only to be murdered for their creed. Do I think God blesses one and not the other? I do not think so. It is easier to turn one's coat from one side to the other, if the coat's lining fits better with one's surroundings. After all, faith, like all flags of conviction, is a fickle badge... simply another reason to court hatred of your neighbour. Man seeks God's grace, I accept, and devotion needs its form, I accept too, but ultimately faith is of man's design, not of God's.

'So even with five years in a religious war, you still have not found your Faith's path?'

'I have belief, that is enough.'

'You sound more like Henri Hueçon, than my student. I think that sorry soul has influenced you far more.' The Tutor thought a little. 'So, would you kill a protestant priest if he burned catholic babies?'

Jack did not hesitate to reply. 'Certainly.'

'You hold to a code of conduct sir above religious fervent. Is it chivalry?'

'I am no knight. I am a soldier. I have no nobility, just tools and a killing craft.'

'Soldiers do as their generals instruct, even murder perhaps?'

Jack nodded. 'True, I have seen and committed murder in the name of war and duty.'

'So do you agree that holy war does commission murder, and that murder is not simply the right of soldiers, but also of God's own soldiers? By that I mean priests.'

Jack's face formed a frown. 'Tutor, I don't know where this conversation is heading, or for what reason, but I thought God had angels to fight his wars, and I have never seen an angel. Priests are appointed by the Church, and the Church is appointed by kings and emperors, not God.'

'Some will call you a heretic, John Brownfield, and God will judge you harshly... You *will* go to Hell.'

Jack simply smiled in agreement. Then the Tutor's inquisition changed as he scanned Jack's gear, stowed in the corner of the room they shared. He looked at his shield, sword and scabbard, a large cloth bag, folded cloak, armour, pistols in their leather holsters... and a tall axe.

The Tutor sighed and walked over to the equipment to pick up the axe, and said, 'Bendback's axe. I feared to ask about those I did not see around you tonight. I hoped they were elsewhere.' There was a short silence before the Tutor spoke again. 'Bendback, is he dead?'

Jack waited awhile before replying, his sorrow preventing easy words. 'Yes, in France. With his dying breath he handed me his axe well bloodied, his opponents well killed.'

The Tutor replaced the axe reverently back exactly where he found it. 'Henry Musgrave was a good man.'

A tear formed in Jack's eye, his voice broken and weak. 'He was a man in a shape cruel, but he had a heart stouter than any I know.'

The Tutor returned to his beaker and raised it high. 'To Bendback Bob. His ancestors can be proud he bore the name of Musgrave.' Then he threw back the beaker's contents into his mouth.

Both men rested their conversation a while. They took more wine and pleasure in the warmth of the fire, in the security and privacy of the dimly lit room.

Jack gazed deep into the open fire and he thought on their conversation, and without raising his face from the heat, or alteration to his demeanour, he spoke once more. 'I suspect, Tutor, you are not what you pretend to be.'

The Tutor, wine in hand, hesitated to finish the last dregs from his beaker. He then completed his thought and threw the deep red liquid to the back of his throat, as if to flush impropriety from his mouth. 'And what do you think I am, John *Brownfield*?'

'Not wholly a scholar, but a man in the guise of a scholar.'

The Tutor set his empty beaker almost silently on the table. 'Am I not learned, not a faithful servant of education and of God? Indeed, am I not a good scholar?'

'No sir, you are a good agent, even a spy perhaps.'

The Tutor did not seem disturbed by the accusation. He simply sat looking at Jack, who remained fastened in his position leaning over the fire, eyes lost in its flame.

Jack, not hearing a response to his charge, then turned his head to face the Tutor. 'Are you a spy?'

The Tutor smiled, relaxed and lucid. He stared at his companion for a moment to determine his mood and said, 'And John, what brings you to such a foolish conclusion?'

Jack's expression showed no enmity towards his friend, only the quiet realisation of a truth long hidden from him. 'My conclusions are, at best, the product of supposition. But if you require my suspicions in order for you to admit the truth to a friend, then I shall share them.' Jack paused awhile in the hope that the Tutor would save him from further reveal and admit to his accusation. But nothing came. 'Your lack of response to my accusation tells all. You hide the truth badly, as if you no longer care to hide it from me.'

'No, John, I am simply lost to an answer to your charge,' replied the Tutor.

Jack with a sigh continued, 'I once thought you were my wife's lover. But deep in my heart I knew you were not. But whom else would she keep so close, other than her physician or her astrologer. No, you were simply a good friend who could help a woman make enquiries in those places a woman's word would not be heard. A woman seeking the truth of her parentage.' Jack continued after the Tutor offered no response. 'You never married. I never knew you with a woman. I know you liked women, and I know you are no sodomite. No woman bound you into matrimony, you, so attractive a man in most every woman's eyes. It was as if you had pledged celibacy. I also remember the thief on the road that day, many years ago. The one who mistook you for kin, the one you despatched so coldly and with great skill. But he was not your brother. He simply remembered a kind monk's face from a monastery perhaps. A kindly place which had provided him alms in better times. Were you a monk, displaced by King Henry's edicts perhaps?'

The Tutor said nothing, refilled his beaker and took a long drink. He seemed to savour the wine longer on his tongue, as if it was a first taste of good wine in a dry mouth. As if he had been a long time waiting for this wine. As if this was to be his last ever taste of it too.

'All very good, John, and supposition as you say. But you called me a spy, not a monk.'

'Yes I did. I remember all those years ago when I was a boy, when I first met Henri Hueçon and he took so much heed in my maturation. He was indiscrete that night at Wharton's dinner table, to toast the password, and you too for your correct response to it.'

'The password?'

'Yes spy, the password, *Per aspera ad astra;* through difficulty to the stars. You see, *Guild Brother*, I too am an agent of the *Black Merchants Guild.* The Frenchman recruited me as an apprentice into the Guild soon after the occurrences on that infamous *Truce Day*, when I was still a boy. I had always wondered how Henri warmed to me so quickly after such an indifferent initial meeting at Wharton's table. I know now you had alerted him to my potential, and thus awakened his appetite for my company. So you see, I too know the password between its agents.'

'Then why did you not announce yourself to me as a *Brother of the Guild* sooner?'

'Because you know the precept… Announcement of one's association to another in the Guild, is only permitted if it is essential to do so, or as directed by a Guild Overseer.' Jack then shook his head. 'Henri should not have announced the password so publicly, or you to respond likewise with, *Semper paratus, semper fidelis*; always ready, always faithful.'

The Tutor let out a deep sigh. 'Then deception, so long held, is no longer appropriate… I am glad that truth be out between friends. I am an agent of the Guild. So you know I have no allegiance to any sovereign power, but to a greater power, commerce. I am sorry, John. Henri lied… He told me you were unsuitable for training into the Guild. I did not know you had become an agent.'

'That is the way in secret societies. Secrecy even within itself.'

The Tutor continued. 'My role was to keep an eye on the Northern Marches, to report on matters of interest to the Guild; matters that could see further unrest in the realm. Unrest means war. War means weapons. Weapons means gold and Royal favours for the Guild. And as you know, John, the Guild are very well placed to supply weapons.'

'This is true. But why were you in Captain Traquere's employ?'

'Sir Thomas Wharton was an important figure in Border affairs. A man who could effect major conflicts in the area and control the passage of goods. Henri's relationship with Wharton was not on firm ground and the Guild wanted more tangible blackmail to hold over Sir Thomas… to coerce him into Guild thinking. The Captain hated Sir Thomas Wharton, and the Guild wanted to know why. So I was placed as his Tutor.'

Jack's face lit up with a new understanding, and an annoyance of a truth that should have been long known to him. 'Ah, so the Captain suspected Mary was Sir Thomas' child, hence her marriage to me. Not to spite me, but to further spite the Warden and his deputy, who had directed the marriage in the first-place. But the marriage the Warden directed was of the Captain's eldest daughter Eleanor, the girl he knew I was courting. The eldest daughter is always to be married first. Did Wharton know Mary was his bastard?'

'We never found out the truth of Mary's parentage. Truth is, Mary suspected it, but she never really wanted to know. Our trips to Carlisle and Cockermouth took us back to a time when Wharton was titled as Captain of Cockermouth, and to rumours of a relationship with Mary's mother. But rumours they remain, no truth we found.'

'Rumour murdered Mary, and I murdered Will. Seems like foul actions grow from foul roots. From seeds sown in rumour,' announced Jack, his face seeking solace in the fire's flame.

'No, Will was deranged. He needed little to blame an innocent for his woes. You simply ended his misery.'

'Aye, and sent him to Hell, no doubt,' replied Jack.

'What will you do with Mary's maid, Catherine, and her child?' asked the Tutor.

'I will place her in the care of a goodly soul. One who owes me his life. I cannot take her in myself, because I travel to Antwerp in two days with my men hungry for foreign gold, and a kinder climate. My troops bolstered by a few boys, given to me to learn a soldier's craft. If Catherine's child is born, I will take the baby as my ward, and her mother into my company.' Jack poured himself another drink and took only a sip, remembering lives lost and lives taken. Then he focused attention on the Tutor. 'Francis and Tom, reported a well dressed foreigner, the night they found you here in the Herded Goose. Was it Henri Hueçon?'

'Hueçon, yes. He was disappointed that I had no scandal regarding Sir Thomas Wharton. He even wished me to fabricate a lie around Mary's death to implicate him. I could not do it. I loved Mary. I would not have her memory tied to lies.'

'So how does it sit with you and the Guild?' asked Jack, with concern in his voice.

'Uncomfortably. I have no new assignment from the Guild, which may be indication of their foul intentions towards me. So I either stay and hope for the best, or run and hope it is not you they send to murder me... No, I will return to the Cistercian Order, but in Spain.'

'So Tutor, do I call you *Reverend Brother*, or *Guild Brother*?'

'Neither. Call me… *friend*.'

[Mary and Will's story can be read under the title,
Truth and Madness.]

I cannot say when my dreams became my reality. I do not know when my acceptance of him begat my mania; my vagary observed in the eyes of those around me. All I know is that his death was not the end of him. But in my defence, when one dreams a dream so real, a brother killed in fact and now alive in an invention of one's fancy. And that dream of him is the same dream for a score and more nights, and peaceful sleep is deprived. Then it is easy to blend the dream into day, and fantasy into truth. One believes the brother is alive and is not a fiction of the conscious, a bereavement of the soul.

So may God have mercy on me. May he heal the wound and remove the itch from the scar it leaves behind. But I suspect the wound and the scar I have inflicted on myself will ache and itch for the remainder of my days. So while I remain on Earth, I will remember him each and every day. And when my time on Earth is over, I will seek his forgiveness in Heaven.

John Brownfield, MDLX (1560)

Chapter XXI

The quayside at Newcastle was full of activity, with a sniff fouler than any Jack had under his nose previous. A lesser man would have wretched up his guts at the smell of it, but not Jack. He was not man to lose his refection easily, unless of course the ale was tainted, or his consumption of it was unrestrained.

Four tall ships stood against the quay and spilled out their goods, while a further two, taller and broader, sucked them in. All served by many men loading and unloading, dirty and work worn. Jack felt sorry for these beasts of burden working this foul landscape, and he raised his face from it to seek a new vision, one less busy, one less dirty. But the sky was no help, it was as grey as the quay landscape, as grey as the imagined sea that lay beyond the grey river.

Jack had sent his men to secure passage to Antwerp, to sell their horses and find provisions enough to last them a while. Jack fretted a little. There were too few of them, and Jack thought on Robert, Tom, Francis and Finn; too few to negotiate a good commission in a foreign war, but enough perhaps for another commission—with a generous paymaster of his acquaintance.

In the distance, a familiar figure picked his way through a maze of grimy men, stacks of goods, rope and barrel; a man distinctive and exotic in a world of dirty work. Jack looked on amused, as the man tried to maintain a good distance from those around him that might soil his suit. Jack thought on the poor man's shoes, the soles scuffed and blackened by tar and grease, the soft white leather soiled by the puddles of dirty water that stood around his passage. Jack waited and grinned at the man's mincing steps, as he avoided all—and as he took his time to reach Jack.

'No gentleman should be allowed in such a place. *Mon dieu*, my stools are cleaner and smell far sweeter than this foul stench.'

'It is good to see you, Henri.'

'And it would be good to see you, *Jacques*, if my eyes could see. My poor peepers are watering with the pain of stink in this… *Mais non,* I cannot describe it!'

'After all these years, Henri, is it not fitting for you to drop your French veneer? I have known you to be a Dutchman since I learned the nature of your true tongue, and recognised the words you used at Wharton's dining table when I was boy, and you were not my paymaster.'

Henri Hueçon smiled. '*Mais non, Jacques*. Like my clothes, my word is my show. I'm beautiful in both sight and in sound.' Henri then moved to stand alongside Jack to share his view, and to hide their conversation a little better from their surroundings. 'Have you passage to Antwerp? It is *très important…* your new commission awaits, and your new master is not a man to be kept waiting.'

'My men are arranging it as we speak.'

'*Bon!*'

'Will you be joining us?' asked Jack.

'*Non*, I have duties elsewhere. Responsibilities to the Guild, which regrettably press me to leave you.' Henri shook his head mournfully. 'My heart grieves at so short a reunion.' But Henri quickly relocated his smile, as he looked around at the dirt and bustle of the quayside. 'Although I know one who will not be sorry to see me leave you here.'

Jack looked puzzled. 'Who be that, Henri?'

'My suit of course.'

Henri turned to walk away, but as he did, he cast a disapproving eye down at Jack's baggage; two meagre leather bags with weapons attached, wrapped and tied in woollen cloth. 'Is this all you carry, *Jacques*? Have you learned nothing about gentlemen's baggage?'

Jack replied the gentle scold, 'I'm afraid I cannot afford the excess of a trunk to carry my clothes.'

'Excess sir, is travelling with three chests for one's clothes. I of course have four.'

Jack smiled, as ever, in response to Henri's wit, and raised his hand in salute to Henri as he walked away. But within six paces, Henri turned again for another last word.

'*Jacques*… what does your tutor plan?'

Jack replied, 'He says he will be a monk—join his order in Spain.'

Henri nodded, and returned Jack's salute with words too low for Jack to hear. 'He will be sorely disappointed then.'

⁕

It was with a heavy heart that Jack looked out to sea. Heavy from the episode of his life he left behind, cautious about the new episode ahead. He could not clear his mind of thought, and the spell on deck did nothing to blow his thoughts away. Robert joined him after a while, concerned about Jack's mood, but he stayed his distance, so as not to disturb Jack's contemplation of the sea. The wind was strong, and it pushed back Jack's shirt and hair in the wind to outline his lean body and face. Robert could not stay his place any longer, because he could see the sadness on Jack's face, and he was anxious to bring him a cloak against the winter wind.

Robert wrapped the cloak around Jack's shoulders, and Jack, with his gaze still on the sea, gripped Robert's hand tightly.

'Is that you, Will?'

'No, Jack… it's Rab.'

Jack turned to see his friend and smiled. But his smile hid a heavy heart, and the corners of his mouth descended under the weight of his hurt. Robert knew of his friend's pain and chose to remind Jack of a better time.

'We've come along way, Jack, from a footba' game in a field.'

'Aye, Robert… but we've been here before. Travelling overseas, perhaps to war.'

'Aye… but things have changed fer us all, Jack.'

Jack sighed, his eyes returning to the sea. 'Why must there be change?'

'Change is fated. A man can seek tae embrace this condition, or seek tae avoid it. Ye can look tae yer castle, and remain content within its ramparts... but there'll be nae fortune tae be had, while ye sit on yer arse. Or, ye can look back tae the path from which ye travelled. The scenery will be familiar, and the destination known, but nothin' will be new, and ye will wither fer lack of new treasure... But a man can also look tae the untravelled road, and hope it may lead him tae better fortune.'

Jack was surprised to hear Robert's words, full of deep thought and understanding, and he countered, 'But Robert, all you can be sure of on the untravelled road, is what you see in the first few footsteps.'

Robert smiled broadly and answered, 'True… but at the end

of those footsteps… is the sight of a few footsteps mair.'

'It is strange to hear you talk like this. More words I have never heard you speak.'

'Aye… I oft mind my words, but some need the sayin'.'

The sea was busy pitching the ship, and grey seas and greyer skies met Jack's gaze as he looked forward in search of land on the horizon. But the haze in the air obscured his vision past a mile, and as he squinted to make out any shapes on the horizon, a shout called out from mast top to halt his scan.

'*Ship ahoy!*' and again, this time with more volume and alarm, '*Ship ahoy… ship ahoy on the port beam!*'

Within moments ship's captain and crew were about the deck, and within the next instant, Captain James Small had his hands to his eyes, to focus his attention on the dark shadow on the horizon.

The words of his boatswain were fevered in anticipation of a possible target. 'French built merchantman, and a big'un, *Captain.*'

Captain Small presented himself atop an iron port-piece; a gun in ship's suite of enhanced ordnance, to better see the shadow in the distance.

'Aye, Poppy, a big'un she is. But what is she, merchantman or warship? Low in the water she sits. Down low. Full of prize perhaps, or laden with too much cannon… Lets hope it's gold, and not iron and powder, eh?'

'She's a galley, Captain. I swear it… Oars, I wager, where we have guns.'

Captain Small strained his eyes to better see the distant vessel. He shifted on his feet to walk the port-piece hall, four feet of barrel, to lean hard out against the ship's rail. His words to Poppy, breathless, as the rail winded him. 'Your eyes have better range, Poppy… Is she French, Spanish, Dutch, or one of our own?'

Poppy pushed his eyes to the distant shadow, to refocus his stare. He held his gaze, until colours could be discerned in the grey.

'French.'

Captain Small's face showed unease. The nationality of the target displeased him. England was not at war with France, only discomfort. But ten years of an uneasy peace, created little charity in a bitter memory. A mind scarred with past slaughter of brothers by a French army. Time did not remove those memories of losses so easily. Then he smiled, and offered, 'But the question, Master Boatswain, is…'

The boatswain turned to his captain, waiting for him to finish. But the captain simply winked.

The boatswain knew his captain. He knew how to finish his sentence, and he returned his captain's wink, and replied, 'Aye, sir… The question is… Is yon ship a pirate; a ship with foul intent on honest ships, making an honest living?'

Captain Small winked again, and smiled at his boatswain. 'So you think she a pirate ship, eh Poppy?'

The boatswain found it difficult to hold an earnest face as he replied, 'Aye she is. I've heard tale of a terrible French pirate operating this sea. It would be God's pleasure that we see it stopped from its theivin' and murderin' ways.'

Commands given. Commands delivered. Men ordered and men responded with haste and purpose, and within minutes ship and crew were sailing towards the French shadow in the haze.

'You had better ready your men, Captain Brownfield,' the companionable English sea captain slapped Jack's back hard, adding, 'They'll be none too fond of our amorous advances, eh Brownfield? They may even decide to slap us, as we raise her skirts and take our pleasure.'

James Small was an opportunist. A merchant sailor authorised by his masters to commit acts of convenient theft. To plunder ship, and harm those who would prevent such a commission. He was a man of ambition—an ambition that lived beyond the sea, and into a life of ease on the land, with a smart house and smarter wife, land and status. His lowly patrimony hindered his goal, but prize money, reward and the stolen treasure he could acquire—and hide from his employers, would buy his dreams. His spoils had made his masters rich, and his prey, mainly the French and Spanish, poorer—especially if their ships were unfortunate to find themselves alone at sea. He cared nothing of inter-nation treaties and alliances, because there would always be a nation, or faction, happy to reward him for the prize of a ship.

His men loved him. He made them rich enough to drink and whore heartily in the port towns, whilst providing financial comfort for their bigamous collection of wives and families. And although he contributed well to his masters' wealth, it was not to the detriment of his own growing fortune.

Skilful piloting brought the English ship, *Devotion,* behind the stern of the French galley. Running to catch the juggernaut, as it tried in vain to manoeuvre to meet the English ship broadside, to bring what cannon it had to bear on the smaller English ship. The Frenchman was clearly a fat merchantman and no warship, for her gun provision was only adequate. Running was no option for her. The three-masted Devotion, at around eighty tons was much faster than the three hundred ton, two-masted French galley, running at six or seven knots at her top speed under sail, or oar.

In only twenty minutes since first sighting, the two bow guns of the Devotion reached the stern of the galley, scarring deep her transom.

As the Devotion chased the galley, the call came to ready the men to board the French vessel, and Jack steadied his men, checking on their readiness to brawl alongside the boarding crew of the English ship. All were ready. All but Tom, who had announced to Jack, as he curled up to sleep out the excitement, 'If ma Daddy wanted me t' fight at sea, he would've taught me t' swim.'

Jack had too much admiration and thanks for Tom's past bravery to call him coward, and order him on to this expedition. Instead, Jack took to his own readiness.

As the noise of men grunting and growling on the deck grew, with the increasing shadow of the French ship, four of the Devotion's crew brought out barrels full of weapons; cudgels, axes, poleaxes, spikes and other dull rusty blades. Jack pulled out his sword and dagger, and felt their weight in his hands. He considered their effectiveness for the forthcoming fight. He judged the restrictions of space and balance he would have in the fray. Better strategy saw him return his own blades to his sword belt. He took off his belt, cap and jacket—just donned, and thrust them into the lap of the sleeping Tom. Jack, in his shirtsleeves, walked to the barrels of weapons and lifted from them two axes, dull of blade, but with sufficient heft to satisfy him of their effectiveness as weapons. Thrusting the handles of the axes down into the tops of his boots, he returned to the head of his men, to calm them before the fight. Robert too, had abandoned his blades for two axes. But his choices were double headed and weightier than Jack's, using the leather lanyards on their handles to affix them to his wrists.

'Aye, here we go again, Jack. Blood afore breakfast.'

Jack placed his hands on the sides of Robert's head, and squeezed hard. 'And I will see that ugly face again afore dinner.'

Robert pulled away from Jack, filled his mouth and spat hard and full on the deck. 'Filthy work my ma would say. Filthy work killin' is.' Robert portrayed a man who was not looking forward to the action, but Jack knew Robert would be the first in, and the bloodiest fighter on the English side.

Following the track of the galley's process in the sea, the

Devotion came alongside the behemoth with a terrible sound. The thunderous thump of timber on timber. A barrage of cannon rang out from both ships. Thunder, smoke and splintered wood filled the air. Ropes flew from the English ship, as English grappling irons sank into French timber, and even French flesh. Captain Small gave a rude shout, which held its bloody note against the racket, and led his men over the side to melee with the enemy.

Soldier and sailor climbed the boarding ramps, their voices screaming louder than the English and French handguns. Jack's men joined in too, voices louder.

Jack followed Robert up one of the ramps pushed against the gallery of the French ship, while English crossbow and gun kept French heads down—whilst the Devotion's company climbed aboard. The sing of bolt and bullet flew overhead as they climbed.

Robert reached the French ship's gallery to be met immediately by a dark skinned French sailor. Robert welcomed him with a head butt, and as the sailor recoiled, the bold Scot leapt from the gallery, to bring one of his axes down hard on the sailor's head, splitting his skull. Robert recovered quickly. Another French-negro sailor ran at him from his left with a poleaxe, forcing Robert to push out his axe to counter the blow. The force of the strike against his axe unbalanced him.

But Robert did not need to recover well to meet this second opponent, because Jack had already reached the top of the gallery. With axes in hands, Jack jumped down from the rail, and sunk dull metal blades into the back of Robert's attacker.

The French sailor dropped his poleaxe in his great pain, but there was no great wound. So Robert finished off the falling second French sailor, with another blow to the head, removing an ear and rendering the sailor unconscious. Both men recovered quickly and stood together. They scanned the scene, Robert volleying spit from his mouth onto the French deck.

'They're big bastards on this boat, Jack.'

Jack looked at the melee around them, and then smiled at Robert. 'They are at that, Robert. As big as this boat, and twice as foul.'

Both friends threw each other a broad smile, and ran into the scrap shouting slaughter. Jack low with axes at French legs—Robert high at French heads.

[The story continues under the title, *Devotion and the Devil.*]

Author's Note

Although *Three Hills* is a novel, the settings are real and the majority of the main historical events that impacted so heavily during Jack Brownfield's fictional life did actually happen, principally the battles of *Solway Moss* and *Ancrum Moor*. The nature of the Marches between England and Scotland were as described, and those famous Borderer 'Names'; *Maxwell, Armstrong, Kerr, Musgrave*, etc, did dwell and perish in the Borders. Many were reivers, stealing a way of life in a land defiled by a cross-border war that had existed in earnest since the thirteenth century.

Those with a keen eye for Cumbrian and Borders places, will be able to pick up the clues to ascertain locations, whether it be *Tr'penoh*, the 'village of no consequence', or to give its modern name, *Torpenhow* (pronounced locally as *Trup-en-ah)*, or the 'Traquere's tower' which exists today as *High Head Castle*, an eighteenth century ruin; a once great house that replaced an earlier late-medieval tower house. The round tower too, Jack's hideout, does exist, unusual in its form in Dumfriesshire, the Borders, as *Orchardton Tower*.

I ask that liberties taken over the occupation of properties for the sake of fiction be forgiven. Although I have housed the cast of characters in properties that they could have lived in if they actually existed at the time, because no record exists to dictate otherwise.

Where actual sites are named, for reasons of clarity, I have used current modern identifiable place names, instead of the names the characters may have actually used in the sixteenth century. For example, the River Esk, the obstacle that contributed to the defeat of the Scots at the battle of Solway Moss, was known on some maps of the time as the Leven River. Locals would have named it differently. Similarly, the battle site area was listed at the time as Sollom Moss, but again for clarity, a modern tag has been used. In fact generally the language throughout the story has been greatly modernised to give only a flavour of the *Cumbric* dialect and rhetoric, for reasons of accessibility, at the cost of historical accuracy.

I have to thank all those 'Names' for my use of their surnames, all taken within context of the story. I have to give my particular thanks to Sir Thomas Wharton for lending himself to the story, the actual Deputy Warden of the English West March during the time of John Brownfield.

This work is written as a saga, purely as an entertainment; a core of a series of adventure, mystery and romantic novels, and not written as a serious salute to history. For those wanting to read more about the intriguing history of the period and the area, I cannot recommend highly enough works by *Alistair Moffat* and *George MacDonald Fraser*. I have, of course, reason to thank many other writers; all those worthy scholars that have painstakingly researched Border history and presented their work for both my enjoyment and research; books that encouraged me to create this work of fiction; too many to mention, too many to praise.

Mark Montgomery, Author, MMXII (2012)

Historical Note

I won't go into the historical background of the conflict between England and Scotland. I will only say it existed, and had existed for centuries before the commencement of our story and the Scottish tragedy on the Solway Moss. I also won't go into the nature of the individual protagonists, as there are much better reference works to learn about the cast of real characters that enabled the background of this story. Differing, well researched histories that will colour your view of the qualities and failings of kings and knights, of nobles and heroes of the day.

Let us say, both the English and Scottish governments had a long history of grievances and snubs against each other, and each incited their own Border peoples to cause their respective cross border neighbours as much trouble as possible.

Borderers were very good at causing trouble, especially the Scottish Borderers. Larceny, murder and burnings were stock-in-trade for the Scottish Borderer, especially cattle rustling, or reiving. The *Border Reiver* conducted his 'trade' with both enthusiasm and skill, and this proficiency for hit and run mayhem made them a very popular choice for the armies of the day.

The buffer between England and Scotland was the Marches;

military and judicial administrative zones set up by both the Scottish and English Governments under agreement known as the *Laws of the Marches* (1249). Each side of the border was split into East, Middle and West Marches, each administered by a March Warden, appointed by their respective governments.

So it was in August, 1542, when the Warden of the English East March, Robert Bowes, in reply to Scottish raids, conducted a reprisal attack with three thousand horsemen with the sole aim to ruin Teviotdale and the surrounding areas of the Scottish Middle March.

During the raid he camped on good open high ground, just a mile or two over the border to the east of Kelso, not far from his own permanent base at Norham Castle, and he sent two forces to raid the Tweed Valley, while he stayed a garrison to hold his camp. However, on their return to their encampment, a small Scottish force, led by the Earl of Huntly, ambushed the two English raiding parties. What harmed the English more was the fact that some of its own Border Horse units, chiefly those formed from families from Tynedale and Redesdale, thought the fight was going against them. They thought better of sticking around to fight and deserted with their stolen livestock, leaving Bowes and his force to be badly mauled by the Scots. The Scottish force, reinforced by Lord Home with a mere four hundred horsemen enlarged the English mauling into a complete rout, the English losing several hundred horsemen and Robert Bowes himself captured, to be held for ransom.

The English king, Henry VIII, was none too pleased. But regardless of the trouncing his forces had received, his invasion of Scotland was already inevitable and he retaliated with a force of twenty thousand northern troops.

Again the poor Scottish Borders felt the pain of conflict and Kelso, Roxburgh and Teviotdale were burnt again. This time

Huntly's Scottish forces were no match, and all they could do was shadow the advancing English army as they destroyed farm, town, church and abbey. The English carried their supplies with them, foraging being lean so late in the year, and with Huntly harassing any attempt to bolster their supplies of food and fodder, resupplying the English assault proved too difficult and the English march of destruction lasted only a week. Short on supplies they returned to their fortress town of Berwick-upon-Tweed. Again in Henry VIII's attempt to punish the King of Scotland, it was as ever the Borderer that suffered the wrath of a vexed king.

In the meantime, the Scottish king, James V, was raising an army to counter the English assault. He ordered a muster to Fala Moor in Midlothian on the ancient Roman road, *Dere Street,* and a force of between fifteen and twenty thousand gathered. But the Scottish nobles, on hearing the English force had retired to Berwick, quickly lost their will for a fight (a will in actuality that was never there in the first place, due to their lack of unity behind their appointed king) and there was full-scale desertion.

History records James V's ongoing relationship with his nobles as not a happy one, and it was suspected many rich and powerful Scottish gentlemen would have welcomed an English invasion just to remove, what was in their opinion, a troublesome and pointless king. Despite this, James was able to raise a force of between twelve and fourteen thousand strong while the English rested in Berwick.

It is with a word of caution that I put a figure on the size of James' army that actually marched on England. Differing accounts estimate, widely, the size of the King of Scotland's army, and it is certain that more men would have joined on the march while others would have melted away.

The meagre Scots army marched from Edinburgh and their muster at Fala Moor towards the English West March. Not south towards Berwick and the English main force, but southwest towards Carlisle and Cumbria, an easier road to hitting back at the English on English soil, avoiding an encounter with the superior English force at Berwick on the east coast.

James V must have thought his entry into England an easy matter, with the English army many miles away on the east coast at Berwick. He only had to overcome the modest garrison at Carlisle, commanded by the English knight of our story, Thomas Wharton, who was at this time Deputy Warden of the English West March.

It was over supper on the evening of the 23rd November 1542, when Thomas Wharton was told of the pending attack by the Scottish force, and he mustered his small force of three thousand in defence of the forthcoming attack. His strategy was to go out to meet the invading Scottish army, despite their overwhelming numbers. This bold move can only demonstrate a little of the character of the man, Thomas Wharton. He was not a man to hide in his castle, to let the invaders pass him by, destroying all as they travelled, or sit inside safer walls whilst they besieged him, or parleyed a kinder outcome for their forthcoming encounter. No, he ordered the beacons lit and called the North Cumbrian Borderers to his side.

That evening, the Scottish army, splitting into two battalions, were moving south. Their lead forces, skirmishers, were already in the *Debateable Land,* firing farms and scattering those locals unwise enough to remain in the path of the Scots. The Debateable land was a long strip of land, about three to five miles wide and about twelve miles long, reaching out from the mouth of the Solway Firth. It was a small piece of territory between the Scottish and English West Marches, neither recognised as Scottish nor English, and as such became the stomping ground for the infamous. Fugitives and those of the worst kind of character used the area's lack of judicial rule to carry out their nefarious activities. The area was greatly responsible for the legend of the Reiver, those families; Grahams, Armstrongs, Bells and Littles, who used the lawless sanctuary of the Debateable Land to launch their crime spree on both sides of the border without favour and without discrimination.

By early morning of the 24th of November, Thomas Wharton stood with his Cumbrian Border Horsemen on a good vantage point on Arthuret Heights (close to Longtown), looking over the point at which the Scots army would need to cross the River Esk. Sir Thomas Wharton was reported to be an able soldier, and it is recorded, as he watched the large Scottish force crossing the River Esk, he observed how the natural landscape hemmed in the advancing troops. Between the banks of the Esk and the surrounding marshland, named the Solway Moss, the Scots army had little space to manoeuvre. So he deployed around eight hundred of his Cumbrian Border Horsemen to attack the Scottish flank.

These Border Horsemen were light cavalry, and their type had been used for thousands of years as skirmishers to forage, raid and to harass the enemy. Locally known as 'Prickers', they were swift horsemen, lightly equipped and well able to cut and run. Armed with light armour, perhaps a reinforced leather jacket or 'jack' with a steel cap or helmet to protect their head, a sword 'suited to the slice', a long spear or lance, and depending on their preference and purse, a small crossbow or 'latch', a 'dagg' (pistol) and/or a bow. When mounted, they rode small sturdy horses, well suited to the bog and hill of the local landscape. Uniforms did not exist for the Border Horseman, but a cloth badge bearing the device of his country's or master's flag would be sewn somewhere on his attire to mark out his allegiance.

It was men such as these that stood with Thomas Wharton,

and no doubt was at the forefront of James V's march towards England. Unfortunately James V was not with his army as it marched. He was not a well man and he remained in Lochmaben. Lord Maxwell, the Warden of the Scottish West March, an able soldier and a noble of much wealth and power in the region was an obvious choice to take over command of the Scottish army, but instead Oliver Sinclair was given temporary command. Oliver Sinclair was a favourite courtier of the Scottish king, a well-born fop and disliked by other Scottish commanders, so his appointment did not go down well. This point of history however was disputed at the time (depending which point of view the historian shared, catholic or protestant) some suggesting Oliver Sinclair's appointment was made in error. It was put forward that Oliver Sinclair might simply have been sent to deliver a message from James V when he was 'caught up' in events that saw him hailed as the new commander.

The English assault was unexpected and, as the Scots army was attacked, confusion gripped the commanders of the Scottish force and their men. The effect of the assault by so few soldiers was devastating and, sensing the growing panic in the Scottish ranks, the English Prickers stepped up their attacks, firing their pistols and crossbows into the Scottish ranks. They followed up their ranged weapons by running in amongst the Scots with lance and sword to hack at the Scots army, before retiring and repeating the attack.

As the Scots army tried to manoeuvre and escape the vicious poking and pricking by Wharton's skirmishers, they crashed into their own men and the panic to escape brought misery to those men stacked up behind, who were then trampled and forced into the bog and river as the outer ranks tried to flee the point blank assault of Wharton's Prickers. Many Scots simply drowned.

Leaving behind cannon and standards, weapons and the

wounded, the Scots retreated and ran. Twelve hundred prisoners were taken. Lords and earls, barons and some five hundred gentlemen and landowners (including Oliver Sinclair), were all taken for ransom as was the custom dating back hundreds of years. Included in the spoils were three thousand horses, thirty standards, twenty cannons, one hundred and twenty guns and four cartloads of lances.

As the poor Scots army fled, running disordered back into Scotland, it found more misery as the dispossessed Graham clan and other Scottish Border families took their revenge for previous wrongs and plundered the shattered army.

James V died soon after on 14 December 1542, leaving a six-day old infant girl, Mary Stuart to succeed him. The nobles that were captured at Solway Moss and interred in the Tower of London in December, were later released in the same month after they accepted Henry VIII as the guardian of the baby girl, Mary, signing a secret contract of betrothal between Henry's own son, Edward and the infant Scottish queen; Henry being the successor in the event of Mary's death. That agreement failed to see fruition, as did many agreements and pacts of the time. The Scots reneged on the pact, but Henry was just as bad at keeping agreements.

Wharton's victory was to earn him a peerage (First Baron Wharton) and elevated the reputation of the Border Horseman beyond measure, placing them into many European armies as most valuable mercenaries., because who could argue with the skill of the Pricker, when a mere eight hundred horsemen smashed an army twenty times their size, with only a handful of causalities sustained. Stories would be maintained and embellished of their feat at Solway Moss, even though they had more than a little help from an able English commander and his incompetent Scottish counterpart.

History may have been disingenuous to our King James V and

his shameful defeat of his army on the Moss. After all, historians are as good as the completeness of the events they record, and as fair as their own prejudices allow.

The fame of the Border Horseman may have been cemented on the Moss, but history would seek, not to celebrate the skill of the warrior, but more so his exploits within the deeply ingrained clan system of the Anglo/Scottish border, where families engaged in survival of the fittest—and theft, kidnap, murder and reiving were the daily trades of the able Border Horseman. But in all his criminality, the Reiver word was his bond; his reputation was all he was. And so we can call the Borderer noble, even in his villainy. Nobler perhaps than those of noble birth, whose word was often worthless—their nobility being born and rarely earned.

Printed in Great Britain
by Amazon